INDIGO: STORM

ADRIAN J. SMITH

Copyright © 2022 by Adrian J. Smith

All rights reserved.

No part of this book may be reproduced in any form or by any electronic or mechanical means, including information storage and retrieval systems, without written permission from the author, except for the use of brief quotations in a book review.

Cover art by Miblart

AUTHOR NOTE

Thank you so much for joining me on the adventure that is the *Indigo B&B Series*.

This author is part of iReadIndies, a collective of self-published independent authors of women loving women (WLW) literature. Please visit our website at iReadIndies.com for more information and to find links to the books published by our authors.

CHAPTER 1

THE MAPS and satellite readouts streaming across the computer monitor screamed at her. Violet shuddered as she stared at them, abandoning the exams she had been grading. Her stomach clenched. It wasn't an awful storm, but the highs and lows, the ramping up, could easily be seen. She'd be willing to bet a tornado would show its face in the middle of all that.

She could hardly tear her gaze from it, the itch to be out in the middle of the storm stronger than anything. It had been months since she'd been able to slide into the Hummer and chase. The thrill it sent through her was a shudder of excitement and even a little arousal every time.

The knock on her door startled her. Jerking back, Violet glanced up to find one of her favorite students filling the doorway—not that she allowed herself to have favorites.

"Hey, teach."

"Lando." Violet's lips curved up. "See this?"

Pointing at the screen, she expected Lando to lean over her shoulder and stare at the monitor. What she didn't expect was the scent of Lando's cologne, her hand on Violet's desk to prop her up as she leaned in to get a better look.

Violet held in the shiver, but goosebumps ran along her arms.

Lando squinted at the screen, and Violet had to work hard to tear her gaze from her soon-to-be-former student to her computer monitor.

"It doesn't look too bad."

Violet clicked her tongue. "If you follow these lines, see? The spin is just not forming."

"This is real time?" Lando asked.

"Mmhmm." Violet pointed at the screen again. "Oklahoma. I've been following the weather cell for a few hours now."

"You want to be there, don't you?"

The question caused tension to ripple up Violet's spine. She hadn't realized it was that obvious, or perhaps she suspected most of her students were oblivious. Violet's lips parted, and she shifted her gaze to her student, a woman who by any means was young and ready to take life by the horns and ride it until she had to get off.

"Yes," Violet answered simply, a wispy tone to her voice.

"You storm chase in the summers, right?" Lando's gaze turned to her.

Violet hummed her agreement. "But I'm taking the last quarter off this year to chase in the spring."

Lando didn't move, her thick forearms and biceps still holding herself up as she leaned over Violet onto the desk. "I've thought about finding an internship, maybe going out this summer."

"You'll love it." Violet hit a few buttons on the monitor to change the parameters and run another analysis. She wasn't in charge of planning their chases—that would be Diane's business —but she was excited to join in earlier that year than she had since she was a student.

"Finding a team isn't as easy as I thought it'd be," Lando commented, still looking at the screen.

Violet's stomach clenched. She'd run into the same when she was a student. First it was because she had no experience, but the second issue, which rapidly became a third issue, was that she was a woman, and a woman attracted to other women at that. Storm chasing was often in the most conservative parts of the country, and when she'd been younger and dipping her toe into meteorology, womanhood had not been a common attribute of storm chasers.

She and Diane had managed to break through those barriers, and she was glad. It meant it was easier for students like Lando to join in, but there was often still an undercurrent of sexism and homophobia were in the teams. Lando, by the very fact of being a woman (because Violet didn't assume anyone's sexuality anymore) would have an easier time than Violet had but would still have issues finding a team willing to hire her on.

"I have a few contacts. I can see if they have any openings."

"I would really appreciate that." Lando finally shifted, straightening her back.

Violet tore her gaze from the monitor and stared up at the stocky build, wide hips, and hair that seemed always perfectly in place. Lando had a preference for keeping her hair short, which would help in the storms, though Violet suspected she wouldn't have time to gel it into the perfect style as she did every day for classes.

Lando shoved her hands in her pockets and leaned back on her heels, her tone flirtatious when she spoke. "I did come here for a reason, and an extra lesson in meteorology wasn't it."

Violet flushed. "What did you need?"

"My final paper."

"Right." Violet looked at her desk, which was a mess. She had to clean that up before she left for the quarter and summer. The finals were...somewhere. She hadn't expected any students to actually come get them. They so rarely did and never before the following quarter.

They were in a folder. Violet just had to find that particular folder. Lando plopped into the extra chair that sat in Violet's office, crossing an ankle over her knee. Violet tried to ignore Lando and focus on finding that paper. By this point, she was pretty sure every student she'd had was used to her scattered organization.

"Here it is!" Violet grabbed the folder like it was a prize she'd won. Flipping through the different papers in there, she landed finally on the one she was looking for. *Heather Sutherland.* Sliding it out of the stack, she glanced it over and handed it to Lando.

Lando skimmed it, wrinkling her nose when her eyes lit on the grade at the top.

Violet's heart went out to her. It was an odd turn for Lando to receive only a passing grade in one of her classes, but Violet had graded as fairly as she could. She wouldn't give special treatment to anyone, except perhaps Diane. When they'd been in school together, Violet had often let Diane cheat off her.

"I was surprised when I flipped the coversheet and saw this was your paper." Violet easily slipped into professor mode. She relaxed her shoulders and stared at Lando's face, her chunky cheeks, her soft baby-blue eyes. She looked...sad. Perhaps it was disappointment. Violet couldn't quite read the pinched expression, but she didn't seem surprised.

"Lando," Violet said softly. "Is everything okay?"

Lando's eyes welled up, and she didn't make eye contact. The air in the room thickened, and Violet had a choice to make about what she did with it. Reaching forward, she put a hand on Lando's knee to get her attention, immediately pulling back as soon as those blue eyes filled with water focused on her.

"What happened?"

"It's nothing. Thank you for giving this back to me." Lando shifted as though she was going to leave, but Violet put her hand up to stop her.

"Lando, you're one of the best students in my classes, not because you have the best grades, but because you give it your all. This paper—" Violet tapped the top of the pages "—is not your best work or even near it. I don't think it's because you didn't understand the subject matter. In fact, that's the only thing you seemed to do well in it. What happened?"

Lando's nose reddened, tears slipping down her cheeks. She wiped them away haphazardly. "My grandma died earlier this month. It's nothing."

Violet's heart shattered, her own tears welling in her eyes at the remembrance of pain from her own losses. "That's not nothing. You could have asked for an extension."

"I didn't want special treatment."

Pressing her lips tightly together, Violet leaned in and touched Lando's knee again in a tender move. She'd gotten to know this young woman far better over the course of the last two quarters when Lando had been in classes with her, but that didn't mean she was heartless when it came to her students' struggles. "That is exactly what special treatment is for."

"It's fine," Lando muttered and wiped at her eyes. "Thanks for this."

"Well, it didn't tank your grade, if that's what you're worried about."

Lando swallowed hard, her gaze finally lifting to reach Violet's eyes. "It didn't?"

"Still a B plus." Relief flooded through Lando's face, her shoulders relaxing. Violet wasn't going to tell her that if she'd gotten a B or even an A on the paper then she would have had an A in the class for the quarter. It would have only added salt to an already very raw wound. "Next time, come talk to me. I'm serious, Lando, that's what extensions are for, and I would have gladly given you one."

Lando nodded, although Violet wasn't convinced she'd do it. Some students were as stubborn as they came, and Lando was certainly one of them. Violet rested back in her chair and stared at her student. She would miss Lando's enthusiasm over the next six months as she traipsed across the countryside and hunted for storms and tornados. She always found students' inquiries and learning inspiring. It was part of what had pushed her to teach—that, and needing a more consistent paycheck than six months of storms could give her, which wasn't much to begin with.

"I'll ask around about an internship," Violet supplied.

"Thank you." Lando sounded far more steady than she had before, which Violet was glad for.

Giving Lando a small smile, Violet turned back to her monitor, finding the storm had indeed turned out one tornado. She hissed and pressed closer, her nose close to the screen so she could see clearly. "One touched ground."

"Really?" Lando's eyebrows raised up, and she was back leaning over Violet to see the screen herself.

"Right here." Violet pointed to the proper spin of the air currents. "See it?"

"I do. Is that another one there?"

"Could be," Violet murmured, zooming in to try and get a better view. "But I don't think it's one yet."

"I have so much to learn."

Violet snorted lightly. "We all do, Lando."

When she shifted into her seat again, the back of her shoulder brushed Lando's chest, but Lando didn't move sharply away like Violet would expect her to do. Instead, she stayed put, still focused on the computer screen. Lando always managed to keep her on her toes, but still, it sent an unsettled feeling into the pit of Violet's stomach. Turning her chair to break the physical connection, Violet glanced up at Lando.

"I guess I'll see you in the fall, then."

Lando frowned. "That's a long time to go without my favorite teach."

"But time well spent," a woman's voice echoed into the room.

Violet tensed sharply. She'd nearly forgotten Diane was supposed to come by. Lando raised an eyebrow at Violet before slowly shifting to stand up with a straight back and her hands shoved in her pockets. Her jaw was tight as she stared across the room at their interruption.

Violet needed to figure out what to say, something to break the sudden tension. Her lips parted as Diane eyed Lando up and down, a sly look in her eye that made Violet's stomach churn. "Diane, this is Lando, one of my students."

"I imagined she was." Diane reached her hand out, waiting for Lando to take it.

Lando had a blank look on her face as she reached out, fingers connecting. "Good to meet you."

"You as well," Diane responded.

Violet's stomach twisted even more. "We were looking at the maps from the storm in western Oklahoma."

"Oh?" Diane raised an eyebrow, glancing at Violet before facing the computer. "Anything come of it?"

"Small tornado, at least one for now."

"Let me see." Diane reached into her purse and grabbed her reading glasses, sliding them on before she bent over Violet's chair, much in the manner Lando had just been doing. This feeling was entirely different. Instead of an unsettled feeling, what swarmed Violet was pleasure and heat to her cheeks. She was embarrassed that no matter what Diane did she seemed to have this kind of reaction. She'd tried to control it for as long as she could remember, but she'd never been able to.

Violet leaned back in her chair, looking over Diane's backside to make eye contact with Lando, except Lando's gaze was quite pointedly locked on the curve of Diane's ass. The very same ass that Diane popped out in Lando's direction. Violet sighed and pressed her lips firmly together, trying to figure out what to say or do.

She was too late because Lando jerked her chin up, making eye contact with Violet and the no doubt disappointed and jealous look on her face.

"Lando is one of my best students." Violet kept her gaze on Lando, making sure Lando understood that she had seen.

"Is that right?" Diane answered, popping a look over her shoulder to Lando, amusement flashing in her eyes.

Everything about the moment put Violet in a state of unease. The way Lando eyed Diane, the oddly flirtatious undertones

Diane was giving Lando, a woman easily fifteen years their junior. It wouldn't be good for anyone to have the moment continue.

"Yes," Violet said, hopefully breaking it up. "She's quite smart."

"My recent paper disagrees with you," Lando answered, holding up the offending paper with the C written in bright red pen.

Violet cocked her head to the side. "Extenuating circumstances. The only thing that proves is you need to ask for assistance when necessary."

Lando grinned broadly. The moment warmed Violet's stomach, warring with the discomfort she still felt over the entire situation. Diane's and Lando's gazes locked. Violet felt like the third wheel in some silent conversation happening over her. Diane turned to stand upright, and immediately, Violet followed suit. She couldn't take sitting down any longer.

Keeping close to Diane, Violet eyed Lando and tried to figure out just what was going on. Lando shoved her hands back in her pockets and rolled onto her heels. "I guess I'll have to take you up on that offer, teach."

"Offer?" Diane reiterated, a thin blonde eyebrow raised. "Did you offer for her to come with us?"

Lando's eyes widened, and Violet cursed inwardly. "No, not the offer she is referring to."

"If she is the best student you've had..."

Violet shook her head. "I thought Erik was going to come with us."

"He is, but..."

"Then we don't exactly have room, do we?" Violet gave Diane a pointed look. "Besides, Lando surely has to take classes this upcoming quarter."

Lando lifted one shoulder and dropped it in response. Violet wasn't quite sure what that meant, but she also wasn't sure she wanted to ask. The air sizzled in the tiny office, and the unsettled feeling swam back through the pit of Violet's stomach.

"Doesn't seem like she is," Diane commented.

"Our team is full."

Lando shot Violet a curious look, and Violet ignored it, focusing on Diane as everything seemed to spiral out of control. With what was happening currently, she did not want Lando to join them. A flirtation or a fling would only complicate the next six months, and Violet wanted to get work done. She wanted the time spent to be a success, and she wanted Diane for herself.

Diane stepped forward, pushing Violet to the side. "Tell me about what classes you've taken. What are you studying?"

Violet bit the inside of her lip. She'd seen Diane do this before, the sudden interest in whatever new plaything was around. Lando didn't stand a chance.

"Oh, I just finished meteorology with Professor Myers. I've taken quite a few earth science classes."

"Looking to be a teacher?"

"No, ma'am." Lando bent her knees before straightening them out again, her look slightly demure and one Violet had never seen before. *Was Lando playing at coy?* It seemed so unlike her.

"A weatherman?"

"No." Lando seemed to be enjoying this.

"Weather woman?"

"No." Lando shot Violet a quick glance. "I want to chase storms."

"What would possess you to risk your life for very little reward?" Diane's gaze was sure as she stared Lando in the eye, waiting for an answer.

As much as Violet hated to admit it, she was equally curious about Lando's answer. They'd briefly discussed Lando's ambitions, but never in any depth. She really should probably take the time to get to know some of her students better.

"I like to work with my hands." Lando stared right at Violet.

Violet shivered under the scrutiny. "I don't want to stand in a room and read maps. I want to work and put my skills to good use."

"So go stock a grocery store," Diane's quip was sharp.

Lando frowned. "I've done that, ma'am. What interests me in storms is beyond that. I love the science behind it, studying the chaos that comes from a storm and moves into the devastating effects that we find in the middle of it and after it. But what really strikes me is that balance of fear and absolute amazement."

Violet's chest filled with pride. She understood that feeling Lando had so accurately described. It had taken her years to begin to put words to it, but she'd always been fascinated by the nearly unbelievable. She'd grown up in the high plains, had witnessed the aftermath of so many storms she'd lost count. When she'd taken up photography as a child and into adulthood, she'd often gone in search of those devastatingly beautiful moments when the earth turned against itself. She'd gotten away from the photography in the last decade as she focused on the science and reasoning behind those moments, but she could recall that pull of the storm. Something she'd never been able to give up.

"That's exactly what I wanted to hear." The predatory tone in Diane's voice unnerved Violet. She'd heard it one too many times in the decades they'd known each other, and nothing good ever came of it. She would have to step in soon if she didn't want Lando to end up falling under the same spell she was doomed to live out.

"Well, it's the truth, ma'am."

"Enough with the ma'am." Diane cut her hand across the air. "We're all friends in here, yes?"

That word stung, though Violet didn't let the pain flicker on her face.

"Call me Diane." Once again, Diane reached her hand out for

Lando to take it. "Thank you for putting so succinctly what I think all of us in the chasing community feel."

"Uh...right." Lando shook Diane's hand but flicked a nervous glance to Violet.

Violet drew in a sharp breath, needing this to end sooner rather than later. "Diane has been chasing storms for the better part of fifteen years."

"Oh?" Lando seemed more curious now than before.

That line of conversation had clearly backfired. She'd meant to point out the stark age difference between the two of them in order to put the sexual tension to a stop. Instead, it seemed as though she'd only increased it.

"What got you started in it?"

"That one right there." Diane pointed at Violet. "She dragged me into the center of a storm one morning, insanely early, and I've never been able to give it up since."

"Were you chasing then?"

The question was directed at Violet, but Diane answered. "No, we weren't chasing then. We were barely old enough to drive."

"I didn't realize you'd known each other so long."

"Violet, here, is the girl next door."

Violet grimaced. She hated when Diane talked about her like that. It carried so much undertone about meaning, a meaning that had never come to fruition. For all the years she'd pined after Diane, they'd never once done anything that would push them toward more than mere friendship. That was probably Violet's fault in the long run, since she'd never brought that line of conversation up, too scared it would ruin a good thing.

"Not really next door," Violet interjected. "I lived down the street, but we met when we were kids and have been best friends ever since."

"Yes, friends." Diane slid Violet a look, a simmering one, the same one Violet had dreamed about for years but had never fully experienced.

Lando looked between the two of them, her gaze flicking back and forth as if she could read the tension in it. Violet's lips parted as she focused on her student again. "We started officially chasing storms when I was in graduate school."

"Sounds like an interesting story," Lando commented. "But I think it'll have to wait for another time. I have to get to work."

"Oh." Diane pouted, her lips pursing together.

Violet held back her disdain for the moment. "Well, I was glad to see you in my classes again this quarter."

"Yeah, teach. You, too." Lando knocked her chin up, grabbing the paper she'd put on the desk at some point. Violet wasn't sure because she had completely missed it. "In the fall?"

"In the fall," Violet answered, not saying anything more than that.

Lando left, and Diane turned to Violet, a saccharine smile on her lips. "She's interesting."

Violet refused to acknowledge her.

"We should invite her along, see if she wants to join us."

"I don't think that would be a good idea," Violet murmured as she sat back in her chair to look over the maps flashing across her screen.

"Why not?"

"I think our team is fine the way it is."

"Vi," Diane's tone dropped, and she sat on the edge of the desk, crossing her legs and tilting her chin down. "If she's as good as you said she is…"

"That was for her benefit." Violet left it at that. It was a true enough statement. She always wanted to uplift her students when she could, and Lando was her most dedicated that semester. However, she wasn't going to explain why to Diane, and she certainly wasn't going to lie and tell Diane that Lando wasn't smart.

"Oh." Diane pouted again. "Are you ready to leave tomorrow?"

"Not really. I'll pack tonight."

Diane snorted. "Always last minute for you."

Violet shrugged. "If you want it to be less than last minute, scram. I've still got to finish some grading and put in the final grades for the registrar."

"I never understood teaching."

"You never had to," Violet clenched her jaw. That was borderline rude, and she hoped Diane didn't push at it. "Was there something you needed?"

"Just checking to see if you were ready."

"A phone call would have sufficed."

"But then I wouldn't have met the wonderful Lando."

Violet snorted. "Her name is Heather."

"Heather?"

"Heather Sutherland. She goes by Lando."

"Suits her." The wistful tone in Diane's voice took Violet off-guard, and when she glanced up at her friend, the faraway look meant trouble.

CHAPTER 2

THE LAST WEEK had been lonely and depressing. Lando hadn't done much other than lounge around the house her grandmother had left her, puttering here and there and pretending like she was doing something productive. The week off from school had been such a change to her routine, and she wasn't looking forward to the next week, when everyone returned and she was left with nothing to do.

The place she'd worked prior to the winter had fired her. She couldn't blame them. Three days was not enough to grieve her grandmother's death. Maybe for someone who hadn't been that close, but her grandmother had raised her. Twenty-three years they'd spent together, and Lando was devastated it wouldn't be more.

The house was so quiet without her.

Tears stung Lando's eyes as she collapsed onto the couch in the center of the living room, not bothering to turn on the television or anything. Loneliness had never bothered her much before, but after her grandmother had gotten sick, she'd been so caught up in trying to take care of her. The end had been swift, which was a blessing, but the rest was too much for Lando to comprehend.

She was going to need to find a job soon. She'd done a few applications, but the problem was without a degree, being in school, and with the firing on her record, it was harder to find one than she'd thought. Since school was out for at least a quarter, if not longer, Lando at least had the time. If only she could figure out how to motivate herself to open her laptop and start filling out applications.

It was such tedious work, and often there was little to no reward since she rarely heard back. She was lucky the house was paid off, but that didn't mean she didn't have other expenses, and those student loans would come due soon. The weight of the world rested on her shoulders, and Lando could barely breathe from the pressure.

Deciding she had to do something, Lando dragged herself off the couch and toward the kitchen. She'd bought the paint before her grandmother had died. They'd talked about redecorating and renovating the kitchen for years, and just when she'd gotten ready to start that project, her grandmother had gotten the diagnosis. The least she could do was get that project done while she had the time.

She was halfway through emptying the cabinets when there was a knock at her door. Furrowing her brow, Lando stood up and brushed her sweaty and dirty palms over her thighs to try and clean them off. Peeking her head around the corner toward the door, Lando tried to see who it might be. She didn't expect visitors. They'd mostly stopped the week after her grandmother passed, and had left her alone. They were her grandmothers' friends anyway, not hers.

Lando brushed her hands again when she couldn't see who it was. She put her hand on the doorknob, opening it slowly, wishing she wasn't dressed in her run-down pair of sweats and a T-shirt, but again, she hadn't expected anyone and she'd been set for hard manual labor. As the door swung open, she had to hold back the strangled gasp that wanted to escape.

Diane leaned against the door frame, her arms crossed and

pulling her suit jacket tight across her breasts. Her eyes were locked on Lando, a single blonde eyebrow arched perfectly over her questioning gaze. Her lips were plump with a pale-pink lipstick, her makeup perfect. Diane was sex on a stick if Lando had ever seen it. She'd noticed it in Professor Myers' office, and she was witness to it here.

Lando could play this one of two ways. She could flirt with the woman who clearly flirted with everyone. Or she could be standoffish and try to figure out why this virtual stranger would show up at her house without warning. Diane clearly wanted something. Lando just wasn't sure what it was.

Keeping silent, Lando eyed Diane again, the black suit jacket giving way to a pair of tight dark blue jeans. She was the quintessential example of business casual. Lando kept her hand on the door, holding it tight, giving Diane a pointed look as she waited for the other woman to make the first move.

"Imagine my surprise at discovering your real name is Heather."

Lando pressed her lips together tightly. She despised that name. Her mother had given it to her in honor of her best friend, and they'd had a falling out shortly before Lando's mom died in a tragic car accident. All the name had brought with it was a memory of death and family she never had.

"Imagine my surprise at discovering an unwelcome woman on my porch."

Diane's lips curled up into a brilliant smile, and Lando feared she'd walked right into whatever trap Diane had set. "May I come in?"

"No."

Diane pouted. "It's about your internship."

"I don't have an internship."

"Yes, you do. May I?" Diane straightened and tried to push her way inside.

Giving up, Lando let her in but didn't offer any refreshments. Her grandmother would kill her for being so hostile toward a guest, but she still couldn't figure this woman out. She was attractive for sure, and Lando would enjoy flirting with anyone who gave her the time of day, but there was a sense of underlying expectation that Lando didn't quite feel privy to.

They sat together on the couch, which boasted a messy blanket. Lando picked it up and threw it onto the chair next to the coffee table where a couple of cups were. She found herself staring at Diane again, attempting to decipher every action and facial reaction she had. Yet she couldn't. Diane's expression and body were perfectly schooled.

"What internship?" Lando asked.

"As I'm sure Violet told you, we're going chasing this spring and summer. She's taken extra time off work in order to spend more time with the team. We're hoping to make progress in terms of tracking the movement of storms, specifically smaller rope tornados and the damage they can do."

Lando thought it sounded good, pleasant enough, as though it might be interesting, but she still failed to see what any of it had to do with her. She hadn't been able to find an internship with a team in the month she'd known she had access to the funds, and if she didn't find one in the next two weeks, she was going to be out those funds, out a potential job, and likely out of work and school as well.

"Sounds like an interesting project."

"It is." Diane flashed another seducing grin. "Violet does more of the analysis than I do."

"So what do you do? For the team, I mean." Lando crossed her arms and leaned into the couch, pretending she was far more confident in the conversation than she was. She wanted to come off as strong and put together even when she knew she was falling apart at the seams.

"I mainly drive and track the storms overall so we know where we're going."

"Sounds reasonable." Lando wasn't quite sure how other

teams worked, but she suspected it was similar. "Who takes the data?"

"Violet does most of that—and our other team members."

It all seemed simple enough, though Lando still couldn't fathom why Diane was there in the first place. "How did you get my name?"

"Violet shared it with me after you left her office."

"Shared it for what purpose?"

"Not this." Diane blushed, a gentle pink rising to the pale skin. "In fact, I'm not sure she'd be too pleased that I'm asking you this."

"You haven't asked me anything," Lando countered.

"Not yet." Diane lowered her gaze, acting coy, but Lando suspected it was just that, an act. "I don't think she'd like it if I took you from your schoolwork."

Lando didn't answer, because the truth was, she didn't have schoolwork to go back to. She couldn't make the payments for the classes, and without her grandmother and those extra funds, she had no idea when she'd be able to do that. She'd been far too embarrassed to mention that to Professor Myers the day before, so she'd pretended like she would be there in the fall.

"I'd like to offer you an internship."

"What?" Lando's eyes widened, dragged back to the conversation at hand.

"You have the approval, yes?"

"I do, for two quarters of field education."

"So you could come with us. It'll be an excellent learning experience. You'll get to work one-on-one with one of your professors."

"Are you serious right now?" Lando frowned, thinking it couldn't be real. Never in her life had things just fallen into place when she needed them to. She was always the one who struggled to get from point A to point B without backpedaling sixty times in between. It was just the story of her life.

"Completely." Diane's lips curled upward again, this time the smile slightly predatory. Lando would have to learn to read these moods of Diane's rapidly before she felt comfortable enough revealing anything of herself.

"You want me to join your team." Lando clenched her fists, still not quite sure she could believe this dream might be coming true.

"Yes. I do."

Grinning broadly, Lando bounced in her seat. "This is amazing. Thank you!"

Diane looked pleased with herself and with Lando's reaction. She held out her hand, and Lando readily took it. "So does that mean you'll join us?"

"A thousand times, yes. But wait...didn't Professor Myers say there wasn't room on the team?" A stone grew in the pit of her belly, as though this dream come true was about to fall through the cracks again and she wouldn't be able to have it. That was how it so often worked. One minute the dream was within her grasp and the next it was snatched back.

"We have room on the team. Though, I would like to talk to Violet before you show up, so please don't talk to her about this."

That uneasy feeling deepened. If she was going to be working closely with her teacher for the next six months, shouldn't they talk about that first? Get some sort of game plan in play for what was going to happen and when? Still, it was an opportunity that Lando wasn't sure she could pass on. She needed the income, but to have income and advance toward the career she wanted at the same time? It would be damn near perfect.

"All right," Lando replied. "When will you talk to her?"

"Soon." Diane patted Lando's knee. "I promise. We're leaving tomorrow—got delayed a day but that can't happen again—so I need you ready to go."

"Oh." Cold washed through Lando. She hadn't expected to leave so soon, but she supposed that was what Professor Myers had talked to her about at some point, if she recalled the many conversations they had about it over the past quarter.

"Will that work for you?"

"Yes. Isn't there some paperwork we need to fill out or something?"

"Don't worry about that." Diane waved her hand in front of them. "I'll take care of everything."

"Okay. When do we leave?"

"Meet me at this address, and we'll take off from there." Diane fished in her pocket for a business card. It had her name and an address on it. Lando knew of the road, and it wasn't far from her house. "Pack light. There isn't much room in the vehicle for personal items with all of our equipment."

"I can do that. I'm not a very heavy packer in general."

"Good. Then I look forward to seeing you tomorrow." Diane stood up and held out her hand.

Lando followed suit and took it, shaking. She gave her thanks for the opportunity again and saw Diane to the door. Staring down at the card in her hand, giddiness swelled in her chest. She had to tell her aunt. Someone would need to watch the house for her while she was gone, take care of certain things. Grabbing her cellphone, Lando immediately made a phone call.

"What's up?"

"Aunt T, you got time for a visit tonight?"

"Uh...not really, but I can. Why?"

"I need you to come over." Lando could barely keep the excitement out of her voice.

"Is this an emergency?"

Having to think that over, Lando immediately nodded. "It is. Not major, but I do need to see you."

"I'll be there as soon as I get off work."

"Awesome. Bye, Aunt T."

"Bye, Stinker."

That gave Lando three hours to put her kitchen back in order, pack, and do everything she could to close up the house for the next six months. It was a monumental task, but one Lando was happy to undertake.

When her aunt arrived, Lando had the house cleaned and mostly shut down. She'd called all the utility companies, put a stop on her mail, and was ready to begin packing for the next six months of her life. Aunt T walked right into the house and called out to get Lando's attention.

"Hey," Lando said and she came around the corner. "I'm just packing."

"Packing?" Aunt T dropped her keys on the kitchen table, following Lando into the back bedroom. Her scrubs were dirty, and Lando knew she'd be tired, but there was no one else she could ask for this favor.

As soon as Aunt T was settled on the edge of the mattress, Lando stared at her closet. Packing light was harder than she'd anticipated, especially when packing for six months of the year. She could always purchase things she'd forgotten, but she didn't even know how often they'd have access to laundry facilities.

"What's this all about?" Aunt T glowered, and Lando knew she was going to have to do some good explaining to make up for the lack of information and the quick decision.

"Remember a few months ago when I applied for that internship?"

"Yes?" Aunt T still looked suspicious.

"Well, I ended up getting one today, and we leave tomorrow."

"Tomorrow!" Aunt T's eyes went wide. Lando's stomach churned with guilt. Aunt T was very easily like the third mother for her, her grandma being the second, and she didn't want to cause any unnecessary worries or fears. "Who are you going with?"

"A woman named Diane and her team."

"Does Diane have a last name?"

"Uh…yeah. It's on that card on my nightstand."

Aunt T leaned over and grabbed the business card, staring at it. Lando focused on packing, knowing she didn't have much time before she'd have to crawl in bed and attempt some sleep. "Do you even know this woman?"

"Not really, but she works with Professor Myers. She's the one that hooked me up with her." It was a small lie, but Lando knew it'd ease her aunt's discomfort.

"Will your professor be going with you?"

"Yes." Lando firmly shoved a rain jacket into her duffel bag.

"Isn't that the one you have a crush on."

Lando froze in the middle of grabbing another warmer jacket. Spinning on her toes, she eyed her aunt carefully. "Excuse me?"

"Don't you have a crush on her?"

"I don't know what you're talking about." She'd thought she'd managed to keep that a secret from everyone, including herself. Having a crush on the teacher was a bad idea from the start, and Lando had worked her hardest to keep those feelings at bay and focus solely on her school work. She didn't need any more distractions that quarter.

"Sure, you do. You talk about her all the time, get this flushed little look in your cheeks."

Lando glared and rolled her eyes, focusing on the task at hand.

"That look!" Aunt T pointed at her. "That's the one right there."

"Oh hell," Lando muttered. "Yes, Professor Myers will be going out chasing with us, but I do not have a crush on her."

"I don't believe you, but we'll go with what you said for now. Are you sure this is wise? I mean, won't you be spending a lot of one-on-one time with her?"

"The entire team will be together most of the time. It'll be rare any of us will be without the other."

Aunt T frowned. "How much are you getting paid?"

Lando shrugged. "The internship pays most of my salary. It's only two grand a month, but it's supposed to be supplemented."

"That's not a lot."

"No, but housing and food should be taken care of while we're out chasing."

"Should be?" Aunt T raised her eyebrows at the card, flipping it over. "Didn't you talk details before saying yes?"

"Sure." Lando slipped that lie in again. She'd taken it because she needed it. Two grand was more than she was making then, so what did it matter if she had to leave the state for it? They could hash out details as soon as she had Diane in the car and they were driving. Surely there was a lot of time spent getting from one place to the next.

"I don't know how I feel about this."

"Well, I'm going," Lando said firmly. "I need you to check in on the house when you can. I've shut everything off, but just to make sure it doesn't fall over, you know?"

"Or burn to the ground?" Aunt T slid her gaze upward, those cool sea-glass eyes locking on Lando's form.

"Yeah, or that." Lando shoved in a pair of sweats for sleeping into her duffel. "Thanks, Aunt T."

Aunt T hummed, though it didn't sound like she was too pleased. "What would Nan say if she could see you now?"

"She'd tell me to go, what are you talking about?"

"She might, but I'm pretty sure she'd give you a good whipping if you made a mess of it."

"Can't hardly make a mess of a job when I'm living that job."

"One can only hope," Aunt T murmured. "You'll call?"

"Yeah, and I'll send damn post cards from every town we stop in. I promise. I know how much you like them."

"I'll add them to my collection." Standing, Aunt T stretched her calves before stalking over to the duffel. She fiddled around with the edge of it. "Got everything you need?"

"Mostly."

"I'm serious about calling. Don't make me come out there to find you."

"I promise."

"Good." Aunt T enveloped Lando in a hug, tightly pulling

Lando into her chest and holding her there. "Next time you need to give me more damn warning."

Lando chuckled. "I'll try."

"You know your mama would be proud, right?"

Tears stung Lando's eyes. Aunt T always tried to do that, bring her mother into the conversation, but Lando hadn't even been two years old when her mother had died, and she barely remembered her. Most of her memories were because of Aunt T and Nan. It was far more for Aunt T's benefit than hers. "I know."

"Nan, too, as much as she was a stubborn old fool, she loved you with everything she had."

That did make tears fall. Lando sniffled and buried her face in Aunt T's shoulder. She was easily six inches taller than Lando, but it didn't matter. Any time Aunt T hugged her she felt like she was home. Her life would have been so different if her grandmother hadn't taken her in and she'd ended up with Aunt T. Both their lives. It likely would have ended in disaster. Aunt T wasn't ready twenty years ago to be a parent. Hell, she'd barely been ready ten years ago.

"I miss her," Lando whispered.

"Yeah. Me too. Old bitch had too much opinion in her to keep it quiet."

Barking out a laugh, Lando pulled back. "I'll see if there's a break at all when we can come home and visit, but I do promise I'll call."

"Like I said, if I don't hear from you at a minimum weekly, I'm siccing the marshals on you."

"You do that." Lando winked. "I'm going to finish packing."

Lando saw her aunt to the door and locked it as soon as she was alone. She was going to miss the old house she'd grown up in, but this adventure was going to be the best decision for the career she wanted. It had to be, because she needed the break in life she'd never gotten before.

CHAPTER 3

THE AIR WAS crisp that morning when Violet made the last pot of coffee in her apartment for the next six months. She'd always dreamed of chasing storms full-time, but it was rare to find someone who could afford to do it. She'd allowed only the summer for so long that adding in the extra quarter was going to be a shock to her system.

Six months was a long time to be gone, but it would be perfect for her soul. She needed it. The time to reconnect with nature and the outdoors, to do something she was so passionate about aside from teaching. Violet sipped her coffee, staring out at the horizon as the sun meandered its way upward.

It was late March, and they'd already missed several raging storms throughout the plains, but that wasn't going to deter her. A few storms were nothing compared to six months living among them. The bitter brew hit her tongue, waking her up and warming her. Six months with Diane was going to be a feat she'd have to work through.

In all the intervening years since they'd met, Violet had never been able to end the crush she had on Diane. There was no reciprocated interest, no matter how much they flirted. Diane marched to the beat of her own drum, and unfortunately, Violet was caught up in it, always one step behind.

Scowling, Violet clenched her jaw. She was nearing her mid-forties, and she'd been enamored with her best friend for too long. She really needed to find a way to work through that and spending this length of time with the woman, confined in small spaces with no relief, could either help that cause or make it worse. Either way, it was going to be six months to remember.

She could barely wait to get the old team together, working hard on finding storms, gathering data, and analyzing it. It was a lot of work in a small amount of time, but worth every minute of it. Violet finished her coffee, cleaned the pot and mug, and set them back in place. She took out the trash, grabbed her bags and locked up.

In ten minutes she was at Diane's, lounging on the edge of the bed while Diane finished packing. Diane always was a last-minute person with just about everything, even as much as she teased Violet for it. It used to drive Violet crazy, but she was determined to take the next six months with as much patience as she possibly could. The second cup of coffee was welcome, and warmed her fingers.

"Where are we going first?" Violet asked.

"Western Oklahoma, out around Guymon. I figure we can easily go north into Kansas or south into Texas or west into Colorado from there depending on where the storms are."

"Makes sense." It would take them about a day to get there, which wasn't bad. The run-down hotels they would stay in along the way when they did stay somewhere would be good enough to sleep in but not much more. "Have you been tracking the weather stream going into that area?"

Diane nodded curtly, grabbing another piece of clothing and folding it into her small suitcase. "It looks promising."

Violet lifted her shoulder in a slight shrug. She'd followed the same stream, and while it had some promising attributes to it, she wouldn't bank teaching a course on it. It wasn't very strong, and while it did have the potential to grow, it hadn't picked up any speed in the process."

"Did you talk to Erik?" Diane asked.

Shaking her head, Violet set her cup on the edge of the footboard. "No, why?"

Diane's lines thinned. "Nothing."

"Why?"

"It's nothing."

"Diane, you can't leave me hanging, what did he say? Is he not coming?"

"He's not." Diane bristled. She finished with her suitcase, zipping it shut and drinking her coffee as she stared at Violet over the rim. "And it's probably for the best, honestly. There were some issues last year that I wasn't very happy with."

"What issues?" Violet's shoulders fell. She liked Erik. He was spry and always good for a joke, probably one of the most jovial people she'd ever met.

"It doesn't really matter now. He won't be joining us for the season."

Violet pressed her lips tightly together, nearly in a pout. She could barely look Diane in the eye, but forced her gaze upward. "I guess that means more time for just you and me together."

The hopeful tone in her voice was unbelievable, and she hoped Diane didn't pick up on it, but how could she not? Violet had been desperate to get Diane's attention in that way for decades, and she'd never been able to rid herself of the feelings roiling around inside her. She wanted Diane to notice her, notice them.

Diane gave her a pitying glance, and Violet knew she hadn't been able to hide it. Cursing inwardly, Violet stared into the dark liquid of her coffee, hoping it would swallow her up whole.

"I did hire a replacement."

"That's probably for the best. I can't imagine running a team with only two of us. It'd be next to impossible."

Diane frowned. "I think we could handle it if needed."

Violet shrugged. "For a short time, perhaps. For the entire season? I'm not sure."

Diane reached forward, sliding a hand along Violet's thigh. The shudder was involuntary, and Violet cursed herself again. *She'd never get over the damn crush, would she?*

"Please tell me you didn't book that same fleabag as last year," Violet interjected, trying to change the subject as swiftly as possible.

"Absolutely not. That place was disgusting."

"Thank goodness." Violet gave her a wry smile. "The bedbugs followed us for weeks."

Diane frowned. "They did. We need to raise our standards some, don't you think?"

"Always." Violet couldn't read the look Diane was giving her, but she didn't quite think they were talking about hotel rooms anymore. "When are we leaving?"

Diane checked the small gold watch on her left wrist. "Now, I suppose."

"Good. I'll clean these up." Violet grabbed the mugs of coffee and brought them to the kitchen. As she washed what was left of the dishes, she rolled her shoulders. This was it. It was decided. She was going to take this season to either make a very pointed move on Diane or she was going to take it and get over the damn feelings she'd been harboring for so long. They both needed freedom from it, and Violet clearly was the one struggling the most so she was going to have to make the move to fix it.

They moved Violet's things from her small sedan into the Hummer they took for chasing and then stashed Diane's suitcase in the back. They walked to and from the garage several times, getting all their equipment and setting some of it up so they could do recon while driving to Guymon. Once they double-checked that everything was working, it was nearly eight in the morning.

Violet stretched her back, both palms planted squarely just above her butt as she eased into the move. Diane watched her appreciatively as she turned when another car ambled down the long drive. Violet frowned.

"Who's that?"

"I suppose it'll be our third party."

"Just who exactly did you hire? Do they have any experience chasing?"

Diane didn't have a chance to answer as she stepped closer to the small SUV and pointed to where she wanted the vehicle to park. Violet's heart clenched tightly before it raced, her entire stomach dropping as the short woman stepped out from the driver's side. Her hair perfect gelled and combed, her bright blue eyes holding the mystery of the world in them.

Absolutely not. Diane did not hire *this* woman to join them. Diane walked over, shaking Lando's hand and making small talk, but the rushing wind in Violet's ears from her anger prevented her from hearing anything. Her entire body was frozen on the spot. Utter betrayal coursed through her.

She'd told Diane no. Hell, she'd told Lando there wasn't room for her on the team. What the hell had happened in the interim? Nothing about the way the two of them had interacted for that brief moment in her office made her feel warm and fuzzy from this. It was not going to go well. Diane would lavish all her attention on Lando, and Violet would be tossed aside and forgotten. *How could Diane do this to her?*

Diane brought Lando over, a hand wrapped in Lando's arm as they walked together. Violet glared at the connection. Diane used to touch her like that, used to walk with her like that. Holy hell, this was going to be an absolute disaster. *Where the fuck was Erik?* She needed him back.

"I know you've meet the astute Professor Violet Myers," Diane said, her voice trying to smooth ruffled feathers.

Well, Violet wasn't going to let her have that satisfaction. Crossing her arms, she glared, first at Diane, but then at Lando. Two could play at this game, and Lando was by far the weaker link in this scenario. Violet clenched her jaw tightly. This entire season was going to be a disaster.

"Hey, teach."

A shiver ran along Violet's spine. She loved it when Lando called her that, but still, she couldn't give in to the chaos that rampaged its way through her. She was really mad at Diane, not Lando, and she had to keep that thought strongly in the forefront of her mind. Saying nothing, Violet spun on her toes and walked to the passenger side of the Hummer, sliding into the seat and slamming the door shut. She booted up the computer and let work consume her.

~

Lando had never seen Professor Myers that mad. The glare was enough to burn the sun. Clenching her jaw, Lando tried to figure out just exactly where she had gone wrong, what she could have possibly done to warrant that kind of reaction.

Lando looked to Diane for some kind of assistance, but Diane just bristled and said nothing. *What the hell was going on?* Lando was pretty sure she'd just accidentally ambushed Professor Myers, and it was absolutely clear Diane had not talked to her prior and let her know Lando would be joining them.

Diane told Lando to shove her stuff into the back of the Hummer. Soon enough she was settled into the back seat of the vehicle behind Diane, who was driving. Unfortunately, it gave her the perfect view of Professor Myers—the woman who couldn't hide her anger worth shit. Steam rolled off her in waves as Diane turned the engine and left the driveway.

They were thirty minutes into the drive after stopping for gas and coffee, and Lando wasn't sure how long she could take the silent treatment. The tension in the vehicle was through the roof. She eyed Professor Myers, the stark line of her profile with her chiseled jaw, her wide nose that had clearly been broken a time or two, her thin lips that were pressed so tightly together they nearly disappeared.

"P-professor Myers." Lando tried that at first, hoping to get her attention. Diane shifted slightly in the driver's seat but didn't move or encourage the professor to speak. Lando wondered if perhaps she hadn't been heard. "Professor Myers, I just...I wanted to say that I'm happy to be on the team with you."

The look Professor Myers shifted to her was slow and tedious. As soon as her gaze landed on Lando, it was filled with smoldering hatred. Whatever the hell had changed between them, it had happened swiftly, and Lando wasn't sure she would be able to get back to where they once were. Lando leaned forward in her seat, trying to use whatever charm she had left in stock to win Professor Myers over.

"I'm sorry it was such a sudden decision."

"Don't mind her," Diane butted in. "She's just sore over not getting her way. She'll get over it, and I think you should call her Violet, since we're going to be working so closely together. Professor Myers is so long to say."

Lando didn't tear her gaze from Professor Myers. She wasn't going to do anything Diane said unless Professor Myers approved it.

Professor Myers' scowl deepened. Lando was pretty sure this was supposed to be how it went. Her good luck had immediately turned to bad luck. If she was doomed to live this way for the next six months, so be it, but she needed this internship to get a job in the line of work she wanted. At one time she'd thought Professor Myers would do anything possible to help her with that. But she'd been wrong. Once again, Lando was all on her own.

It wasn't anything she wasn't used to, but she'd hoped, perhaps dreamed, that she'd found a friend in Professor Myers, someone who would stand up for her, be nice to her, someone who cared about her. She could see how she'd been wrong. Still, she should try to be nice. Shouldn't she?

"I'll call her what she wants me to," Lando answered stubbornly. "And until she says otherwise, it'll be Professor Myers. It's a sign of respect, and I do respect her."

Professor Myers' lips twitched. Lando barely caught the move, it was so subtle, but she was glad to see at least that little bit of humanity in her. A sign the woman Lando had come to know over the last few quarters was under a deep layer of anger. Lando could work around that. It might take some digging, but she'd be glad to do it.

"You may call me Violet." Her voice was so smooth, like whiskey on a humid summer night.

Lando had to work hard to hold back her grin. She had seen a crack, and she'd worked it until it opened just a little. She would have to continue in the same vein until she won Violet over again. No matter how long that took. Inwardly, Lando cursed her inner need to please everyone around her. She'd grown up the kid who never had a place in life, and she'd spent the better part of her twenty-three years on the planet trying to find it by pleasing the adults around her.

"Violet, then." Lando turned toward Diane. "Where are we going first?"

"Guymon."

Violet and Diane shared a look, one Lando couldn't read, but it did hold some surprise in it. Lando pulled in to herself. She needed to take a break from the intensity of the conversation, which she had started, but every day couldn't be like this, could it? They'd end up arguing the entire time instead of getting anything done.

Another four hours of silence and another pit stop. Lando climbed out of the back seat, stretching her legs and her back. She would be so thankful for the days when they'd be chasing instead of traveling, so she wouldn't be squished in the back with all the equipment instead of making progress toward their research.

She used the restroom and wandered around the gas station,

trying to find something to snack on. Diane still hadn't talked to her about pay, so she mentally added up how much she had left in her bank account, which was next to nil, and debated if she could purchase the small bag of Twizzlers in her hand or not. If she did, she wasn't sure she'd be able to make her phone payment, and then Aunt T really might kill her.

She must have stared a little too long, because a hand swiped down and grabbed the bag from her. When Lando looked up, Violet raised an eyebrow, her jawline set and her look hard. "It doesn't take a genius to buy food."

She didn't have a quick comeback for that one. Normally Lando had no problem with speaking her mind, but when it came to Violet, she stuttered nearly every time. Violet was her professor, she was supposed to be someone who was kind, gentle, who cared for her students, and yet, outside of the classroom that was not who this woman was. The stark difference was impossible to deal with.

Lando snatched the Twizzlers back and dropped them onto the shelf. Without a word, she stalked out of the gas station and slid into the back seat of the vehicle. Her heart raced the entire time, but she had no idea what to say to either Diane or Violet. This was a disaster. Coming on this trip, this internship, was an absolute disaster. Day one and it was already done.

The front passenger door opened and slammed shut. Lando huddled into the corner of her seat, trying to be as small and inconspicuous as possible. She wasn't sure how well it worked, considering she was the only other one in the vehicle. Violet drew in a deep breath and sighed.

"She didn't tell me she hired *you*."

"I gathered," Lando responded, plastering her hands together.

Violet turned in her seat, her gaze falling onto Lando, and behind the look, Lando swore she saw sympathy and kindness, but it was quickly masked. "I didn't want you on this trip."

"Obviously." Keep her answers short and sweet and she might

make it through six months. Six months seemed so long. Six months with no one on her side. It wouldn't be that much different than back home, but it surely was going to suck. She'd always dreamed of having a team who became her family—especially since she really didn't have one, no one other than Aunt T.

Plastic rustled in the front seat, and Violet pulled out a sandwich from a bag. Lando's stomach rumbled, but she ignored it. She hadn't eaten anything since that morning. She'd packed a few snacks to bring with her, but that was it. Most of the food she'd had at the house, which wasn't much, didn't make for good travel food. She'd rather save her funds for caffeine than sugary snacks.

Violet ate slowly and in absolute silence. It didn't take much longer for Diane to join them, her bubbly facade back in place. She ignored the tense air, and grinned as she sat down. "Only a few more hours and we'll be there."

Neither Lando nor Violet answered.

Diane reached into her own bag, pulling out Twizzlers and a Dr. Pepper. She handed them back, and Lando took them, surprise ringing through her chest. She wondered if Diane had seen the interaction with Violet or if Violet had told her about it. Either way, she was thankful for the treat she wouldn't normally allow herself.

Lando remained as quiet as possible for the rest of the drive, not wanting to poke the bear in the passenger seat. Hopefully tomorrow would be better, when they actually did some chasing and Lando learned the ropes better. She could prove that she was the right woman for the job, even if Violet didn't want her to join the team.

CHAPTER 4

THE SMALL HOTEL only had about ten rooms, and Diane, of course, picked a single room for herself, leaving Violet and Lando to share. Shivers ran up Violet's spine. That had been why Diane wanted them to break down the formalities of the student-teacher relationship. She was going to do this at every place they stayed. Violet knew it.

When it had been Erik, she hadn't minded. They had worked together for years, and he knew she didn't care for men in that way. But with Lando? A woman she didn't want to come on the trip to begin with? Violet was hardly going to sleep the first few nights until the exhaustion from the days seeped in. Even then, the whole situation would undoubtedly get under her skin.

Violet stood outside the main lobby of the hotel, not having dared go inside the room she'd been assigned yet. Lando was already in there, and she stared at the vehicle that had brought them here. Their Hummer stood out like a sore thumb in the entire parking lot, but it normally did wherever they went. There was no doubt to those around that they were storm chasers.

This was her life. This was what she'd always wanted to do since she was a little kid, and she had worked hard to have the financial freedom to do it as often as she did, and particularly for the extra three months that year. Shuddering, Violet gritted her teeth. She would not let some young kid, new to the world of being an adult, ruin that for her. She had to find a way to get over whatever it was she'd felt since discovering Lando was their new team member. The very least she could do was be cordial.

Lando pulled open the back of the Hummer and grabbed her bag, shutting it immediately. She walked with squared shoulders to the door of their room, not even sparing a glance toward Violet. It was going to be a long six months if they didn't find some sort of balance—if Violet didn't. She wasn't so obtuse not to know that she was the cause of all this. Still, she couldn't help herself.

Diane sauntered her direction, her hips swaying side to side in the nice pair of dark blue jeans, a tight t-shirt showing off every aspect of her figure. She was one of those women able to dress up or dress down and still be drop-dead gorgeous. Violet, however, had never been one of those people. Despite her name, she did not look like a beautiful flower.

"You're going to have to ease up on the girl," Diane started, leaning against the wall of the hotel room with her shoulders and not even bothering to look at Violet.

Tensing, Violet gritted her teeth. "You should have told me."

"It was a last minute decision, and there wasn't time to tell you."

"You had all damn morning to tell me. That's not an excuse."

Diane sighed, crossing her arms as she stared toward the two rooms she'd booked for the next week. "You're right, I probably could have slipped it in there in the thirty minutes you were with me this morning, but you still would have been mad about it."

"Would have had more time to digest."

"I don't think you've even begun to digest it. You told me yourself she was your star student. Why would you be so upset that I asked her to join us?"

Violet had to think on that one. She'd known Lando had an internship, that she'd wanted to do some type of chasing while in school and beyond school, and if she'd been on a team with anyone other than Diane, Violet probably would have been perfectly fine about everything. But she really couldn't tell Diane that, could she?

"Look at it this way too, instead of Erik being here, and Lando being a part of the team, that gives us more finances for the trip in the long run. Part of her salary is paid."

Violet couldn't argue money, and Diane knew that. Still, she was sure Lando wouldn't be making any kind of livable salary even with the supplements from the internship. No crew member who was green at the gills did. She couldn't decide what to say first, that Diane was taking advantage of a young student who had her parents' backing financially or if it was a smart decision to allow them more wiggle room for the six months they would be out there. It would be nice if they could purchase some new equipment along the way or even stay in a nicer place for a night or two.

"Violet, what are you thinking?"

"That you're a bitch sometimes."

Diane grinned, her eyes lighting up with humor. Violet shifted her gaze from Diane down toward the room she was going to have to share with Lando for the next week. She was going to be walking on eggshells the entire time, no doubt. Lando was only an added complication to her plans with Diane that season. She'd have to work around their constant flirtations, but she could do that if she wanted. She wasn't going to leave this season without letting Diane know how she really felt. Decades of pining was enough.

"You may be right about that." Diane pushed off the wall, turning so she stood against Violet, pressing her tightly between the hotel and Diane's hot body.

These were the moments Violet longed for. Diane's smile turned salacious. Her hand just above Violet's head, the lean in, the proximity of their breasts, the brush of Diane's breath on her cheeks. Violet suppressed the shudder but only barely.

"You need to give the kid a break."

"Do I?" Violet pushed back. "She's an adult. She can take care of herself."

"She's our new team member." Diane's gaze dropped to Violet's lips. "It's your job to take care of her."

"So you don't have to?"

"Exactly." Diane's grin broadened. "You're so much better at teaching than I am."

Diane patted the wall and stepped away. The heat she'd brought with her remained, and Violet dragged in a breath as she tried to find her balance again. She hated that Diane had the ability to do that to her. She'd always had it, and she'd always used it to her advantage in more ways than one. Diane sashayed a few steps away, sending a look over her shoulder.

"Come on, *teach*. It's your turn."

Growling under her breath, Violet moved off the wall and followed Diane toward the Hummer. They were going to need to make some adjustments to the programming that year, and she could easily get a start on that, perhaps show Lando how to do it so when they were in the field she could do it while Violet helped navigate.

They unloaded their personal items, and Violet helped Diane bring what she needed into her room before daring to turn toward hers. "What are we doing about food for the week?"

"Charge it. I don't have time to figure out low-key meals right now."

Violet scrunched her nose and sent Diane a pointed look. "You didn't figure out meals prior to us leaving?"

Diane shrugged. "There wasn't time."

"Did you plan any of this season?" Diane looked offended, and Violet immediately wanted to backtrack that complaint. She hadn't meant to be so brutal with it. "Sorry."

"Go figure out dinner with your new best friend, and I'll deal with it for the rest of the week. Fair?"

"Fine." Violet crossed her arms, once more looking at the

door and wishing she didn't have to leave Diane's room. It would have made so much more sense for her and Diane to share and to leave Lando on her own, but Diane had never shared in her life.

"Violet, she's not going to bite you."

If only you would, Violet thought before chastising herself. She'd spent far too long pining over someone she considered her best friend from childhood to want to push that boundary tonight when she was in such a tizzy over Lando. Soon, she vowed. Soon Violet would take the next step to find out if Diane really wanted more than mere friendship, and it might be the end to what friendship they had, but she couldn't live in Diane's shadow much longer.

"Go on. I'm hungry." Diane had a whine to her tone, and Violet knew she was being too quiet. Diane didn't do well when she didn't have interaction.

"Fine." Violet grabbed her suitcase and backpack. She raised an eyebrow as she pushed the door open with her butt and took the step down. "But since we're picking, I don't want to hear any complaints if it's not up to your standards."

Diane was about to retort, but Violet turned and let the door slam shut, spinning around and walking face first into Lando. She dropped her backpack, but Lando reached down with amazing reflexes and caught it before it hit the ground. Violet's heart raced as she stared wide-eyed at the backpack and then into Lando's ice blue eyes.

"Uh...thanks." She was damn lucky Lando had managed that. The pack held her laptop, and if that broke, they'd be out a couple thousand to replace it and the time while they waited for it to come in, not to mention transferring all the data and reprogramming everything.

"No problem." Lando straightened her back but held onto the backpack. "I don't know the routine, sorry. What are we doing about food?"

Violet sighed heavily. "Queen magistrate over here has

demanded we figure it out for tonight, which means ordering out or going somewhere. She says she'll figure out meals for the rest of the week, but I have my doubts."

"Okay. Is it..." Lando stuttered. Violet cocked her head, wanting to give Lando the time to finish her question before assuming where it was going. Lando glanced to the ground, not making eye contact. "Is it buy your own? Sorry, Diane didn't have a lot of details for me."

"She never does," Violet murmured. "It usually is, but we'll charge tonight since it's her problem she hasn't dealt with."

Lando nodded. Violet couldn't quite read the look. For a few more seconds, they stood awkwardly together outside Diane's room. Violet curled her toes in her boots. "I'm going to bring this stuff to the room. Did you have anything specific you wanted to eat?"

"No, I'm really game for anything."

"Fine." Violet snatched her backpack from Lando's warm hands. She stepped around Lando's stocky form and toward the room next door. Pushing open the door, she saw Lando had already claimed the bed farthest from the bathroom.

Plopping her stuff on top of the mattress, Violet pulled out the computer and started a quick search of food in the area, even though she already knew what she wanted. There was a little Mexican restaurant they'd ordered from before. Diane would hate it, but if she made the mistake of leaving the food choices in Violet's hands, Violet was going to get food she wanted while she could.

～

Violet sat on the bed, her feet stretched out in front of her as she leaned against the headboard. She'd sent Lando out to fetch the food, and the silence in the room was pure bliss. The television next door echoed, but it wasn't annoying. She knew Diane was watching the news, trying to catch up on the storm since Violet had the main computer they used for tracking.

She was better at it than Diane anyway, so it made more sense. She rubbed circles into her temple. In twenty-four hours her chasing world had been turned upside down. She could not believe that Diane had gone behind her back to hire Lando. Grabbing her cell phone from the nightstand, she dialed Erik, wanting to know what was up with him. Diane hadn't even given her a heads up he wouldn't be joining them.

When it went straight to voicemail, Violet frowned. She left him a message and asked him to call her back, though she didn't expect he would. Tensions had been high during the last season, so she wasn't overly surprised when he hadn't shown up for this one. Working on a team with all women would be equally interesting. It could either go well or be a disaster, though Lando didn't strike her as someone who thrived on drama. Diane, however, was.

Waking up the computer in her lap, Violet pulled up the maps of the area they were in. Weather forecasters had been trying for decades to predict tornados and severe weather storms. They were always looking to improve their skills, their technology, anything so they could predict deadly nature faster and more efficiently. Violet had taken up that call years ago when she was a child, working every moment of her schooling in that specific direction.

The door opening was her sign she wasn't alone anymore. She hadn't realized more than twenty minutes had passed. Lando used her hip to hold the door open as she held the bags of food tightly in her hands.

"Where do you want me to put this?"

"Desk should be fine." Violet stayed still, watching every move Lando made. She'd never been such an observer before. In class she looked for enthusiasm, smarts, if her student was understanding the concept. But they were far outside the classroom in some ways. In others, Lando was stepping right into the center of an in-depth class she had no escape from.

Lando set the bags down and rolled her shoulders. She went to the door, but instead of shutting it, she started to walk out of it.

"Where are you going?" Violet asked, her voice sharp and demanding, far more than she'd intended.

Lando raised an eyebrow, her pale blue eyes searing into Violet's heart. "To get Diane."

"Leave her. She'll just bitch about the food anyway. I'd rather eat in peace for a few minutes before I have to listen to that racket."

"O...kay." Lando shut the door.

The tension in the room rose. Violet said nothing as Lando moved to the food and started unpacking everything she had ordered. She figured they should eat well when they could, since sometimes they'd be out in the field for longer than they slept.

Lando was methodical. She put everything in order on the desk and then grabbed a plate, turning to face Violet with a questioning look on her face. "Are you going to eat or stare at my ass?"

Violet bristled. She had not been staring at Lando's ass. She was about to object but decided last minute it wasn't worth her time. Tearing her gaze from Lando's young face, she stared down at the computer screen which had gone black again from lack of use. Cursing under her breath, she slid it off her thighs and put it on the bed next to her. She could grab some food, and then teach Lando what to look for while she both ate and worked on the programming. It would kill three birds with one stone.

Tearing the plate from Lando's fingers, Violet stacked it with food. She moved back to where she'd been sitting before, and when Lando stood with her plate piled high, Violet gave her a doubtful glance.

"Up here. We can figure this out while we eat. I'd like to get some sleep tonight."

Lando said nothing as she shifted onto the mattress, trying not to spill her overfilled plate.

"Don't get any of that on my bed."

"I won't," Lando muttered.

As soon as she was situated, Violet woke up the computer and took a bite of her fajita. It was exactly what she'd wanted. She hummed in pleasure as the flavors hit her tongue. Taking another bite, Violet scarfed down the food. The mere snacks she'd had on the drive down were not enough to sate this kind of hunger.

"This year we're working on finding three rope tornados that will pull up our equipment so we can follow trajectories with it."

"Three?" Lando raised an eyebrow.

Violet nodded sharply. "That's the hope. In reality, I'll be pleased if we have one. Rope tornados are notoriously hard to catch."

"Because they don't move in a straight line."

"Right."

They seemed to find a rhythm, almost like they'd never left the classroom, although Violet kept her answers shorter and to the point, letting Lando make the conjectures and bridge the gaps between information and learning. They had no issues until Diane knocked on the door.

Lando stood up and opened it, greeting Diane with a large comfortable grin. Violet's stomach sank. Diane eyed Lando like she was a piece of candy she was going to swallow whole if given the opportunity. Unfortunately, Diane would do that. Violet watched every interaction with as much keen observation skills as she'd been taught in school.

Diane's eyes crinkled as she made eye contact. Lando blushed and broke the connection. It was a dance as old as time. Lando clearly had feelings for Diane, even in the short period of time they'd known each other, and they would deepen. Everyone became smitten with Diane, and it never turned out well.

Diane's hand skimmed down Lando's arm, and Violet's

stomach twisted. She wanted that hand on her, not on Lando. The attention Diane would give to anything new that walked into view was absurd. Diane murmured something, but Violet didn't catch it through the raging anger in her ears. Shaking her head, she clicked a little too hard on her laptop to try and change the view of the weather map in front of her.

It looked like there was a small storm on the horizon. Going to Guymon could either be a lucky break or a devastating disaster. Only time would tell. Clenching her jaw, she tried to ignore Lando helping Diane to choose what was best to eat. Seemed the attention lavishing went both ways.

Violet glued her eyes to the screen in front of her, but her ears were attuned to the room. Diane wove stories of chases they had done in the past, glorifying them, making her seem like the hero for every single one. She always did that when she wanted to impress someone. Violet sneered. She would want to sway the young impressionable student to her side because soon enough Lando would figure out the secret. Violet was the brains behind the operation. Diane took care of finances, food, and driving.

While driving was no task to balk at, it certainly wasn't science, and Violet lived in the realm of hard facts and data that could be collected. Diane sat too close to Lando on the opposite bed, their thighs touching. Violet burned.

This was the worst it had ever been for her. Something about deciding to make her move that season must have set it off, because all she wanted to do was stand up, yell at the two of them, and toss Lando out of the room. She was getting all worked up into a tizzy, and over what? A twenty-something kid who had nothing going for her yet?

Violet snorted.

Lando was no competition. She could take on the younger woman any day of the week. She had decades of friendship to back her up. She knew what Diane was like when she was at her worst, and Violet still wanted her.

"Why did you have to get Mexican?" The strong whine in Diane's tone irked her.

Violet shifted her gaze slowly from the computer monitor to Diane's pouty lips. God, she could kiss those lips. Clenching her jaw, Violet hardened her stare. "You told me to order what I wanted. Since that never happens, I did."

"But Mexican? You know it doesn't settle right with me."

Violet shrugged. "Your one day of pain for six months of mine seems like a fair trade."

"What do we normally eat?" Lando chimed in.

Violet could curse. She wanted a fight, an argument, anything to piss Diane off to the point that she'd leave the hotel room. "Whatever she wants."

Diane huffed. "Healthy food."

Violet scowled. That was one way to say it. Expensive was another. Rolling her shoulders, Violet tracked the storm that was hours away. It wouldn't hit until the next day, sometime late morning if her mental calculations were correct. She'd have to double-check that with the computer next, but she'd wait until she had a bit more data to verify.

She lost herself in the numbers as they scrolled across her screen, trying her best to ignore Lando and Diane in the bed next to her. Six months of this was going to push her over the edge. She may just have to move up her timeline on coming clean with Diane about her feelings. As disastrous as that may prove to be, it might be the quickest solution to the problem at hand.

"You should turn in early," Violet commented, accidentally interrupting the conversation they were having. "Looks like a storm is coming in early tomorrow, so we should be ready."

Diane nodded curtly. "Will you talk to Lando about the equipment and what her duties are? I think we should get started with it as soon as possible."

Violet gave her a flat look. As much as she wanted to point out that Diane could equally show Lando what to do, Violet was the only one who could explain why they were doing it. It would be a better educational experience from her, no matter how much she hated to admit it. This was an internship for Lando, and certain criteria needed to be met in order for it to be successful.

"Fine."

"Good." Diane clapped her hands. "Then I'm going to try and get some rest. The two of you should do the same."

Violet grimaced. Diane set her nearly full plate on the desk as she left the room with a wink and a note of good luck to Lando. Again, Violet's stomach twisted. Long night indeed.

CHAPTER 5

VIOLET STANDING over her in the pitch black room was the last thing Lando expected. The hand on Lando's shoulder shaking her was equally odd. Blinking rapidly to clear the sleep from her brain, Lando moved to sit straight upright, Violet shifting to avoid a full head-on collision.

"What's wrong?"

Violet's eyes were wide, but it was too dark for Lando to read them properly. "Storm. Get ready. We're leaving in two."

"Two?" Lando's brain was still trying to catch up.

Violet stepped away from the edge of the bed, stripping right in front of Lando. The creamy smooth skin of her shoulders and bare back enticing. Lando swallowed down that thought hard and flung the blankets over her legs.

"Did you wake up Diane?"

"Yes, Miss Priss is up." Violet dropped her sweats to the ground in favor of a pair of jeans.

Lando had to force herself to drag her gaze away. She grabbed what she hoped was a suitable outfit and stepped into the bathroom, changing as fast as she could. A light brush of her teeth and swipe of deodorant, and she felt mostly ready to tackle her first storm. As she opened the door, Violet stood right on the other side of it with an angry look in her eyes.

"Jesus," Lando muttered. "Give a girl some space."

"There isn't time."

"Whatever." Lando rolled her eyes and found her shoes, shoving her feet into them while Violet did whatever she needed in the bathroom.

Sure enough, in a few minutes they were all piled into the Hummer, Diane driving wherever Violet told her to go. The sun was rising, painting the horizon beautiful hues of red and crimson. They drove for an hour west. Boredom was the only thing Lando could think about. There was nothing for her to do unless they stopped for a storm. Then her job was to get out, grab the odd-shaped little white devices from the cardboard box in the back, and put them exactly where Violet told her to.

She honestly wasn't even sure they needed three people for this, but if Diane wasn't willing to step into the path of an oncoming tornado to get data, she supposed they did. She still couldn't really figure out what Diane did other than drive.

Finally, they approached the storm. The sky was dark, rumbling even though the sun was almost fully over the horizon behind them. Lando had to squint to see where the clouds started and ended. Violet muttered something, but Lando didn't hear it from the back. Instead, she was mystified by the beauty of the night storm where the only thing they could see was lightning as it struck down. Diane powered forward right into the center of it.

"There's already one touching down," Violet nearly shouted.

"Where?" Diane questioned.

"Take the next right. It's going to be hard to see in the dark."

Lando's stomach clenched tightly. This was going to be her moment—when she really became part of the team, when she could do something that would be helpful rather than feel like a total leech.

Violet sounded so confident as they drove through what felt

like fields. It was so dark it was hard to see, nothing other than the headlights and the flashes of lightning to guide them.

"Pull off here." Violet's voice lowered, and Lando barely heard it over the storm outside.

Lando's heart raced, but she grabbed the box and started turning on the small devices so they would connect up with the computer sitting in Violet's lap. They worked without speaking as Diane ignored Violet's plea of where to stop and drove deeper into the heart of the storm. The second device lit up with life. Violet clicked on her computer, cursing as the vehicle jerked sharply and she mistyped.

Lando's shoulder crashed into the door, and it took her a second to get resituated and turn on the third device. They were limited in how many they had. Diane told her no more than five each time. If a tornado took it up, then that was perfect. If not, she didn't want to lose them to other damage if they could avoid it. Focusing on her task, Lando listened as Violet muttered to herself as the devices connected to the computer.

"Stop!" Violet shouted.

Lando froze, her hand hovering over the fifth device. Diane stomped on the brake, the car skidding to a halt in the middle of whatever backwoods road they were on.

"It's just west of us."

The window was dark, and it was so hard to see. Lando squinted, and it took her longer than she wanted to admit to find the funnel, but she couldn't see where it touched down.

"Is it on the ground?" Diane asked, thankfully.

"I don't know," Violet murmured. "Lando, are you ready?"

"Yeah." Grabbing the cardboard box, Lando shifted toward the door of the vehicle. She pushed her way outside, wind whipping across her face. Cold air slapped her, goosebumps rising on her arms and her neck.

Violet rounded the front of the Hummer and took Lando by the elbow. "Do you see it?"

"Not where it's touching down."

Holding her hair back with her hand, Violet surveyed the field before them. It was so dark outside. Night storms were different than any other storm Lando had experienced. She was thrown into the pitch black, unable to confidently make out anything. Rain pelted down, sometimes digging into her skin like sharp little points, it hit so hard.

"I'll help you over the fence."

Violet held onto her arm as they walked, trudging through the small ditch to the wooden and barb-wired fence. Lando's stomach twisted at the thought of trespassing, but she did as she was told, climbing as carefully as she possibly could—although the slice on the back of her forearm told her she hadn't been successful. The box was thrust across the fence line, and she gripped it firmly.

"Go about a hundred feet west, drop the box, and run. It's all up to luck now."

"Right." Lando gritted her teeth as she trotted off to where she thought the tornado might be. Violet stayed put behind her. She'd never felt so alone before. Wind whipped the wheat around her ankles and her knees, and she was glad she'd chosen jeans instead of sweats. They offered far more protection.

Fifty feet seemed like a mile in the middle of a storm before the sun was good and truly up. If she faced east, she could see the light trying to peek through the clouds, but it was so dark, it was next to impossible. The temperature dropped, and the sound of rushing wind filled her ears. She couldn't hear anything else.

Walking another twenty feet, Lando looked around to see if she could find the funnel she'd lost track of, but it was nowhere in sight. She stumbled, her foot catching on a rock or something, she wasn't sure. She only had another thirty feet to go, or so she thought. Lando straightened her shoulders and kept her eyes peeled for the funnel. Her ears hurt so badly from the drop in pressure that if her hands were free she would have reached up to grab them.

The sound got louder. She had to be close. At some point, Lando could hear nothing, not even her own breathing or heartbeat. She dropped the box on the ground and spun on her toes to head to the Hummer, but she couldn't see it. Nothing but darkness surrounded her.

Panic welled in her chest. She screamed out for Violet's name but couldn't even hear her own voice. Stumbling again, Lando stepped forward in the only direction she could think to go. She lost count of how many steps she took, but the roaring eased up a bit. Prying her chin up, Lando looked ahead of her, seeing light in the distance and following its path. She had to be going east, which meant she was going toward the Hummer.

Her ears rang loudly as the rushing noise came back toward her. Cursing, Lando picked up her pace, not wanting to lose sight of the horizon. She was so focused on making sure her feet planted in the right spot, she didn't notice Violet until arms surrounded her and dragged her down to the ground. Violet lay next to her, their bodies pressed tightly together in a small divot in the field. Violet's chest rose and fell sharply. Lando closed her eyes and drew in as deep a breath as possible to calm herself.

She was safe. She was right where she was supposed to be. She'd found her way back to the car. It didn't take much longer for what sounded like a roaring train only inches away to dissipate and move off into the distance. Violet was the first to move, pushing her palm deep into the ground as she sat up and looked around. It was already lighter than it had been when she'd left the Hummer. When Lando looked up into Violet's gaze, disappointment riddled every feature.

"What the hell were you thinking?"

Lando's lips parted, but shock entered her chest, and she couldn't find any words to respond.

"Do you realize how close you were to it?"

She hadn't. Not until then. Not when she'd been walking out into that field. Lando had just been doing what she was told, trying to prove to Violet that she was useful and was there for a reason, that she could be part of the team.

"Do you even value your life?"

That one stung. Lando clenched her jaw tightly, sitting up and staring at Violet with no idea how to defend herself. She should have been far more careful. She shook her head. "I'm sorry."

"Sorry?" Violet's eyes went wide. She stood up, towering over Lando. "Sorry for almost killing yourself? If you want to be useful, be useful, but don't get yourself killed, because that is far more work for us in the long term."

Anger surged in Lando's chest. She would not sit there and be chastised. Climbing to stand, she glared at Violet.

"The least you could have done was get the damn things where they needed to go." Violet pointed to the box still sitting in the middle of the field. "If you're going to die for it, make your life worth something."

Lando's lips parted. Any retort she'd been thinking vanished. She'd never seen Violet be this cruel before. Whatever had happened between the end of the quarter and now, this was not the woman who had taught her for nearly a year. This was someone Lando didn't even like, someone angry, cold.

"And of course you're hurt." Violet lifted Lando's hand, dropping it.

Confused, Lando looked down to blood pouring down her fingers onto the ground below.

"That's going to be a trip to the doctor." Cursing again, Violet turned toward the fence line no more than five feet away. "Expensive as crap."

Swallowing, Lando remained silent and followed Violet toward the fence. Violet stepped through the barbed wires like she had all the experience in the world, and Lando struggled to get over the top one, poking herself several times with the metal. Gritting her teeth, she finally stood on the other side.

Violet tossed a towel at her and wrenched open the car door to find Diane. "It missed. I'm going to go get the box."

Lando missed Diane's response, but Violet glared as she stalked by Lando. "Waste of time and effort. Go home if you're not going to be helpful."

Lando's heart sank. Violet angrily climbed over the fence again, rain still pelting down on her. Staring off at Violet as she walked, anger in every step, Lando shivered. Diane got out of the car, grabbing the towel and wrapping it around Lando's arm.

"She'll cool off in a minute."

"Right," Lando mumbled.

"I'll find the nearest doctor who can look at this."

"It's fine."

"It looks like stitches."

Lando grimaced. First storm and she may already be out for a chunk of the season. She kept her mouth shut but found pity in Diane's gaze as she checked the injury and looked out at Violet as she grabbed the box.

"Next time, don't lose the funnel."

~

Forty-six stitches and so much local anesthetic that Lando could barely feel her hand. Exhaustion hit her as the doctor finished cleaning her wound. Her eyes drooped from the weight of everything. She'd barely spoken to anyone except for the necessities. *Not allergic to latex. Not taking any medications. Don't give me pain killers. No insurance.*

Violet had glared about that one.

With the final directions given—not to get it wet, and that the stitches could come out in twelve to fourteen days—Lando grabbed her bloody towel and stalked out of the small clinical office. Violet stood, leaning against the wall of the small waiting room. Diane sat primly in one of the chairs, her neck bent to look at her phone.

Lando eyed each one of them before stepping toward the front door and pushing her way outside. The rain had let up, but it was still damp and cold. At least it was light enough she could see clearly. The door behind her opened and closed. They rode in silence to the hotel room.

Climbing onto the bed after changing, Lando closed her eyes and released as much tension as she possibly could. Violet was nowhere to be seen, thankfully, and she hoped they wouldn't be going out again that day or even the next day. She could hear mumbling through the wall, but she tried to block out the words until she couldn't.

A door slammed, and Diane and Violet yelled miserably at each other. Lando shuddered, wanting to fall asleep and let the pain in her arm come back full force. She'd been given a prescription for narcotics, but she refused to take them—not to mention she couldn't afford them even if she wanted. The door slammed again and two seconds later the one to her room opened and shut.

Cringing, Lando stayed still and hoped Violet would think she was asleep already. Instead, Violet rounded the bed and turned on the lights as she went, making it incredibly bright inside. Lando tightened her jaw and glared at Violet, who stood two feet in front of her next to the bed with her hands on her hips and a pissed off look on her face.

"I'm sorry."

Lando snorted but said nothing in response.

"I don't even know why I'm apologizing," Violet muttered, turning.

Sitting up sharply and using her good hand to do it, Lando shook her head. "You could try sounding like you're actually sorry if you're going to apologize. If not, save it for someone who gives a shit."

Red tinged Violet's cheeks, her gaze narrowing. "Diane told me to apologize. Said I was being a bitch."

"Well..." Lando sighed. "She's not wrong."

Violet crossed her arms. "Excuse me?"

"You've been a bitch since we left Kansas."

"You shouldn't be here." Violet bent down, getting into Lando's face. "You should be home, attending your third quarter classes, having a normal job."

"What's *that* supposed to mean?" Swinging her legs over the side of the bed, Lando prepared for battle. She wasn't going to let some teacher who knew next to nothing about her dictate what she could and couldn't do. She hadn't even allowed her grandmother to do that.

"It means you're not ready for this kind of work."

"I'm not a fucking kid," Lando shot back. "And frankly, if you weren't such a bitch lately, then maybe we could work together as a team. Diane has no problem with me. So what's yours?"

Violet's lips pressed together.

"You don't even know, do you?" Scoffing, Lando moved to the fridge to grab some of the leftovers from the night before. When she spoke again, her voice was softer, imploring. "What happened, teach?"

Something in her tone must have hit a chord with Violet, because the angry look she seemed to always wear lately had a crack in it. "Nothing happened."

"Sure it did." Lando used her bad arm to hold the Styrofoam container close to her chest as she grabbed a fork and mixed up the leftover fajitas. They had no microwave, so she'd have to eat them cold, but she'd survive. "You've been a total bitch since we left. You know, I used to look up to you, thought you were the bee's knees. Now? I think you're just cold-hearted, lonely, and pathetic."

Violet hissed. Lando kept her chin down as she eyed Violet carefully to see what kind of dent she'd made. Violet didn't seem perturbed by the comment. Shrugging, Lando sat on the edge of the bed and put her food down to make it easier to eat.

The bed moving surprised her. Shifting, Lando looked up to find Violet next to her, a sorrowful look in her eyes. "I am sorry."

"Are you?"

Violet nodded. "You scared me. You were easily within five feet of where it was touching down."

Lando clenched her jaw. She'd known she was close, but she hadn't thought it was that bad. "And still I missed the damn thing."

Violet snorted lightly. "I sent Diane to pick up your pills."

Lando's lips parted. "Oh. I uh...I won't take them."

"You've got to be in pain."

"Tylenol."

"Not going to touch that, I'm sure." Violet's gaze softened even more. "You should take them."

How did Lando explain this without revealing too much information? She could just have Diane give her the bottle and then immediately take it to the dumpster or flush them down the toilet. "Are you going to take the stitches out or are we going to have to find another doctor in two weeks?"

Violet raised an eyebrow, her cool blue eyes wide. "I can do it if you want."

"Good. I'd rather not go back to another white coat."

Violet looked confused, but Lando didn't elaborate. She was glad the tension in the room seemed to have calmed down. She grabbed her fork and took another bite, putting an end to that line of conversation. Violet finally moved, finding her own dinner and pulling the computer over. Instead of sitting on her bed, she sat on Lando's, leaning against the headboard with her legs out in front of her, laptop precariously balanced on her thighs.

Lando eyed her cautiously. It had been an apology, but she still sensed there was something else going on under everything. "You know you haven't just been a bitch today."

"Drop it, Lando," Violet muttered, flicking through something on her computer screen.

Debating whether or not to listen, Lando shifted so she mimicked Violet's position. Her arm was already aching in ways it hadn't before, whether it was because the adrenaline from that morning was wearing off or the anesthetic was, she wasn't sure. It pounded under the gauze the doctor had wrapped it in.

Lando ignored it and continued to shove forkfuls of food between her lips, knowing she'd need it to keep her stomach steady later when the nausea from the pain hit. Especially in the morning. Violet hissed as she stared at her computer screen, forgetting all about the food in front of her. Lando remained quiet, watching the graphs as they flashed across the screen. She caught some of the information in them, but certainly not everything, not without studying them closer.

Violet groaned and tensed. Curious, Lando tried to lean in and see just what had Violet's attention. The door to the room opened, and Diane stepped inside, a pitying expression on her features. Lando's stomach churned. She did not want pity—ever. She'd grown up with pity at every turn, and she was done with it.

"Here." Diane sat on the edge of the bed running her hand up and down Lando's leg. "Does it hurt much?"

Lando clenched her jaw. "Not at all."

"She's lying," Violet murmured.

Diane and Violet shared a look, and Lando cursed her inability to read it. She wished she knew them better, because what she'd known of Violet seemed far off the mark if the last forty-eight hours was anything to go by.

"Does it hurt, Lando?" That pitying tone was back in Diane's voice.

"Not much." Lando ignored the food next to her, hoping they could move on to a different conversation. She focused on the computer still sitting on Violet's lap. "What did you find in the data?"

Violet frowned, eyed Lando carefully, before giving in. "It was a small tornado. You were lucky. Any bigger and both of us probably would have been damaged by it."

That was it, wasn't it? Lando was damaged. She had been since the day she was born, since her mother's death, then her father's. She'd always been damaged goods to everyone. She wished she could take a shower, a bath, anything to get the dirty feel off her, but she also suspected Diane wasn't going to let her get up from the bed any time soon.

"I'll get you some water for your pills." Diane stood.

Lando panicked. She hadn't anticipated they would try to make her take them in front of them. She glanced at Violet who eyed her curiously before she shifted to sit and stand up. She'd take them with her into the bathroom and flush them. Diane popped a bottle of water into Lando's hand and the pills in the other.

"Don't want you to be hurting tomorrow."

"Yeah," Lando muttered. She walked into the bathroom and shut the door. Staring at herself in the mirror, Lando blinked back tears as they threatened to overtake her. What was she supposed to do with herself? She was too much of a mess to be doing this.

The pills in her hand were warm, small, and white. Just like she remembered them being. As if on cue, the pain in her arm radiated into her chest, tightening all her muscles. It took more effort than she dared to admit to turn to the toilet and drop them into the bowl. Hitting the handle, Lando watched them spin down the drain and disappear. She'd have to do that with the rest of them later, when Diane and Violet weren't watching her like a hawk. Drinking the water, Lando squared her shoulders and walked back out to the bedroom.

Diane still had that pitying expression on her face, her lips pouted slightly, her eyes trailing all over Lando's body. Violet couldn't even be bothered to look up. If she wasn't still sitting on Lando's bed, Lando would turn over on her side and go to sleep. The tension in the room was clear as she sat down and tried to look as though she wasn't hurting as much as she was. It was going to be the longest night of her life.

CHAPTER 6

VIOLET STAYED on the bed with Lando until Diane stopped fawning all over the poor girl and left. As soon as Diane was out of the room, Lando seemed to relax and settle. It had taken her another thirty minutes to shift everything to her own bed, and by the time an hour had passed, Lando was asleep. Violet left her alone.

It wasn't every day they experienced a near-death situation before eight in the morning. She was sure Lando was exhausted. Violet reveled in the quiet. Diane sent her a few text messages, but she ignored them as she worked through the data on her computer and followed a few small storms nearby. Unless there was a good one coming, they'd stay in for the rest of the day.

By morning, Violet ached in places she hadn't since the last chasing season. Climbing the fence so quickly to get to Lando and pull her back had not been ideal. Her thighs hurt the most, then her back. Sleeping on a hard-as-rock hotel bed wasn't helping her any either. Groaning, Violet turned onto her back and stretched each one of her muscles as she went. She missed her morning yoga, but there was no space or time for it in the middle of the season.

Sun streamed in from outside, lighting Lando's delicate

features. She was so damn young. Violet had to keep reminding herself of that. Wet around the ears and inexperienced when it came to chasing. She should have gone with her in the first place, made sure she was safe from when she left the vehicle to when she came back. Guilt filled her belly, and she knew she was going to have to make it up to Lando somehow.

Lando groaning caught her attention. Violet shifted, lifting up on her elbow to see her former student rustling in the covers. Curious, Violet got out of the bed and stepped around to the other side. Lando had her face scrunched in pain. Violet's heart raced, and she shook Lando's shoulder slightly.

"Lando, wake up. I'll get you some more pills."

"No." Lando's eyes clenched tightly.

Violet's stomach plummeted. "You need something for the pain."

"Just get me some ice."

Straightening her back, Violet grabbed her jacket and left the room with the ice bucket under her arm. It didn't take long until she was back. She took a plastic bag, shoved ice into it, and tied it tightly. "Sit up."

Lando moved around until she leaned against the headboard, her face paler than it should have been. Violet checked the injury, but from what she could see, it didn't look bad, though it was still wrapped in gauze.

"You need to eat for the antibiotics."

Sighing, Lando grimaced. "In a bit. I don't think I can stomach anything right now."

Violet settled the bag of ice on Lando's forearm, making sure it covered as many of the stitches as possible. "Why won't you take the pain killers?"

"I don't like how they make me feel."

Not for one second did Violet believe that lie. In fact, she believed the opposite was true. "Where's the container?"

"Dresser."

Standing up, Violet found the pill bottle on top of the dresser near the television. She stared at the prescription label. "Do you want me to throw them out?"

Relief flooded Lando's gaze. Without hesitation, Violet left the bedroom again and walked down the row of rooms until she found the dumpster. Lifting the lid, she tossed the bottle inside. She was a horrible teacher. She should have known, should have paid more attention.

Bolstering herself to go back into the room, Violet stared longingly at the door. When had she gone so wrong as to not pay attention to her students? They were the entire purpose of her teaching—the learning, the mentoring. Bile swam in her stomach at the thought she'd missed Lando's struggle with addiction.

As she walked into the room, Violet shut the door. Lando looked better already, though she still seemed rather pale. Pursing her lips, Violet said nothing as she went into the bathroom. After a quick and refreshing shower, she wrapped her hair up in a towel and tied a second one around her breasts.

Without a second thought, she walked into the main bedroom to grab her clothes and stopped short when she found Diane hovering over Lando with food on a plate. They both looked guilty. Violet's stomach twisted again, only this time it wasn't because of guilt or shame. She said nothing as she wrenched open her suitcase lid and grabbed clean clothes.

Disappearing again, she dressed slowly. She was going to have to get used to it. She should have anticipated it really. Diane was always attached to whatever was new and Lando was new. But it meant a deeper conversation with Lando about the drugs wasn't going to happen any time soon. It was probably better in the long run anyway if they didn't talk about it. Violet didn't want to get that invested, not if she could avoid it. If Lando was still her student, that was one thing. She'd be obligated then. Just as coworkers? Violet could maintain her distance.

Diane was feeding Lando. Violet resisted the urge to roll her eyes as she grabbed her computer and sat on the other side of

Lando's bed so she could work and teach at the same time. Lando needed to learn the ropes better so they could avoid more accidents later.

With the maps pulled up, Violet studied them. Lando keep stealing glances at the screen, and Violet could tell she was interested. Diane kept fussing and making a big deal over Lando's injuries, wanting to pull off the gauze and see what it looked like. Lando begged her not to. Violet tried to ignore them until Diane asked the one question Violet hadn't been expecting.

"Did you take your pills?"

"Not yet," Lando said. "I needed to eat first."

Violet's shoulders stiffened, and she risked a glance in Lando's direction. They shared an unspoken look, and Violet made the decision not to divulge what had happened earlier that morning. It was nothing Diane needed to know, and clearly, Lando would be embarrassed by the confession.

"Give it another thirty minutes and let your stomach settle before you take the antibiotics." Diane glared at her. Violet let it slide and focussed on her computer. "When you've got a minute, come look at this. I want your opinion on it."

"Me?" Diane asked.

Violet nearly smirked but held it in. "No, Lando. If you're driving, she needs to understand this to help out."

Diane's jaw clenched hard, and Violet felt as though she'd won an unexpected battle. It took some maneuvering, but Lando was sitting next to her after a minute, their thighs and shoulders touching as she leaned over to see what was on the screen.

"This here. Do you see that?"

"Yeah."

"Pressure is dropping."

"Where?" Diane butted in, coming to Violet's other side and pushing her nose into the computer.

Violet tensed but kept her finger where it needed to be. "Willing to bet there will be a storm."

"That's two hours from here."

Humming her agreement, Violet switched to a temperature map. "Here and here."

"Cold and hot," Lando murmured.

Pleased with her student, Violet held back from showing her pride. The bad grade on the last paper truly had been because of personal issues and not lack of knowledge. Violet stared at the map, watching the temperature lines move and then flash back to where they started. She was well-practiced in reading these after years of studying them. Lando had quite a bit to catch up on, but she was smart enough that Violet was sure it wouldn't take too long to manage.

"I'm betting there will be at least one or two tornados there. A nasty storm at least."

"Are we going?" Lando looked as though she was about to vomit, though Violet recognized the hint of excitement underneath it all.

"No. It's too far for today. You're not up to it."

"I can be."

Diane clucked her tongue. "No, not today. We can take today off."

Anger surged into Lando's countenance. Violet wasn't surprised. She would feel the same way if it were her, had felt that way before.

"We can go if it's important."

"Not as important as you." Diane leaned over Violet and placed a hand on Lando's good arm.

Violet's chest constricted, and she moved just enough to break the contact between them. She couldn't stomach Diane's fake concern. She was only doing it for Violet's benefit, she knew. If it had been Erik who was injured, Diane wouldn't have batted an eye.

Watching the screen with more determination than before, Violet caught sight of another storm coming in. It'd take a day to get to them, but they could wait it out, and that would be the perfect one to take Lando to next. She'd have more time to recover and wouldn't be in as much pain when they did travel.

"Look here," Violet murmured and pointed to the screen.

Lando's eyes lit up like she'd won the prize. "Think it'll hit tomorrow evening?"

"I bet it'll be the next morning, honestly. Look how slow it's moving." Violet shivered as Lando shifted in closer to see the screen better. "See this?"

"Yeah, I see it." Lando's breath was hot on her arm. "It is slow."

"Not sure if it'll kick up anything for us, but it'll be pretty to watch nonetheless."

"Should we head out there?" Diane asked.

"It'll get to us in enough time, I think. I want to see if it's going to gain momentum or lose it."

"What do you think, Lando?"

Lando looked surprised at the direct question. Her gaze flickered from Diane to Violet before she nodded. "I think it's good to wait."

"Then we wait." Diane stood up and walked around the room, picking up things here and there and putting them someplace else. It always irked Violet when she did that. Doing her best to ignore Diane, Violet focused on the maps, teaching Lando more about each one and how to predict the storms better than a regular meteorologist.

∽

Lando sat in the back seat of the vehicle as usual. They'd packed up all their bags and shoved them into the car, moving west into Colorado to follow the eye of the storm that was coming. Her arm still ached, but it was at least manageable so long as she didn't hit it on anything. If they stayed on the highway ,that would be fine.

Violet's profile looked calm, for the first time in a while.

Lando wasn't sure if calling her out had been the right course of action, but ever since the morning after the accident, Violet hadn't made any harsh comments in her direction. She'd also tried to stay as much to herself as possible. Diane, however, had been fussing over her ever since, and it had been nice to have Diane's attention on her, something she missed from being home and surrounded by her family.

Her grandmother would have fussed in much the same way. She relaxed into her seat and was just about to close her eyes when Diane caught her attention. "Where did you grow up, Lando?"

"Oh...just outside of Kansas City. Near the school, actually."

"You've never lived anywhere else?"

Lando swallowed. "When I was very little, I lived in Kansas City."

Violet twisted and looked her up and down. Lando raised an eyebrow back in her direction but let it drop as she leaned over the center console so she could hear Diane better.

"I've never lived outside of Kansas."

"Have you traveled much?"

"No." Lando shivered. She couldn't tell what the questions were about, but it was at least nice to have some normal conversation going. Violet's muscles tightened all through her jaw and down her neck. Lando couldn't fathom why.

"Never traveled, huh? Violet and I used to travel all the time."

Violet shifted a glance to Diane, one full of curiosity and disdain.

"Remember when we went down to Florida to chase that hurricane?"

"Yeah, I do," Violet muttered, anger lacing every word. "Utter failure."

"How did you fail chasing a hurricane?"

Violet was about to speak, but Diane interrupted her. "Vi had to leave right before it hit landfall. Her grandmother had fallen ill, so she went back home instead of staying it out."

Diane looked as though she was pleased to share the story. Violet, however, looked even more angry than before. "She died that week."

"I'm so sorry," Lando offered.

"Don't be," Diane butted in again. "She didn't care much for Vi, anyway."

"How can anyone not care for their own flesh and blood?" Lando's mind spun, although she knew some answers to that. Her own father hadn't loved or cared for her much, but mostly because he'd been addicted to drugs. Violet, however prickly she had been with Lando lately, wasn't someone she could see arbitrarily hating.

"Because Vi's gay."

Lando tensed. She glanced over at Violet, whose jaw was clenching so hard she was probably going to break a tooth. Lando's heart raced. She'd thought it but to have it confirmed was another thing entirely.

"That really isn't for you to share," Lando stated, crossing her arms and cringing the instant she hit her stitches.

Diane shrugged. "It's true. Her grandmother hated her for it, took her out of the will, and left her with nothing."

"That's not something you just share with other people when it isn't yours to share, Diane. If I wanted to tell you that both my parents died when I was little or that my mom was a young mother or that I was an unplanned pregnancy, that's my choice. You just took that choice away from her." Lando surged forward, making sure Diane heard her. "We all have our own stories, and they are ours to share with whom we want when we want."

Diane wrinkled her nose, and Lando's stomach lurched. She couldn't handle someone who would dismiss someone they'd been friends with for years so easily. Violet looked absolutely offended.

"And for the record, I like women, too. So it's not a huge

fucking deal."

Flopping into her seat, Lando shifted so she wouldn't have to talk to Diane anymore. The car was silent until Diane pulled off at a gas station. Reluctantly, Lando got out of the vehicle and trudged inside. She needed to find something to eat so she could take her next antibiotic. The things always made her nauseous no matter what she ate with them, but at least if she ate she was less likely to puke.

She grabbed a bag of pretzels that was under five dollars and went to pay for them. Violet strutted through the store and toward the bathrooms. Diane came right for her. *Great.* Lando paid for her food, and Diane followed her to the car.

"Hey, I need you to pay me back for the pills."

"Oh...sure. How much were they?"

"Just about a hundred dollars."

"Okay. I'll just...go to the ATM then." Lando dropped her pretzels inside the vehicle before she went back inside. It didn't take her long to pull the money out, but seeing the balance dwindle to double digits was not fun. Through the window she could see Violet glaring at Diane as she got into the car. It was going to be a long, fun car ride the rest of the way.

She should have brought headphones. Violet came back into the gas station, flexing her fingers as she walked around looking for something. Lando pocketed her wallet and stayed away as much as she could. She didn't want to be stuck between them any more than the next person, but she had a feeling that was going to be her job for the rest of the drive at least. She never thought being part of storm chasing team was going to come with so much drama. She'd always thought it'd be focused on storms and nothing else. That they would live, breathe, and sleep by storms.

When Violet moved to pay, Lando walked outside and handed Diane the twenty she'd pulled from the machine. Diane took it and slipped it into her pocket like they'd just made a drug deal, which Lando supposed they had. She glowered as she got into the backseat and opened her pretzels to try and get some food in her belly before the antibiotic had to be washed down. God, she hated those things. She wouldn't have gotten them if she'd had a choice, but since Diane had done it without her knowing, she'd take them. And technically, she'd now paid for them, so why not. Violet was the last to get in the car, and Diane pulled out of the gas station and onto the road in no time.

It was nearing nightfall when they stopped, Diane claiming she was too tired to keep driving. Violet hadn't said a damn word to her in hours. Lando wondered when she was going to explode, because she knew without a doubt that it was going to happen. Violet had lost her temper more times than Lando cared to count in the few short days they'd traveled together. It was a side of her old teacher that Lando had never been privy to before.

The hotel arrangements were the same as before. Diane got her own room while Lando had to bunk with Violet. Once again, she gave her the bed closest to the bathroom and with the best view of the television. She got her own ice for her arm and settled in as Violet stared at her computer screen. *What was going on in that head of Violet's?* Lando had never seen someone so withdrawn from general conversation with those around her.

They were stuck together in close quarters for the better part of six months, and if this was going to be Violet for the rest of the time there, it was going to be a struggle. Diane was at least personable. Lando shifted the ice and lifted her gaze, finding Violet awkwardly staring back at her.

"How did you say you met Diane?"

"Grade school," Violet answered, succinctly.

"And you stayed friends?"

Violet shrugged. "Not many options of friends where we grew up."

"Yeah, but you have options now," Lando muttered.

"What do you mean by that?"

Lando grimaced. She'd poked the bear. She hadn't meant to, but she'd done it. Now she was in for it, and there was no way to avoid Violet's wrath. "I never would call someone a friend who outed me without my permission."

"It happens all the time."

"Whatever." Lando shifted onto her back. "When's the storm supposed to hit?"

"Morning."

"Wake me up then." Lando closed her eyes purposefully and drew in a deep breath to relax all her muscles. Diane still hadn't brought up how she was going to be paid, which meant until that happened, her bank account was going to be slim. She'd have to find a way to extend the life of it as best as she could.

Violet ignored her, but the silence in the room was thick with tension. It took Lando an hour before she gave up and went to the bathroom. She craved a shower, anything to make her feel clean. She found a plastic trash bag and the tape, then stared at Violet. This would be so much easier with another pair of hands.

Daring to poke the bear again, Lando made eye contact. "Do you mind helping me?"

"What?"

Lando held up the items. "I want to take a shower."

"Oh." Violet shifted the computer off her lap and moved to the edge of the bed. Instead of sheathing her hand like Lando would have done, Violet wrapped it tightly and then taped all the edges, which gave Lando access to her hand. "That should do it."

"Thanks, teach."

The term of endearment slipped out of her lips before she could stop it. Violet's gaze jerked up until it met Lando's eyes. Lando held the moment, wondering just what trap she'd walked into that time. When Violet said nothing, Lando headed for the bathroom. Violet had gone from one person she'd known in school to a completely different person in the field. It was next to impossible to know who she was going to get next, the woman who was kind-hearted and helpful, the teacher, or the raging bitch on steroids.

CHAPTER 7

THE NEXT MORNING came earlier than Violet had expected. She hadn't been able to sleep well—thoughts of the conversation in the car running through her mind repeatedly. Not just what Diane had revealed about her to Lando, but all that Lando had shared in her own anger. That soft look Lando had given her when she needed help wrapping her arm and then unwrapping it when she smelled clean and fresh.

Violet rubbed her eyes as she stared at the ceiling in the dark room. Lando's deep breathing next to her was a sure indication that she was still asleep. A child by comparison in age perhaps, but Lando had certainly lived in ways a normal twenty-three-year-old hadn't. Turning on her side, Violet watched the gentle rise and fall of Lando's chest as she slept.

What was she supposed to do with the trip? She'd had all these plans for how she was going to confront Diane about her feelings, her long kept feelings, but every time she turned around, Diane hovered over Lando, lavishing attention on her or throwing Violet under the bus. Some days she couldn't figure out why she was so attracted to Diane. Perhaps it was because Diane was her first love, her true love, even if they'd never done anything more than kiss one time.

Violet rustled around and grabbed her computer. She went through some of the raw data they had gotten in the last few days and tried to make sense of it. She could concentrate for a few minutes, but then her mind spun back to Diane or Lando. She had been quite mean to Lando since she'd joined their team. Lando had been right to call her out on that, as much as she didn't want to admit it.

Rubbing her temple, Violet narrowed her gaze at the bright computer screen. She had to focus on something, do something, because she couldn't confront Diane like she wanted to until Diane was awake, which would be a bit. She rolled her shoulders to get back to work but was finding it nearly impossible.

The text came in unexpectedly. She stared at Diane's name for a full thirty seconds before she opened and read it. The call of coffee was too much to ignore, so Violet slid out from the blankets and put her laptop to the side before dressing in silence and slipping out the door as quietly as possible. She found Diane right next to the door to her room, coffee in hand as a peace offering.

Violet took it even if she didn't want to make friendly with her just yet. Violet was still pissed about the day before, the sting of betrayal strong. She took the first sip, noting Diane had at least thought to get her favorite to-go coffee, the expensive, frilly one she barely admitted she liked.

"How's Lando?"

"Sleeping," Violet muttered, waiting for the other shoe to drop and knowing she was going to be the one to drop it.

"Think she'll be up for the storm coming through?"

Violet shrugged. She wasn't going to give Lando a choice, because it wasn't a storm they were going to miss. They just had to find the right place where the tornadoes were going to hit, where they would land and touch down, and then they would be able to move on to the next one. Data was all she sought, and sorting through it, like she'd attempted to do that morning, was where her strengths were.

"She better be. I'm not paying her to sleep her days away," Diane's voice turned cold.

Violet's back went up. With all the fawning, she hadn't expected Diane to speak so harshly. The poor girl had forty-six stitches in her arm, which she'd gotten during an accident while on the job. She expected Diane to be sympathetic. They'd all been hurt at one time or another. Their job wasn't an easy one, not one that was without risk, as much as they attempted to minimize it.

"She'll be ready," Violet answered, knowing she'd be sure to make Lando ready even if she wasn't. She wouldn't let their team flounder or let Diane do an about-face on Lando if she could prevent it.

"When is it supposed to hit?"

"Couple hours. I need to check the mapping and data since it's come in this morning and see where it's at."

"You haven't done that already?"

Violet slid her gaze to Diane, wondering just where the anger was coming from. She was used to this type of tension toward the middle of the season, not so close to the beginning of it. They were usually able to avoid it for longer. "I was a bit busy."

"Doing what? Sleeping in?"

"It's six in the morning, Diane. Give me a break."

"No. We missed our opportunity two days ago. I'm not going to miss another one."

Snorting, Violet tightened her grip on her paper cup. The conversation was rich coming from Diane, who did hardly any of the work in the grand scheme of things. Driving was not something to look down on, but Violet was the one who analyzed, who put things together, who decided where they were going. Diane just rode on her success most days.

"There will be other storms."

"Not always, and not like that one. We were so close."

"And it nearly cost Lando her life." Violet tensed, her need to defend Lando overwhelming.

"That's part of the job." Diane's features hardened as she stared at the parking lot.

Violet sighed. "Is it also part of the job to throw your team under the bus?"

"What are you talking about?"

Her anger hit, and Violet let it lash through her to Diane. "What makes you think it's okay to out me to my student?"

Diane snorted. "That's rich, like Lando didn't already know."

Shaking her head, Violet pushed off the wall. "That's not the point! You don't just tell people I'm gay. You don't tell anyone that."

"There was no harm done." Diane tried to brush it off, but Violet wasn't going to let her have this one. She was still too mad about it, too angry to let it pass. It wasn't the first time Diane had pulled something like this, but this time she'd put Violet's first career in jeopardy. It could cause so many problems for her at work if they knew, if they didn't like it.

"How do you even know that?"

"Because she likes girls."

Violet flung her hand out to the side. "It doesn't matter if students do, Diane. If I get on the wrong side of the dean, I'm screwed. I can't cause any more issues. It was hard enough to take this quarter off as a leave of absence without repercussions. But if they find out about this? What's to say they won't allow me to come back?"

"They'll allow you back."

"You don't know that!" Violet's voice rose until she was nearly screaming, and right outside the bedroom window, where she knew Lando was sleeping only feet away. If she wasn't careful, she would be the reason Lando woke up that morning, again.

"I do know it. And come on, Vi. It might be good for you to get out a little, date someone, get your mind off me."

Violet froze. She shot Diane a dirty look, glaring the whole while. "What do you mean by *that*?"

"I mean I'm not interested in you, and you know that. I

never have been, and I have to break it to you all the time. Why don't you listen? Go find someone else, maybe try out Lando."

"She's my student," Violet hissed.

"So? She's not your student right now. You're not teaching her. She's not taking your class."

"I can't do this." Violet crossed her arms. "You told her I'm gay because you thought she and I should hook up? Is that why you hired her to come along with us?"

"No." Diane shook her head vehemently. "That was just a happy coincidence. We needed a third person for the crew, and she was available."

Violet didn't believe her, not for a second. She'd seen this side of Diane before, although it had been years since. She needed to get out of there before she said something she regretted. Violet walked inside and shut the door, probably a little too loud. Checking to see if Lando was still asleep, she sighed when she saw the woman hadn't moved an inch from when she'd left.

Taking her coffee, she settled on her bed and closed her eyes. She needed a few minutes before she dove into the data, before she tried to forget what Diane had said. Closing her eyes, she held back the tears that threatened to come. Diane could be so cruel sometimes, especially when Violet least expected it.

The first tear that slid down her cheek burned. Violet swiped at it, trying to make it disappear as though it never existed. She hated that Diane had brought her to this again. After so many years she would have thought she'd learned better by then, learned to stop letting Diane have her heart when she so very clearly didn't want it.

The second tear hurt even more. She couldn't believe she was crying. It was stupid. She shouldn't feel this much betrayal over it. It shouldn't hurt this bad. Curling her fingers into her palm until her nails bit at the skin, Violet let the emotions wrack through her, shake her, consume her. She likely wouldn't get another chance just to feel, just to let the world be silent around her when she could allow the hurt to affect her.

After thirty minutes, Violet pulled up her computer, ready to avoid. She skimmed the storm maps, checked the data, and panicked. There was a cell close to where they were, one that looked promising. They had to get there. At least this time it would be daylight.

Sniffling, she jumped out of her bed and moved to Lando first. Diane was ready to go, and Violet had zero desire to even talk to her although she knew she couldn't avoid it. Violet sat on the edge of the mattress, trying to decide how best to wake Lando, except...when she looked at Lando's face, her eyes were wide open.

"Hey," Lando whispered.

Violet's lips twitched. "How's your arm?"

"Fine."

"Don't lie to me."

Lando shrugged, the blanket falling off her shoulder and revealing smooth, creamy skin. "It hurts, but it's manageable."

"Want some ice for the drive?"

"What drive?"

"Storm's in. We need to head out."

Lando sighed, reaching up with her good arm and brushing it over her eyes. "Yeah. I can handle it."

"Good." Violet went to move but stopped when Lando's soft voice reached her ears.

"You going to tell me why you were crying?"

Staring down, Violet's stomach clenched. So Lando had been awake far longer than she'd suspected. Violet wondered if she and Diane had woken her up when they were outside arguing. Steadying herself and taking the time she needed before answering, Violet straightened her back. "No."

"Your choice. Just know if you want, I'm here."

Without another word, Violet stood up and packed up what they'd need for the day.

The storm came more quickly than Violet had anticipated, which was not a good sign. There was something she'd missed in the data when she was analyzing it, and that could easily mean life or death for one or all of them. She skimmed through the reports on her computer screen as she gave Diane directions.

Lando sat in the back, perfectly quiet as she normally had been since the start of the trip. Violet had never seen her be so quiet before. In class, Lando always studiously paid attention to everything, but she asked questions and she instigated conversation and discussion, which she wasn't doing out in the field. It unnerved Violet in a way she hadn't expected. Yet, so far, the entire season had been a bit of a disaster.

Lightning slashed across the sky in front of them as they drove right into it. Rain hadn't hit them yet, and Violet had a feeling that hail would join in the mix soon enough. The air temperatures were calling for it, and that was going to be a hellacious mix. It would be big and heavy and could likely ruin equipment faster than a tornado would.

Violet turned to look over her shoulder at Lando, who sat stoically in her seat. She still looked pale and ashen, but far more "with it" than she had the last couple days. Whether the pain was mitigating or she was moving beyond the initial resurgence of her addiction, Violet wasn't sure, but she was glad to see Lando return closer to normal.

"There's a high moisture content and freezing temperatures."

Lando's gaze locked on Violet's, confusion at first in those pale glass-blue eyes before it turned into recognition. "How big do you think?"

"Not too bad. No more than quarter-sized I'd imagine."

"What are you two going on about?" Diane muttered as she stepped on the gas.

Violet's lips twitched as kept her gaze on Lando, sharing an inside conversation. Diane was never one for details or information. No matter how many times Violet had explained how hail was formed, Diane never paid attention. She was there to drive and take photos if she could. They used to make good money off some of them, but over the years Diane hadn't done as much of it as before.

Violet waited to see if Lando would answer Diane, let her in on the secret. Lando, however, remained silent in the back seat. Frowning, Violet turned forward and flicked through some of her screens, murmuring, "Hail."

"Great. How much damage is that going to do?"

Violet wanted to roll her eyes. They were in the business of damage control, whether it was on the Hummer or in the fields they were accessing. The entire purpose to chasing was to gather information to prevent future damage. It was expected they were going to have some to the vehicle, equipment, and unfortunately people.

Not answering, Violet watched the storm brew on the screen in front of her. This was going to be their perfect opportunity. She could feel it in her bones. Facing Lando again, Violet raised an eyebrow, giddiness working its way into her chest. "Get those ready."

"On it, teach."

She loved it when Lando called her that, when it was welcome and said as an endearment. It was also a good reminder of the once calm relationship the two of them had had, something Violet hoped they could get back to even if it wasn't in the classroom. Lando had been right, her mood had been all over the place since they'd started chasing, and it had nothing to do with Lando and everything to do with Diane.

Diane pulled off the main road, following a dirt road deeper into the fields surrounding them. Violet navigated as best as she could, but at that point, there wasn't anywhere else they could go.

"I see a funnel," Lando stated, her voice growing louder. "Actually, I see two!"

Violet flung around, trying to figure out where Lando was

looking, and sure enough there were three funnels forming. One looked promising. "See it, Diane?"

"On it."

"There's a crossroad about a thousand feet up, take it north."

Diane drove, and Violet tracked the funnels. Excitement grew in the pit of her stomach, and she sensed the same from everyone in the vehicle. They had to push aside whatever animosity was between them to get the job done, and done safely. Then when they finished for the day they could go back to discussing the problems between them, if Violet was up for that. She still wasn't sure she liked what Diane had told her.

Diane turned the car, and they had a full view of the funnels out the front windshield. The sky had an eerie glow to it, lighting up from the storm. Lightning was far off in the distance even though the storm was right on top of them. Thunder boomed through the Hummer, settling in Violet's chest. This was what she lived for. The chase.

They stopped, and Violet shoved her computer onto the front dash as she got out of the vehicle. Diane grabbed her camera, surprisingly, and stepped out as well. Running around to the back, Violet helped Lando with the box of devices they needed at least one tornado to pick up. At least two had touched down, but only one was close enough to matter.

She grabbed Lando's shoulder and hunched down against the wind as it picked up. "I'm going with you."

"I can do it."

"Sure you can." Violet gave her an encouraging smile. "You did just fine last time."

That last comment may have been a bit harsher than necessary, but Violet wanted her point to get across. They shouldn't have sent Lando out by herself the last time, and she wasn't going to do it this time. They were a team, and they worked together, not separate. Her tech wasn't going to tell her much more than her own senses could at that point anyway.

Lando's face hardened when Violet didn't give in. Violet let her carry the box as they walked toward the fence they'd have to jump. Rope tornadoes were notorious for not following their original path and often swung around wildly, which made them far more difficult to catch and collect data on. That was partly why Diane and she had chosen those specific kinds of tornados to focus on.

Violet held the box as Lando hopped the fence, and then handed it over. As soon as they were both on the other side, they jogged toward the one funnel they could see getting close to touching down. Violet's feet were sure as she ran. They weren't that far off.

The first pelt of hail slammed into the dirt only two feet from her. Violet cursed inwardly as she focused on moving closer to the tornado. They had to get as close as possible to it, drop the box, and then run as fast as they could back to the vehicle. Lando kept pace easily enough, and Violet wondered if she was holding back for Violet's sake.

Shaking that thought, she pointed ahead and shouted, "Over there should be good."

A small rise in the ground would hopefully allow the tornado to get close enough. It hit ground about two hundred feet in front of them, kicking up dust and debris. Violet stopped short, debating whether they could make it or not, but Lando kept moving. Picking up her pace as the tornado roared, Violet made sure she didn't let Lando get too far ahead.

Lando dropped the box on the rise and dug her boot into the ground as she pivoted and ran back toward Violet. Taking the cue, Violet turned around and raced toward the Hummer. They needed to put more space between them and the tornado. The hail started immediately, pelting Violet on the head, arms, and shoulders as she moved. Risking a glance at Lando to check on her, Violet stumbled.

Lando caught her arm and helped her to stand just as the floodgates opened and the hail pounded around them ruthlessly. Violet hunched her shoulders, but there was no way to hide from it. They helped each other back to the fence, Diane already inside the Hummer as they climbed in.

Violet spun around to try and make out where the tornado was. She put a hand over her eyes, her back against the side of the Hummer to try and protect some of her body as she gazed out into the field around her. She couldn't see anything except the hail. Hands on her arms dragged her over and then backward into the vehicle. She reached out and slammed the car door shut to protect herself from the hail that seemed to be growing in size.

"Are you all right?" Lando's voice was laced with worry as she practically had to yell to be heard over the hail on the metal vehicle.

Violet sat up, pushing some things off the edge of the seat as she realized she was in the back, sitting next to Lando who had wide, fearful eyes. "I'm fine."

"I didn't know because you didn't get in."

"I wanted to see the tornado."

Lando sighed, but she didn't have to say anything. Diane butted in. "How could you see anything in that mess?"

"I couldn't, unfortunately. Give me the computer so I can track it so we're not right in the line of fire."

"It's not going to move this beast."

Violet clenched her jaw, and when Diane didn't hand her the computer, she reached over the seat and took it. She flipped the lid open and found the tornado on her radar maps. Violet whispered, "It got them."

She looked at Lando first, then Diane.

Shouting, Violet's excitement rose. "It got them! It picked them up!"

Lando grinned, the smile blooming on her lips beautiful, and bigger than any Violet had seen on her. She stared at the computer as data filled her screen, telling her exactly where the tornado was as their devices swirled around in the vortex of air.

Lando leaned over, her eyes glued to the screen, seeing the same information as Violet.

The tornado moved away from them, but Diane didn't take the car toward it. She didn't have to now that they could track it in real time. Lando pointed at the screen, to a secondary funnel they had been following that touched down briefly and then left. Violet vibrated with excitement. Diane was on the phone, calling in the storm, tornado, and hail sizes to local meteorologists so they could get the warning out, but Violet ignored her.

Her shoulder brushed against Lando as she stared at her screen, glancing outside every once in a while to see if she could find the storm through the hail. When it started to let up, Violet moved outside, still finding hail hitting her although far less frequently. Lando joined her as they stared at the trail of destruction through the field in front of them. Lando grabbed her cellphone and snapped a picture of the now white field and long trail of dark dirt where the tornado had taken the hail back up with it.

If Violet had a real camera, she could make some definite money off that photo. Diane was still inside on the phone. Lando showed Violet the picture she'd taken. "I can't believe it."

"Believe it, Lando." Violet grinned, happiness bubbling inside her. "We just had our first break of the season."

"That was awesome."

Violet chuckled, wrapping her arm around Lando's shoulder in a congratulatory side hug. "It was, and you know what, it's damn addicting."

They shared another long smile as they stared out at the field. This was what Violet lived for—the storm, the chase, and everything in between. This was what she wanted to be doing every season. And the best part was she couldn't stop smiling.

CHAPTER 8

THE CHATTER in the Hummer all the way to their small hotel was filled with excitement. Lando wasn't sure she'd ever seen Violet smile that much, riding the adrenaline high. But as soon as Violet and Lando walked into the hotel room, aches started in her head and shoulders.

Violet spun around grinning broadly, her eyes still wide with that excitement. "That was amazing."

"It was," Lando answered as she stepped in closer to Violet, trying to ease into that same excitement again, but her body was telling her to sit down. She'd probably done too much after her injury. Still, it had been worth it. Anything was worth it to see Violet as happy as she was.

Violet pulled her wet shirt off and dropped it onto the floor near her suitcase. Reaching behind her, she went to flip the clasp of her bra, but Lando tensed. "Teach!"

"What?" Violet spun around, the beige bra still firmly in place, something Lando was thankful for.

Walking toward Violet, Lando hesitantly reached out and ran her fingers along Violet's shoulders and upper back. Small dots littered her skin. Some of them were red and pink, but others were already darkening into what Lando could only suspect were bruises. Littered among them was a smattering of freckles she tried to ignore.

"What's wrong?" Violet asked, turning her neck to look over her shoulder at where Lando stood.

"You're covered in bruises."

"Oh, yeah, from the hail. You probably are too. Here." Violet reached for the edge of Lando's shirt and tugged it upward.

Lando firmly put her hand on Violet's and jerked her shirt down. Being half-naked in front of Violet Myers was not something Lando was ever going to do. She could inspect herself in the bathroom with the mirror. She stepped around toward Violet's back so there was less opportunity for undressing to happen.

"You bruise so easily," Lando whispered, focused on the small dots littering Violet's skin.

"It's all part of the job." Violet shrugged, her tone dropping and the bubbling energy from it dimming to a deep simmer. Violet turned around, killing Lando's plan to keep some space between them. Even the top of Violet's chest was littered with the impacts from the hail. "I have some cream that will help them if you want it."

"I'm not sure I'll bruise like you do." Lando had to work harder than she'd expected to raise her gaze from Violet's collar bones to her face, but she got stuck staring at Violet's lips. They were thin, but slightly parted. Lando stood far too close for comfort and backed away, making a point to look into Violet's curious gaze. "I should go check it out and change."

"Probably. Don't need you sick on top of stitches."

"Right. I should probably make sure those are still dry too."

Violet hummed, and Lando took another step backward. She finally twisted on her toes and faced her bag, grabbing a fresh pair of clothes before hiding out in the bathroom. Taking her shirt off revealed the same pattern across her skin, although she was correct, she was not bruising like Violet was. It had been a good thing they'd gotten out of the hailstorm and into the safety of the vehicle as quickly as they had.

The gauze around her arm was wet, so Lando slowly started unwrapping it. She'd have to find some more so she could keep it clean and dry, especially with the work they did. She was halfway through getting dressed when there was a knock on the door.

"Lando?"

"Yeah?"

"Got a second."

"I'm not dressed."

Violet snorted lightly. "Let me in so I can check your arm."

Lando clenched her jaw. "I need more gauze."

"I thought as much. I have some."

In a rush, Lando pulled her shirt over her head and buttoned her pants before unlocking and opening the door. Violet shut it behind her and sat on the edge of the bathtub, an eyebrow raised. Lando sat next to her and held her arm out for Violet's inspection.

"Diane went to get something to celebrate."

"That'll be nice," Lando murmured, Violet's fingers warm against her skin.

"It's alcohol. I wasn't sure...what do you want me to tell her?" Violet's hands stopped, and she made eye contact.

Lando's stomach swam. She hadn't had alcohol in years, but her problems largely hadn't been with it. She wouldn't imbibe, for certain, but that didn't mean she couldn't be around it. "It'll be fine."

Violet's look softened. "Lando, I want you to be comfortable in your own room. Tell me what to do and I can make it happen. If you don't want it here, we can drink in her room."

That would leave Lando all by herself, and she was trying to make a good impression on her team. She wanted to win them over, prove that she could do the job and that she was part of this close-knit family. However, she hadn't grown up with Diane and Violet, so she'd likely never have the relationship they did.

"It's fine, really," Lando murmured. "I won't drink, but I can be around it."

"Are you sure?"

Nodding, Lando said nothing else as she waited for Violet to start in again with her arm. The tension in the small bathroom was palpable, but it wasn't because of how close they sat or even the fact that Violet hadn't stopped touching her. Lando had taken great care not to be in situations where she would be tempted and yet twice in the last week she was already put in those positions. She'd resisted, easily enough, but it would only get harder as the days continued.

"Take some Tylenol, will you?"

"Yeah," Lando answered, absentmindedly.

"Good." Violet patted Lando's thigh tenderly and then lifted her arm to inspect the stitches. "Well, since we took the gauze off, this looks pretty good. No infection."

"I'm on antibiotics."

"Still." Violet's eyes crinkled in the corners as she gave a small quirk of her lips. "I'm glad it's looking good. I was worried."

"Were you?" Enough shock registered in the pit of Lando's belly to get her attention. She'd thought Violet had been far more annoyed with the injury than concerned, but to find that thread of concern was nice. It warmed her.

"I was. I always worry about my favorite students. And frankly, after what you shared the other day, I'm far more worried."

"Don't be," Lando brushed it off. She didn't have time or desire for pity.

Violet wrapped Lando's arm tenderly, making sure the gauze wasn't too tight or too loose. When she was done, she grabbed Lando's hand and gave it a squeeze. "When you didn't ask for an extension because of your grandmother's death, Lando, I didn't think too much of it. You're strong and independent. That didn't surprise me. But am I wrong in assuming that after your parents died your grandmother was the one who raised you?"

Lando could have cursed if they weren't having such a quiet moment. She always forgot how observant Violet was sometimes, how she could connect the dots. How anyone could, really. "Yes."

"So her death was more like the death of a parent." It was a statement, not a question.

Lando didn't dare look into Violet's eyes, already feeling the threat of tears. It had not been long enough for her to process that loss in her life fully, although in some ways she doubted she ever would.

"Lando." Pity laced the word, and Violet reached up, cupping Lando's cheek and turning her chin up so they stared at each other. "You should have told me."

"No." Lando stayed perfectly still. "It wasn't any of your business."

"Grief isn't something to be kept inside. It's something to share. Let me take on some of that load with you."

She wanted to. That was the worst part of it all. Lando wanted to let Violet do that for her, wanted to reach around and find comfort in her arms, but she hesitated. This soft side of Violet was something she'd only ever suspected was there, but she'd focused for so long on the professional side, on the distance between them, and in the recent days that was far easier to do.

"My Nan raised me, yes. My mom died in a car accident when I was about two years old. It was a head-on collision, and my car seat was thrown from the vehicle when it happened."

"Oh my gosh, were you all right?"

"I was fine. Car seat safety!" Lando raised her eyebrows, trying to play it off, but it didn't sound jovial in retrospect. "Anyway, Nan raised me from then on. My dad died when I was eight of an overdose, but he wasn't fit to care for me at any point."

"Jesus, Lando."

"It's just my life. It's how I've grown up, so it's normal to me."

"That is a start full of trauma." Violet's gaze softened, and her fingers curled around Lando's. "And your aversion to drugs and alcohol isn't just because of your father, right?"

"It's not." Lando's cheeks heated with embarrassment. She hadn't admitted that to anyone in a long time. She'd been sober for two years, since she started at the community college, since she'd started getting her life back on track. Aunt T had been essential in that turnaround for her.

"You said you were born in Kansas City?"

"Yeah, Kansas side. My mom didn't want to be too far from home." Lando rolled her eyes, glad for the easier part of the conversation.

"You were two?"

"Well, I was nineteen months. We had just moved to a new apartment, actually. She was supposed to start school in the city, so she'd gotten an apartment—"

"Over by Pittsburg University," Violet finished for her.

Lando's stomach dropped, and she had no idea what to ask. Violet drew in a breath, stared at the ceiling, and let it out slowly.

"Never would have figured that one out."

"Figured what out?" Lando asked. "How did you know where we lived?"

"I was your neighbor."

"What?" Lando wanted to stand up. She wanted to step away, catch the breath that seemed to be sucked from her lungs. She stared at Violet as if her eyes had been opened, as if the woman sitting next to her was not the woman she'd grown to know in the last year.

Violet shifted and stretched her back. "I'd just moved in. In fact, you moved in the same day I did. I just...Heather. I never knew your last name, and you don't go by Heather. Damn it, I should have figured it out sooner than now."

"Figured what out?" Panic welled in Lando's chest, but she had no idea why.

"That day..." Violet trailed off. "We'd only been living there five weeks at the time. That day, you left before me. Lots of times we left at the same time, but I went to Pittsburg and your mom went to the community college. She had a longer drive, and that day, I don't know. She left before me. You left before me."

"What are you saying?" Lando's voice wavered.

"Lando, the day your mom died, the accident, I found you. The paramedics and police were all over that scene, but they didn't have you and didn't even know you were in the car. I knew she had you with her, she always did. You were never out of her line of sight. When I came up on the accident, it was only a few blocks from the apartment, and I saw you in your car seat. I found you." Tears streamed down Violet's cheeks. "I found you."

"How did you...what are you saying?"

"I'm saying that I knew your mom. We weren't good friends, but we were neighborly. I didn't know her very long, and we were both caught up in school. She was a few years older than me I think, and I found you." Violet sighed. "I can't believe you're *that* Heather. I never thought I'd see you again, let alone have you as my student. I just... I never..."

"You found me." Lando clenched her jaw. "Did you read the obituary?"

"It just had your first name in it. I always assumed it was to protect your privacy, and I didn't go to the funeral. It was out of town, and I had classes, and like I said—I didn't know your mom all that well. We moved in the same day, and any time I renewed my lease while I lived there, all I could think about was her."

"You knew my mom." Lando's voice dropped at the end of the statement. "You probably knew her better than I did."

"Never." Violet's hand was back on Lando's thigh. "Never, Lando. You never left her sight. She always had you with her. She loved you."

Tears stung Lando's eyes, grief washing through her. She'd

never known her mother, not in a way she could remember, but this woman, this teacher, sitting next to her had. She had that connection, the very real memories of someone Lando had longed to meet for years. "What was she like?"

Violet's lips parted, but she stopped when the front door to the hotel room opened. Diane's voice filtered through to them, joyous and a stark contrast to the mood in the bathroom. Violet squeezed Lando's knee and brushed her own cheeks. "I'll deal with her and give you a minute."

Without another word, Violet left the small bathroom, shutting the door behind her. Lando was cast into the isolation of the room, the spinning emotions in her chest. It didn't mean anything. Violet was young at the time, her own mother had been young. It was just some weird coincidence. Diane's voice was shrill as she happily chattered in the other room.

"Where's Lando? I want to celebrate!" Her tones were muted thanks to the door, but it was the stark reminder Lando needed that she had to get up and function.

"She's just wrapping her arm up with some new gauze." Violet's voice was a welcoming comfort, calm and confident, and Lando clung to it.

Standing, Lando leaned over the counter and stared at herself in the mirror. Her eyes were red from crying, her cheeks puffy, but overall she didn't look too bad. Turning on the cold water, she splashed it on her face to try and get rid of any signs of what had happened only moments prior. As soon as her face was dry, she squared her shoulders and stepped out into the main area.

Diane looked excited, and Lando couldn't help echoing her grin. Despite what had just happened, it had been a good day. They'd managed to do exactly what they'd gone out there to do. Diane wrapped an arm around Lando's shoulders, tugging her in for a side hug.

"There you are!"

"Here I am," Lando answered.

"How's the arm? It didn't get too wet, did it?"

"It did, but it's fine." Lando brushed it off, her gaze drawing immediately to Violet who had an open bottle of beer at her lips. They shared a look, one full of words neither dared to say. Lando nodded ever so slightly so Violet would know she was fine or that she would be shortly.

"Good! Because I have plans for us." Diane grinned, drinking a long swig from her beer. "First, let's get you a drink."

"Oh, no thanks." Lando shook her head. "I really shouldn't with the pain killers and antibiotics. I think I have enough in my system for now."

"Are you sure?"

"Yeah, I'm sure." Lando stayed right next to Diane, not that she had a chance to move.

"Good." Diane tugged Lando in tightly. "Aren't you glad I hired her, Vi?"

Violet's face revealed nothing, and Lando wished briefly she was able to control her features that well. Resting bitch face did have some advantages, but she was never someone who could manage that. She was so easily read.

"I am." Violet's voice was smooth, gentle, but also sincere. Which Lando had not expected. Ever since she'd been hired on, Violet had been a point of contention, and Lando hadn't been sure they'd ever get over that. It seemed they'd made some progress at least. Lando said nothing as she stayed plastered against Diane's side.

"Excellent." Diane finished her drink, letting go of Lando so she could grab another one.

Lando took advantage and moved to sit on the edge of her bed, relaxing at having some distance between her and other people. She grabbed the water she'd left on the nightstand and took a long sip from that. She'd have to find some way to talk to Diane about getting paid soon, hoping it would happen sooner rather than later. At least she didn't have to worry about a roof over her head, but food was another issue entirely.

"We're going to Kansas," Diane announced as she twisted off the cap of another beer.

"What?" Violet's eyes widened. "We should stay here."

"We're moving in the morning."

"We just caught a tornado," Violet argued, her tone rising with the tension. "We should stay here, try to catch another one or two before we move. How are we ever supposed to catch storms if we keep moving every few days?"

Diane's jaw set. "I told you, we're going to Kansas in the morning. I found the cutest little place we can stay."

"Diane, this is not a good idea," Violet tried again. "There's another storm coming in two days and we can try to catch that one, but they're going to start hitting us daily, and if we keep moving, we're going to miss them."

"I'm the one who decides where we go, Vi."

"No, we decide as a team." Violet shifted her gaze to Lando briefly before sliding it back to Diane. "And we need to talk about this. You can't keep running us from state to state. You're not even following the maps."

"That's your job," Diane fired back.

Lando's chest constricted. She hated listening to bickering like this. She'd caused her fair share of arguments, but listening to others fight always set her on edge. With the last hour in her mind, she knew she was already close to hitting the line when she'd need to escape if she could. Even if it was just for a quick walk outside.

"It is my job," Violet stated. "And I'm telling you, we'd do well to stay here for at least another week before contemplating moving. We can drive for hours in any direction and still hit storms."

"We're moving." Diane put her foot down.

"This is ridiculous." Violet set her drink down on the dresser. "We should not be moving right now."

Diane said nothing but drank her beer as if there was no argument to be made. Which, Lando supposed, if she kept this up, there wasn't. Violet had made excellent points, but Diane hadn't even seemed to pay attention to them. Lando agreed with everything Violet had said, although she wasn't about to voice her opinion. The beef between the two of them was above her pay grade, and she did not have enough of a head on her to begin to formulate an argument.

"Diane."

"This isn't up for debate. We're moving out in the morning."

Violet growled and roughly grabbed her beer, though she didn't drink from it. In fact, she hadn't taken more than a single sip of the alcohol from Lando's recollection. Violet glared at Diane before stalking over to Lando and sitting next to her on the bed. Anger came off her in waves, and Lando wondered what was going to happen next. They'd gone from a celebratory mood to animosity in seconds, and she still couldn't figure out why Violet let Diane make all the decisions like that. Yes, she'd argued back, but Violet could have insisted. There was raw data that could prove it would be useful to stay put.

"What do you think, Lando?" Diane asked, putting her right in the middle of what she was attempting to avoid.

"Oh." Lando swallowed hard, her fingers tightening around the plastic water bottle. "I'm not really sure I have an opinion."

She shared a look with Violet, recognition sliding across Violet's face, as if Lando had also conceded to the fact there was no point in arguing with Diane because she would win no matter what. Lando wasn't entirely convinced of that, but if Violet felt she had an ally for a few seconds, Lando would let it slide without explaining.

"Want to look at some of the data?" Lando asked Violet, hoping to change the conversation so it was less tension riddled.

"Sure. I'll even sit with you in the back on the drive tomorrow and we can go through some more of it."

Diane nearly choked, and Violet's look to her was pure revenge. Lando watched each of them as they stared across the room at each other before Violet got up, leaving her drink on the edge of the dresser and coming back with the computer. They leaned against the headboard as Violet pulled up the schematics and maps Lando had come to realize were her constant companions.

Lando shifted as Diane sat next to her, a hand on Lando's upper thigh. Violet's gaze flickered to it before she focused on the computer. The three of them put their heads together as they looked at the maps. Lando wasn't sure how much Diane understood of them, but at least she knew Violet was well-versed in everything going on. Lando had a lot to learn, which she was willing to do, but she needed the practical experience to do that. Learning in the classroom was only good to a certain point. After that, she needed field experience.

Violet pointed some things out, but Lando was only half paying attention as she was stuck between the two of them. Her mind was elsewhere, flitting from the conversation in the bathroom, the morning chase, to Diane's hand still warm on her leg. She couldn't figure out where she stood with either of them except that oftentimes she found herself in the middle. It was not a place Lando readily wanted to be.

Diane eventually got up and grabbed a third beer, but Violet never went back to touch her first one. After a few hours, the tension dissipated enough that Lando felt comfortable shifting closer to Violet, the entire side of her body pressed against Violet's. Diane was then able to sit more fully on the bed, although she remained very quiet as Violet continued to explain. Lando could so easily fall asleep to Violet talking. The day, the emotional upheavals, the highs and lows had taken their toll, and all she wanted to do was crash. She managed to stay awake until Diane left, well into the night.

When the door clicked shut, the last of the tension Violet had been holding in her shoulders rolled off her and vanished. Lando dropped her head to Violet's shoulder, unable to keep her eyes open any longer. She sighed but didn't know how to ask Violet to get out of her bed so she could go to sleep. Luckily,

Violet shut the lid on her computer and rubbed the bridge of her nose.

"Get some sleep, Lando. We have an early morning."

Lando grunted her agreement but still couldn't pry her eyes open or convince her body to move so that Violet could leave. Instead, she asked, "Why do you let her walk all over you like that?"

Violet hummed and then sighed. Moving, she eased out of the bed and settled the laptop on the dresser. With the leftover beer bottles, she walked toward the bathroom. "That is a story for another day."

Listening to the sound of beer flowing down the drain, Lando smiled to herself. She shifted down on the mattress and promptly fell asleep.

CHAPTER 9

DIANE TOOK the last turn sharp, and Violet smacked her head against the window, jerking awake. Violet had nodded off toward the end of the drive, the rocking motion of the vehicle lulling her into sleep. She'd sat in the back with Lando, going through some of the data and trying to determine just how far they were going to have to drive for storms in the upcoming weeks since Diane finally conceded and promised they would stay put for a while. They just had to move to Kansas first.

Lando had been a perfect student the entire time. However, after a night of no sleep, Violet hadn't been able to keep her eyes open any longer. All night she'd been plagued with thoughts of Laura and her baby, Heather. The car scene when she'd arrived had been awful—broken pieces of the vehicle strewn about the roadway, smoke billowing from the other car, but Laura's had been smashed in the front. Instinctively, Violet had known she hadn't survived that. She'd held Heather tightly as they transferred Laura to a gurney, kept her near her until the social worker had come and taken her.

Violet had never seen her again. Not until a year ago, and she hadn't even known it was the same kid—woman, she corrected. Lando was a woman. She wasn't baby Heather anymore, but a woman who had survived countless traumas and addictions and still seemed to have her head on straight. Violet admired her for that.

The last turn up the road revealed a beautiful whitewashed house. It was two stories, with a red barn just below it on a decently steep hill. Violet sat up a little straighter, blinking the sleep from her eyes. This wasn't any normal place they typically stayed. Her stomach churned at the thought of how much this was going to cost and what kind of dent it would put in their budget.

Diane was usually fiscally responsible, but this couldn't be within their range. Worry welled in her chest, swirling the closer they got. She kept her mouth shut because she didn't want to fight in front of Lando again, as much as she wanted to smartly ask Diane what the hell she was thinking.

Two wooden posts lined the side of the road as they moved in closer, the house coming into better view. The sign over top read *Indigo Ranch & Bed and Breakfast* in beautifully carved scrawl. This was far higher class than Violet was used to, and if she was going to spend the nights at a place like this, she wanted to be able to relax there, not run out at all hours of the day and night to chase storms.

"This place looks nice," Lando mumbled next to her, her sky-blue eyes wide as she stared at the same sight Violet did.

Violet didn't answer, not sure what to say that wouldn't come out as an angry retort. It was a nice-looking house, and she imagined the inside was just as beautiful.

"Elijah Wilson runs the place. She's a rancher, but she said we could have two rooms since she had the space."

Again, Violet didn't answer. Every thought running through her brain wanted to become an argument, but what Lando had asked her last night kept sticking out in her mind. *She didn't let Diane walk all over her, did she?* She did put up a fight each time before giving in. Maybe she really was just a giant pushover with an attitude.

Diane slowed as they reached the front of the house, the well-kept wraparound porch. Violet clenched her fists tightly as they stopped, and Diane rustled around up front. She glanced over at Lando, making eye contact before she opened her door and got out. The air had a bite to it, and the wind brushed against her cheeks and moved her hair. She was used to the wind by that point, enjoyed it because it told her the earth was alive, but today it seemed cold.

They grabbed their bags from the back, Violet leaning into the back seat at the last minute to pull out her laptop. A handsomely beautiful woman stepped out of the front door, shooing an ancient looking dog off the front mat as she went. Her hair was in two long braids down the sides of her head, her plaid cotton shirt tucked sharply into her jeans, and her feet were oddly void of shoes and clad only in socks.

"Come on in," she said with a smile and a wave. "I'm glad you were able to make it in such good time."

Diane marched right up to her, holding out her hand. "I am, too. I think we could use the rest."

Violet clenched her jaw.

"I'm Diane, this is Violet, and Lando is our newest team member."

The woman's eyes landed on each of them before focusing back on Diane. "I'm Eli, please. I'll show you the rooms and then let you do whatever you want. Dinner is set for six, and you're welcome to join or not. I know with your schedule that it'll be hit or miss and without warning when you do make it to meals."

They followed Eli inside, Violet remaining quiet as they stepped through the den. The kitchen was gorgeous, a dream, honestly. Violet was impressed with the eight gas burners, double ovens, and huge fridge. Though, she supposed, if Eli was cooking for people she would need to have all the niceties to survive that.

People lounged in the den near the fireplace but didn't seem to pay them too much mind. Violet made a mental note that they'd have to keep the noise level down, especially if they were leaving in the middle of the night, so as not to wake the other guests.

As they went up the stairs in the center of the house, Violet tightened her grip on her bag. This place had to be way outside their budget, and she still couldn't fathom what Diane had been thinking. The first door off the side opened to a small bedroom with a queen bed inside. Diane walked through it and sat on the edge, apparently claiming that room as hers.

Violet spared a glance to Lando and followed Eli to the room next door, which mimicked the one Diane had perfectly, except for the color scheme. One lone queen bed sat in the center of the room. Violet cringed as she waited with bated breath for Eli to mention something about a third room.

"This is the other room that was booked," Eli stated.

Great. Violet clenched her jaw, her molars grinding as she stared at the sole bed. At least it wasn't a twin.

"I'll let you all get settled, but my home is now your home. So feel free to do whatever you want. I just ask that you stay out of the basement. I keep that to myself."

"Makes perfect sense," Lando said, a slight teasing tone to her voice, and Violet was glad for it.

She wasn't sure she could form words at that point. Eli's retreating footsteps down the hall and then down the stairs echoed loudly in her ears. *What the hell was she supposed to do with this?* She stood stock still just inside the doorway as Lando moved around her, picking her side of the bed and giving the mattress a little bounce with her ass to test it out.

Violet wanted to cry. This had to be some sort of punishment for pushing back at Diane all week. It had to be. There was no other explanation for it. Eventually she managed to force her feet to move, setting her bag by the far wall.

"This place is fancy," Lando commented.

"I suppose," Violet murmured, grabbing her computer and opening the lid. She could dive into work and ignore what she didn't want to see with the best of them. That was until night hit and she had to sleep next to Lando, someone she didn't realize she was so connected to.

Maps filtered over her screen, and it took Violet a second to orient herself on them, figuring out where they were in the relative approximation of the map. She leaned against the headboard as was her habit and scrolled through the different mapping structures. It didn't look as though there was a storm in sight. A few hints of promising bad weather here and there but nothing that looked as though they could get out and go.

It seemed as though she was going to be stuck there.

Violet ignored the fact that Diane was in the room next door, that she could hear her rustling around before she went down the stairs, her heavy boots loud on the stairs. There wasn't much of a barrier between the rooms there, meaning they would have to be quiet when racing out to chase. Violet's head hurt. The ache in the back of her neck and into her shoulders came tenfold, and she was going to have to do something about it to avoid it getting worse.

When she looked up, Lando was gone. *When had that happened?* Violet let out a breath, relaxing into the pillows and closing her eyes, tears stinging. She didn't know why she was close to crying. Nothing big had happened in the last few hours that would set her off, but she knew, without a doubt, that this was one of Diane's underhanded fuck-yous. Violet had ticked her off, and this was the punishment for it.

Finally coaxing her body to move, Violet rummaged through her bag for the container of Tylenol and popped a few between her lips, dry-swallowing them. She settled the computer on Lando's side of the bed, not that there was much room to do that anyway. Lying on her side, she stared at the computer screen and watched as the mapping moved in a short prediction before flashing back to where it started.

Why had she thought she could spend six months with Diane? She never remembered what it was really like, and then even three months of her were difficult. They did much better when they weren't in each other's constant presence. But Violet never remembered that. She always wanted them to be able to be best of friends, like when they were younger, when they were kids, before...before Diane had found out Violet liked girls.

Groaning, Violet closed her eyes and rested against the very comfortable bed. It had been ages since she'd allowed herself to take a nap, but with the headache quickly turning into a migraine, she relaxed her muscles and allowed sleep to pull her under its wing.

∼

Lando left Violet moping on the bed. Honestly, that scared her more than angry-Violet did. Something had come over Violet since they'd left Colorado, and Lando wasn't sure she liked it. Really it had started after the argument with Diane in the room the night before. Violet seemed defeated.

Making her way down the stairs, Lando remained in awe of the house. It was easily one of the fanciest places she had ever stayed in her life. It wasn't some ritzy hotel, but the house was beautiful. Deep rich wood floors, homey yet fancy decor. Lando had no idea how to describe it, but when she was done renovating her house, this was what she wanted it to look like. The kitchen was Nan's dream, honestly. Nothing compared to what they'd planned to do, but an absolute dream.

The people downstairs must have been from one family. There were six of them total, and Lando had no doubt they took up the rest of the rooms in the house. While she didn't mind sharing a room with Violet, sharing a bed was a different ask altogether. She wouldn't lie to herself and say she hadn't thought about Violet in a certain way, but she'd always reined herself in. Sharing a bed with someone she looked up to as a mentor would easily get awkward fast, even if they didn't do anything and Lando kept the feelings and thoughts she'd once had to herself.

Lando avoided the family, wanting the quiet instead of boisterous noise. She wasn't used to being constantly surrounded by people, and while living with Diane and Violet for the week hadn't been awful, it was going to push her limits soon enough. Lando pulled on her jacket and stepped outside onto the front deck. She could see for what felt like miles, though she knew it wasn't that far. The house backed up into a hill, with trees surrounding it to block some of the wind as was normal in that part of Kansas. She'd studied it at one point in one of her classes.

The old dog hadn't moved from where Eli had coaxed him. Squatting, Lando put her hand out so he could smell her. He didn't even raise his head as he took a good whiff of her scent. Chuckling, Lando smiled at him.

"I think you're a big old teddy bear of a dog."

"He is."

Lando jerked with a start at Eli's voice. "Sorry! I didn't realize you were out here. I hope you don't mind."

Eli shook her head and put her free hand out. The other held a coffee mug. "Max is the old man of the farm. He's my weatherman, actually. It's not a bad storm unless he begs to come inside."

"And do you let him?" Lando straightened her back and stood up, eyeing Eli up and down.

"When it's snowy, yes, or below freezing."

"So he likes to be outside."

"Every day." Eli's eyes crinkled at the corners. "You're Lando, right?"

"Yeah. It's a nickname." Lando had no idea why she was explaining this to a perfect stranger except that most people seemed confused by her name.

"I figured as much." Eli rolled her shoulders and turned to stare out at the farm. "Are you from Kansas?"

"Yeah, but the other side. I've driven out here a few times with my Nan when I was younger on some trips, but it's been a long time since I've been to this part of the state. We usually headed east since it's closer."

Eli's lips pressed tightly together. "Most people think western Kansas is Wichita or heaven forbid, Topeka."

Lando laughed, the light noise bubbling up. It felt good to talk to Eli, relaxing in ways being with Diane and Violet wasn't. "Yeah, I used to think that too. Curse of having two drastically different sides of a state, I think."

"Exactly. I've lived here my entire life. Born and raised here."

"Oh yeah?" Lando stepped around the now-sleeping Max and leaned against the railing of the porch. "I bet you see some good storms from here."

"I do. Diane explained you three were storm chasers."

Lando nodded. "It's my first season. I'm not sure they're too impressed with me yet."

"Why's that?"

Sighing, Lando straightened up and pulled up her sleeve to show off her injury. "First storm, forty-six stitches. Barbed wire is not my friend."

"Dang!" Eli set her mug on the railing and took a closer look. "That looks like it hurt."

Lando shrugged, not giving an answer. She didn't want to or feel the need to. "Do people come here to take photos much? There's a perfect view of the landscape from here."

Eli grinned. "Actually, they do. I get a lot of weddings booked in the summer for that very reason. My girlfriend had her last photos taken out here for her next album or something with PR. I don't really understand all that stuff as much as I try to, but the photographers that came out seemed more than pleased with the natural landscape."

"Girlfriend?" Lando's stomach clenched.

Eli nodded and picked up her mug again. "Yeah. We've been together about two years now, and every day is a new lesson with her. We have very different lives."

"Does she not live here, then?"

"She does when she's not on tour, but that's at least half the year, easily. And she does press stuff outside of that."

"Forgive me for asking, but what does she do?" Lando's brow furrowed.

"Sadie Bade."

"You're shitting me." Lando's eyes widened. "She's like the gold star lesbian of music."

Eli chuckled. "I think she'd like that you said that."

"Are you serious right now?"

"I am." Eli drew in a sharp breath. "But she's on tour right now, so I'm not sure you'll see her for the week that you'll be here."

"Week?"

Eli's brow furrowed as she glanced at Lando. "Diane booked you two rooms for the week, yes."

"That's good to know, I guess." Lando rolled her shoulders and tried to brush off that bit of news. Diane, it seemed, did not share her plans with the world often. Communication was clearly not in her wheelhouse. "Do you have a camera at all? I just have my phone to take photos on for now, but I'd love to get a real camera one of these days."

"My sister used to play with photography. I think her old camera might be around here somewhere, but it wasn't something I ever got into."

"I took this awesome one of the tornado the other day." Lando whipped out her ancient phone and pulled up the photo. She leaned over to show Eli, so proud that she'd managed to capture it. It would have been better with a camera that had higher resolution, but for what she had, it was good.

"That is amazing." Eli stared at the photo and then handed it back. "You know, hold on. I'll be right back."

Eli left her coffee mug on the railing and walked inside. Lando relaxed and breathed in the clean air. It felt so good to be outside in nature, as much as she could be. She could see other houses here and there if she squinted to look in the distance, but no one was near them. It felt isolated but in a good way.

When the door snicked open again, Max rustled his head. Eli

came back to where she'd stood before and handed the camera over to Lando. "Take it."

"What do you mean?"

"I mean it's been sitting in a box in my office for the last seven years, and I have not touched it once except to move it. Get some use out of it."

"This is an expensive camera." Lando stared at the sleek black Nikon in her hands. It was an older model, but a DSLR all the same. She'd played with them when she had time and energy to borrow one from the college, but always had to return them before she was ready.

"It's not as expensive as you think, but seriously, it should be used."

"You're giving me a camera that is easily a thousand dollars."

"Was maybe six or seven hundred," Eli countered. "Now it's probably only worth a couple hundred bucks. I'm dating Sadie Bade, trust me, if I want a new camera, I can get one."

Dumbfounded didn't begin to cover what Lando felt. She'd never been given something this nice before, not from someone who was practically a stranger. "What if I just use it while we're here, and then I'll give it back."

"Sure, if that makes you feel better, but trust me when I say you're the only one who's used it in seven years. Even when my sister comes to visit she doesn't use it."

"I don't know what to say."

Eli chuckled lightly as she took another sip of her coffee. "I believe *thank you* would suffice."

"Thank you!" Lando's eyes lit up, her fingers curling around the camera. Having a real camera to use would be amazing. It'd give her something to do, and even though Diane was the one designated to take photos, Lando could as well on the side. Maybe she could practice before the next storm. "Really, thank you."

"Don't think about it. Seriously. Go take some pictures. I've got to get started on dinner."

"I can help you."

"Are you sure?"

"Absolutely." Lando followed Eli inside, and they spent the next hour prepping dinner for all the guests.

As they slid the food into the oven to cook, Lando stared at the camera again. Eli laughed, picked it up, and shoved it into Lando's chest. "Go take some damn pictures already. You're driving me crazy with your excitement."

"All right, all right." Laughing, Lando walked out the back door of the house and stared around the landscape. Surprisingly, the camera still had battery life. She messed with some of the settings, changing it from automatic to manual and adjusting the aperture and shutter speed. Lando took a few test shots of the barn, working on focus. That was something she always struggled with, getting whatever she wanted into focus quickly enough to get the photo she wanted.

Lando spent thirty minutes just figuring out the settings. It had been at least an entire quarter since she'd found the time to check out a camera, and she wasn't used to this particular model. Walking around the house and following the path down to the barn, Lando took photos of random things she could find, focusing mainly on some landscapes.

When she figured dinner would be ready, she turned to walk back toward the house but stopped short. Violet stood on the porch, leaning over the edge of it with her hands folded in front of her. She didn't have a jacket on, and her hair blew around her face in the breeze, her features set. She must have been somewhere else in her mind, thinking and distracted by something.

Without thinking, Lando raised the camera and snapped a picture. She changed the settings, diminishing the light and making it darker when she took the next photo, adding to the mood she thought matched Violet's. In the time they'd spent together, Lando had done nothing but try to decipher what Violet was thinking in any given moment, but she'd never managed to do it. While she was loud when she argued, she rarely revealed her true thoughts on anything.

Lando traipsed up to the house, but instead of going straight inside through the back door, she walked around the porch and caught another picture of Violet leaning over the railing, a perfect profile of the side of her face that Lando had come to know very well in the last week. She held the camera down to her side, debated whether or not to talk to Violet, but opted not to. They would have time that night if needed, when they were sleeping in the same damn bed as each other. Lando nearly groaned out loud at the thought. If this was some kind of punishment from Diane, Lando was going to have to work to get back on her good side.

The house smelled wonderful with the dinner they'd made. Eli was already working on setting the table, so Lando set the camera down and washed her hands before jumping in to help. She could at the very least earn her keep in a place like this. It might be above the bar of anywhere she'd ever stayed before, and she wasn't going to burn bridges where she'd barely even built any yet. She and Eli worked happily together, setting the table and pulling out the food. The other guests filtered in, but there was still no sign of Diane or Violet. Shrugging, they began eating without either of them.

CHAPTER 10

THEY MADE it through the first night, though Violet barely slept. She'd withdrawn, and it was difficult to get out of moments like that for her. Lando shifted in the bed as Violet leaned over to grab her laptop after a long debate over how she would make less noise—working right from the bed or getting up and rustling around.

She had the laptop open and started up her maps. She barely had the programs up and running when Lando shifted again. Violet glanced down, Lando's cheek brushing against the pillow as her breathing became shallow and her eyelids fluttered. So much for keeping quiet. Violet moving on the bed must have woken her, although Lando hadn't come to bed until late into the night.

"I'm sorry if I woke you," Violet murmured, keeping her voice low. The sun wasn't even over the horizon yet, and frankly, most people would consider it still the middle of the night.

Lando cringed but opened her eyes and stared up at Violet. "What time is it?"

Violet glanced at the clock on her phone. "Just after four."

"Fuck," Lando groaned out. "Why are you awake so early?"

Violet chuckled lightly and rested into the pillow behind her back. "I've always been a morning person."

"Really? Or could you just not sleep?"

Sighing, Violet clenched her fists, then her jaw. Leave it to Lando to dive right to the point. Risking another glance down at her student, Violet let the words slip from her mouth that she wasn't sure she'd ever shared before. "I'm not used to sleeping in the same bed as someone else."

"Oh." Lando barely moved, her leg straightening out to where it brushed against Violet's under the covers. "To be fair, I'm not either."

Violet gave her a wry smile. "I mean, it's been a few years since I lived with anyone, in that capacity. It's hard to make that adjustment."

"Well, if you prefer, I can ask Eli if there's somewhere else I can sleep."

Shaking her head, Violet reached out and grabbed Lando's hand. "No. Don't worry about that. I'll figure it out."

Lando sat up in the bed, brushing her fingers through her short dark hair until it stuck up in all different directions. "So… the teacher does have a life outside the classroom."

Violet's cheeks flushed hot. "Yes, just like I suspect you do as well."

"Not much of one." Lando grinned. "Least not anymore since becoming sober. My life is a lot less dramatic now."

Violet didn't know what to say to that. She stared into Lando's cool blue eyes and saw the seriousness under the teasing tone. She couldn't imagine what Lando's life had been like growing up, or the struggles she'd endured so young, but she was proud Lando had seemed to find her feet so far.

"Sometimes the calm is nice," Violet finally commented. "After my ex left me, it was much more peaceful."

"And you got to hog the whole bed."

Snorting, Violet smiled. "Sure, the whole bed, and all the covers."

"Living the dream right there, teach."

Violet paused. The nickname had seemed to turn into something else. No longer did it give them the separation they'd first had, but now it seemed almost a term of endearment with a much deeper quality to it. Especially with Lando's warm body pressed so close to hers. Pushing the stray thought from her mind, Violet glanced at the computer screen that had fallen asleep.

She moved the mouse to wake it up and concentrated on the maps in front of her. Even a little storm would be a welcome sight, but all the storms she found were where they'd left in Colorado. Annoyance with Diane's insistence filtered through her chest and into her belly again. She was going to have to get over that. While Lando had managed to pull her out of herself for a few minutes, the tug to withdraw again was strong.

"Did you sleep at all?" Lando asked as she leaned over Violet's shoulder to see the screen.

"Not really," murmuring Violet, flipped to a map that was closer to where they were in western Kansas. "I can't figure out why Diane brought us here."

Lando didn't answer but pointed at the computer. "Is that a storm?"

Violet's brow furrowed, and she narrowed her gaze to see exactly what Lando was pointing at. "A small one."

"Doesn't look like much activity."

"No, but it's probably the closest we'll get to anything today. The skies are clear for hundreds of miles." The storm did look like it promised to at least give them some lightning. Perhaps they'd be able to get some photos they could sell if Diane let her have control of the camera for a bit. That'd be a new battle to fight if they went out. Better yet, perhaps Diane would stay behind and Violet could go by herself.

"Are we going to go?" Lando's breath was warm on Violet's shoulder. If anyone else had walked in at the moment, surely they would have thought something else was going on. Violet had been getting far closer to Lando in the last few days than she normally would have allowed herself. She and Erik had been close, but not like this. Something simmered under the surface between her and Lando that Violet couldn't put her finger on. It had always been there, a kind of energy she enjoyed. She'd always just thought it was Lando's enthusiasm for learning, but being out of the classroom, she wasn't so sure it was that anymore.

"If you want, we can. It won't be worth much of anything."

"Experience," Lando answered. "Everything is worth the experience."

"Sure. It looks like it'll be swinging our direction in the next few hours."

"I can ask Eli where a good place is to go see it, some place with high ground so we can get a good view before it hits."

Violet was surprised. She hadn't expected Lando to think of something like that. "That's a good idea."

"Since there's no sign of tornados we don't need the low ground."

"True." Violet kept her gaze trained on the computer in front of her. "Let's give Diane another hour of sleep before we wake her. She's not very friendly in the mornings."

"I'm not usually either, but I guess waking up to storms first thing changes my mood."

"I love morning storms." Violet's tone sounded so dreamy. She wasn't even sure it was her speaking, but Lando's echoing grin was answer enough.

"I'm getting dressed. Eli said she gets up early, and I want to catch her before she goes out into the fields."

"You and she seem to have gotten close."

"Sure." Lando slid to the edge of the bed, her legs hanging over the side of the mattress as she turned and looked at Violet over her shoulder. "She's cool."

"Cool?" Violet raised an eyebrow. "Are you sure there isn't something else going on there?"

"I'm sure." Lando winked. "Eli's dating a girl already."

"Well then." Violet clamped her mouth shut.

"They've been together two years, I think she said. She's dating Sadie Bade."

"Am I supposed to know who that is?"

Lando's eyes widened as she dropped her clothes for the day on the bed. "Are you joking with me right now?"

"I don't joke often."

"You don't know who Sadie Bade is?"

"Can't say I do." Violet pressed her lips together, sure she was about to get a lesson of her own.

"She's a musician, but she's also one very out and proud lesbian. She's kind of the voice for a lot of our people."

Violet bristled, though she tried to hide it from Lando. Luckily, Lando grabbed her clothes and was already walking toward the door.

"I'll be right back."

Relaxing as soon as she was alone, Violet brushed her fingers over her eyes. She was going to have to get used to being in such close quarters as someone else. That was the biggest adjustment she was having to make that week.

In under two hours, they were all packed into the Hummer, driving toward the tiny little storm Lando had discovered. Violet had opted to sit in the back and let Lando have the front, since it was her storm they were driving to. She tuned out most of what they were saying, but Diane's tone grated on her nerves. She was overly flirtatious, again.

Eli had directed them to an area with a cliff facing west where they'd be able to watch the storm come in. Violet was somewhat giddy for it. Rarely did she have a storm she could observe without thinking about data or wind speeds or air pressures.

"I loved that photo you took the other day." Diane's voice was dripping with...something. It set Violet on edge. She'd heard this tone from Diane so many times, and it irked her every time.

Annoying her to the point where she'd boil over with anger. Diane knew it, too, that was the worst part.

"Thanks," Lando answered. "It wasn't anything fancy. I only had my phone."

"We should get you a good camera. Would you like that?"

"That'd be nice, but I thought you were in charge of taking photos."

Diane giggled. "I am, but that's when we're going out to a real storm. This isn't a storm."

Violet clenched her jaw, grinding her molars. Every storm was a real storm, and while this one might not have as much danger to it than others, it could still be dangerous. Glancing through the side window, she caught sight of the clouds rolling in from the west. Lightning visibly struck the earth below it. It wasn't overly bright in the mid-morning light, but they could still see it well enough because those clouds were dark.

Her heart raced at the thought of just enjoying a storm for what it was: power, strength, nature at its finest tantrum. Violet was lost in the thunderous clouds off in the distance.

"A storm is a storm, Diane. And I'm just as excited for this one as I was the last one," Lando stated confidently. Lando's defense of her little storm brought a smile to her lips.

She'd said the same thing to Diane before. Sometimes Violet wondered if Diane even liked storms or what she was even in it for. Some days Violet wondered if she should find her own team. Then she'd think about going chasing without Diane's insane organizational skills and nix that idea. She wanted to be with her best friend, with the woman she loved. That was the entire purpose of that season, to tell Diane how she felt, to finally come out with it. Though that had sort of happened for her, but she still wanted to try and get the words out herself.

Diane pulled up at the cliff, and they were all out of the Hummer in seconds. Diane had the camera in her hands, and she took a few pictures before handing it to Lando. They huddled close together, their foreheads down toward the back of the camera as Diane taught Lando something about it. Violet tried to block it out, the age-old ache in the pit of her belly starting up again.

She hated when Diane did this, when she threw herself at other people. She tried to play off being the nicest most helpful person in the world, and sometimes she was. Violet wouldn't deny that, but most of the time there was something for her underneath it all. Violet had forgotten that the last few years when they'd been out with Erik. He'd grown wise to Diane's personality and didn't feed into it anymore. Lando, however, was fresh meat.

Violet scuffed her foot against the ground, shoving her hands into the pockets of her jacket as she stood at the edge of the cliff. The sky was gorgeous. It darkened slowly, the sunlight unable to penetrate the clouds. Violet's heart raced with the thoughts of what the storm would bring. Perhaps they would get hail with it, though she doubted it would be much.

She'd left the computer in the vehicle, the one thing that could tell her what to expect. Instead, she opted to just feel. Diane's giggle disturbed her peace. Violet threw a look over her shoulder at them still huddled together and taking photos.

"That looks good! Try quickening the shutter speed."

"All right." Lando did as she was told, making adjustments on the camera before snapping another photo.

Violet had no idea what the shutter speed was set at, but she wouldn't have lowered it much. It would make the photos dark and hard to see. It would take a lot of manipulation to bring it back to life. She preferred less manipulation and more natural photos as possible. But that wasn't her expertise on the team any longer.

Lando took a few more photos while Violet stared at the storm. Lightning struck down again, and she waited patiently for the thunder to blast her full on. It would echo from where they stood, filling the empty spaces in the air and consuming them for a few seconds before dissipating.

She lost herself in the moment, in the storm, in the nature surrounding her. Violet must have missed when Lando stood next to her, but Diane's camera was gone from her hands, and there was another one between her fingers.

"Where did you get that?" Violet asked.

"Eli gave it to me. She said it was her sister's, but she hadn't used it in years."

Violet raised an eyebrow. "That was sweet of her. Are you sure she's dating someone?"

Lando chuckled lowly. "I am. She was just being nice. But I'm not super familiar with this camera. The ones at the school are Canon."

"They're not all that different." Violet kept her hands in her jacket, wanting to help but also wanting Lando to figure it out on her own. She hadn't specifically asked for help, so Violet kept to herself for now.

"You say that, but then all my pictures turn out like crap. It's better on my phone."

"Phones have some amazing technology these days."

Diane gasped. "Did you see that?"

Violet twisted and faced the oncoming storm. She'd missed whatever was so exciting, and Diane didn't seem as though she wanted to elaborate. Biting her tongue, Violet kept her silence. She was withdrawing again, and while it might do her well in one way, it wouldn't do her well in the long run.

Three bolts of lightning struck down, the clouds rolling as they came closer. Lando hissed and tried to snap a photo, but she wasn't quick enough. Violet understood that. It had taken her months to perfect long-exposure shots, and if Diane had her making the shutter speed faster, there was no way Lando was prepared for that.

"Hold on."

Violet stepped around Lando and back to the Hummer. She pulled open the back and searched for the tripod she knew they had stored there. Walking to Lando, Violet was already setting it up. She planted it on the ground and held her hand out for Lando's camera. With a curious look, Lando handed it over. Violet took it, screwed it on the holder, and then plopped it onto the tripod.

"If you want to capture lightning, the best way is through long-exposure."

Lando shuffled in next to her, but Diane scooted in between them and pushed Violet to the side. Lando flickered her gaze between the two of them, an eyebrow raised, before she listened fully to what Diane was saying.

"You want to make it at least thirty seconds, but you can go longer. The hardest part is getting the focus and making sure that the camera doesn't move." Diane took Lando's hand and brought it up to the camera and then encouraged Lando to lean down and look through the lens. Diane's hand rested at the small of Lando's back.

Violet stepped away again, holding as much of the anger inside as she could. Diane was being ridiculous, but so was Lando in allowing it to happen. Yes, she might be curious about the camera, but Violet could just as easily teach her, and she'd been ready to do it.

She managed to make it through the twenty minutes of Diane and Lando chattering away about whatever. She tried to tune them out as much as she possibly could, but the constant flirting grated on her nerves. By the time they got back in the car, Violet was done with it all. They'd wasted a day traveling to Kansas, a day on a storm that would net them nothing, and all for what? To miss the large storm cells moving across the eastern part of Colorado? She still didn't know why Diane had dragged them there.

It was mid-afternoon by the time they got back to *Indigo*, and Violet stalked out to the back porch without a word to either Diane or Lando. In the silence, she stayed outside as the weather finally hit the bed and breakfast, the large raindrops pinging on the tin roof of the porch. The sound comforted her, the scent of fresh wet dirt soothed her soul.

She had to stop whatever feeling was rushing through her. She needed to find her balance again, tell Diane how she felt and be done with it. Either Diane was going to change her tune or she was going to turn Violet down. Again. But Violet had decided before the season even began that this would be her last chance, and she'd never actually said the words.

She ate dinner mostly in silence, trying to ignore Diane and Lando as they flirted away, Eli as she shifted nervous glances in her direction, and her own jealousy gurgling deep in her belly. She couldn't do this anymore. Something was going to give. As soon as she finished, she headed up the stairs to her room.

She hoped against hope that neither Lando nor Diane followed her. She didn't want to burst in front of the other guests, in front of their host. Snorting, Violet realized immediately why they were there—a buffer. Diane had wanted someone who would keep Violet in line, and who better than a stranger. Lando hadn't done it when they were in Oklahoma or in Colorado, but strangers certainly could.

Violet sat heavily on the edge of the bed and covered her face with her hands. She was absolutely pathetic. Years of storm chasing with her best friend, with the woman she was so hung up on, had gotten her nowhere. The door snicked open, surprising her.

Lando slipped into the room, closing the door behind her and locking it. She leaned against the frame, her hands behind her back, the lines of her body loose as she stared Violet down. "What's going on, teach?"

Violet could have whimpered. There was that endearment again. "Nothing."

"I don't believe you." Lando narrowed her gaze before pushing off the doorframe and coming toward Violet. She sat next to her on the bed. "Talk to me. Seriously. Because you look like something is eating away at you."

Violet couldn't help the obnoxious snort as it left her lips. "It's way above your pay grade."

Lando's lips parted before she shut them quickly. Violet knew she was pushing buttons on purpose, but she couldn't stop herself, even if she wanted to. She wanted a fight. She wanted to make her point.

"You shouldn't be doing anything with *her*."

"With who?" Lando looked absolutely confused.

"Diane." Violet hissed out the name as though it were a curse. "We all work together, we're all in very tight spaces together, and you think it's a good idea to get in bed with her? It's idiotic."

Lando's jaw dropped. "What are you even talking about?"

"It's inappropriate." Violet moved so she wasn't sitting as close to Lando, the unbidden image of Lando springing to mind —pressed against her that morning as they looked at maps, in Colorado when she'd fallen asleep on Violet's shoulder, in the bathroom when she'd look so lost when Violet shared their long connection to each other. She was just as guilty, but she wasn't about to admit that.

"Violet," Lando's voice softened, and she reached out a hand to Violet's thigh.

Standing sharply, Violet moved out of Lando's reach. "It is. You shouldn't be doing it."

"I'm not doing anything."

"Sure you are. I watched it all day. The two of you flirting up a storm."

Lando crossed her arms, giving Violet a hard stare. "What are you going on about? She was flirting. I was not."

Violet huffed. "Sure. If that's all you want to admit to."

"Violet." Lando's brow furrowed. "Why exactly would it bother you?"

"I don't want this team to fail because of your libido."

"My libido?" Anger flashed across Lando's face. "My...that's rich coming from you. For the record, Violet, I am not sleeping with Diane, nor do I want to. You, on the other hand...what exactly is your obsession with her?"

"What the hell are you talking about?" Violet curled her fingers tightly until her nails bit her skin.

"You and Diane. All you do is fight and argue. You, mainly. Any time she talks to me or gives me attention, you flip out. You either get absolutely quiet or you flip out like you're doing now. What is it with you and her? Are you two dating or broken up? Oh God, she's not the one who broke up with you, is she?"

Violet shook her head, the truth coming out before she could figure out how to even answer. She didn't know what to say. They weren't dating. They never had. But that didn't mean they hadn't ever done anything.

"What is it with you two?" Lando asked again.

"Just stop being inappropriate with her."

Lando snorted and rolled her eyes. "Right. I'll put that at the top of my to-do list."

Violet deflated. What was she even doing? At every turn she was picking an argument with someone. Lando just happened to be in the line of fire that night. She went to apologize, but Lando had already moved and grabbed her pajamas, leaving the room. Violet cursed, every muscle in her body tense.

She wished there were somewhere else she could sleep, somewhere away from people, away from Lando and the person she'd just made an absolute ass of herself with. Grabbing her shower stuff, Violet stalked to the bathroom and waited at the door until Lando was done. They said nothing as Lando went to the bedroom and Violet to the bathroom.

In the hot shower, Violet closed her eyes and took deep breaths. She needed to figure this out. She needed to stop being the person she'd become because she didn't even like herself anymore. Lando was right, again. Violet needed to figure out what to do about Diane, and sooner rather than later, otherwise she would be the one to ruin the team.

CHAPTER 11

THREE DAYS HAD PASSED, and Lando was just as confused about Violet's reactions to her and Diane as ever. There had been no further explanation, no more yelling—which had been a bonus—but also no resolution. The tension living in Lando's chest was overwhelming. They'd missed the Colorado storms since they veered too far north and Diane apparently didn't want to drive that far to catch them. That had put Violet in even more of a sour mood, but at least Lando understood that one.

They were there to storm chase, and for the better part of a week, they hadn't done anything except sit on their asses and wait for Diane to decide a storm was close enough for them to take off and go. She'd spent some time with Eli in those three days, some out in the fields, but largely she'd wanted to keep close to the house in case Diane changed her mind and they were able to leave.

Largely, Lando had spent the three days carrying around Eli's old camera and taking photos. She'd stuck to landscapes and cattle mainly, but every once in a while, Violet would show face and Lando would snap a photo or two without her knowing. Lando couldn't figure out why she kept doing it, but Violet looked so sad since they'd left home, as though it seeped from every pore into the world.

Whatever obsession she had with Diane must run deep, because Lando had never seen anything like it before. To her it was clear Diane had no sexual interest in Violet, but they were friends. That much was true. Diane, however, seemed to have a cold shoulder where it concerned Violet, as if Violet was constantly chasing at Diane's heels, nipping at them.

The fire was warm even though it wasn't a particularly cool day. It was nice, beautiful weather—well, for anyone who wasn't a storm chaser. For them it was like the worst lull in work ever. Lando put her feet up on the coffee table and crossed her ankles and arms, staring into the flames licking at the logs. Three whole days of nothing. If she wasn't getting paid for it, she would have called it quits already. Which reminded her, she still needed to talk to Diane about when she was going to get paid.

She caught sight of Diane out on the deck and debated whether or not to join her to ask. It seemed any time Lando tried to bring up that conversation, something else came up and diverted it. The other family staying there for the week stomped down the steps. Lando cringed. *They were so loud.* She'd thought Violet and Diane were loud, but it was nothing in comparison to this family of six. They had all the other rooms at *Indigo*, and it was a tight squeeze for someone not used to living in close quarters with that many other people.

The mother came down with her two daughters, the teenagers sitting on chairs around the fire with their faces in their phones. That had pretty much been what they did the entire time they'd been there. Lando made no comment but did glance toward the mother.

"How has your visit been so far?" Lando asked, trying to make conversation so they weren't all awkwardly sitting together and saying nothing.

The mother smiled, her eyes lighting up. "It's been wonderful."

Her mood seemed so out of tune with that of her kids, but they were teenage girls, so Lando could have been off the mark when it came to reading them. She wasn't that far away from being their age, but her teenage years had been filled with drugs, sex, and alcohol.

"That's good," Lando mumbled. Her visit hadn't been *wonderful*, but then again, she was there for work, not to play and relax. The girls were still focused on their phones, doing who knew what on them.

Lando glanced out the window to see if Diane was still there. Perhaps she could use that as an excuse to get out of talking nicely with people she didn't know. Diane stood by the railing but wasn't looking out at the landscape. Instead, she stared through the window. For a moment, Lando thought Diane was looking at her, but on second glance, she realized Diane's gaze slid farther to her left, right where the mother sat, staring back.

Oh. Lando flickered her gaze a few more times between the two of them and sighed heavily. Now she understood why they were there, and by her estimation, it was a damn good thing Violet hadn't figured it out yet.

Lando stood up and said nothing as she stalked out of the den and up the stairs to her shared bedroom. Violet was on the computer as expected. Lando would play interception as best as she could, because she did not want to witness that fallout or be anywhere in the vicinity when it happened.

She grabbed Eli's old camera and flipped through some of the photos she had taken while sitting on her side of the bed. She said nothing to Violet as they existed in each other's presence. Eventually, Lando stretched her back and glanced over to find Violet staring blankly at her screen, obviously not computing any of the information.

"What photo editing software does Diane use?" Lando asked, trying to keep the conversation professional and also useful.

Violet turned slowly and looked Lando up and down. "Why?"

"So I can try it out if it's cheap enough." She held up the

camera. "I'm going to have to do something with these before we leave here, and while I can put them on my computer for safe keeping, I don't have much to do with them after the fact."

Violet frowned. "She uses Photoshop, but it can be expensive. She's not very proficient with it, either, so I wouldn't be asking her for advice on how to use it."

Lando couldn't decide if that was Violet's jealousy talking or if what she said was true—or both. *It could be both.* Lando bit her tongue. "Is there any cheaper software you'd recommend? I can't exactly use the school's photo lab anymore."

Shrugging, Violet changed the map on her screen. "There are a few programs if you wanted, but I have Photoshop on here if you wanted to play with it."

"No offense, but do you ever let anyone touch that computer other than yourself?"

Violet's look was sharp. "No one's asked before."

"Oh." Lando pressed her lips hard together. "Well, I'd appreciate it if I could, at least until I can save up enough to get some kind of editing program."

Violet didn't answer, and Lando knew they were back to silence and being withdrawn. She didn't like seeing Violet like this, the weight of the world in sadness settled into Violet's shoulders, and it shifted the entire mood of the team. Lando leaned in and pointed at the computer screen.

"Is that one headed our way?"

"What?"

"The storm." Lando raised an eyebrow at Violet in confusion. Violet was never someone who missed a storm, no matter how small, but to see her so distracted was unnerving.

Violet blinked, focusing her eyes and staring at the computer screen. "Oh, yes."

"Are we going to it?"

"If we can convince the princess."

Lando nearly pouted. Prying Diane away from her current interest didn't seem like it was going to be easy, but three days without a storm was weighing on all of them. They needed to get out and have the thrill of an adventure. Perhaps that could put them back together as a team in ways staying in close confines couldn't.

"Is there no way to not give her a choice?"

"I...I don't know." Violet sounded a million miles away.

"You know her better than I do, but I can't imagine we're getting anything done staying here." Lando wanted to amend that statement because at least one person was getting things done, but she was not going to be the one to shatter that wall for Violet.

"Let's see how long we have and where we need to go first." Studying the computer and talking it through, they figured they had about thirty minutes until they needed to leave if they were going to hit it. It'd be an hour drive north, but the storm looked seriously promising for some kind of tornado activity.

The five days of nothing was grating on Lando's nerves, so she knew she was pushing to go, but that was why they were there, wasn't it? She knew it was at least why she was there, why she'd been hired and even applied for the internship to begin with.

"Let's go find Diane," Lando murmured. "Last I saw she was downstairs."

Violet remained quiet as she got out of the bed. Lando could only hope when they found Diane that she didn't have her tongue down someone's throat because that would be a disaster, but for Lando, the possibility of a storm outweighed the possibility of revealing secrets.

Luckily, Diane was alone on the deck still, sipping coffee as she sat on the swing and stared out at the horizon. Lando shoved her hands in her pockets and let Violet take the lead on this one.

"There's a storm northwest of us."

"A promising one?" Diane raised an eyebrow.

"Yes."

"When do we need to leave?"

"In thirty."

"Then let's go." Diane actually looked interested.

Lando breathed a sigh of relief as she walked back into the house. That was likely the least confrontational conversation she'd ever witnessed the two of them have. It'd been nice, but also like there was something simmering under the surface that was about to explode. Lando really didn't want to be present for that.

∼

Lando had her gear ready as she sat in the back seat of the car while Diane drove. She'd barely had a chance to wave goodbye to Eli as they piled into the Hummer and took off. Violet was oddly sitting in the back seat with her, again. Something had shifted in the last week, but Lando hadn't been able to put her finger on it.

Violet had her laptop open and on her thighs as she read out directions. The initial part of the drive was made relatively in the quiet, but once they got closer to the storm and were surrounded by dark clouds, the vehicle came alive with excitement. The adrenaline pumped through her body, every muscle ready to go as soon as Violet said the word.

Yet they were still stuck in the backseat while Diane drove. Violet's nose was buried in the computer, and she was missing the best parts of the storm, the lightning from a distance, the clouds as they rolled in. Shivering against the sudden thought, Lando looked her over. Violet was more relaxed than before, but there was still an intense tension riding in her body. The lines around her mouth and eyes were deep as her neck was bent and her face was down.

No idea why she did it, Lando reached out and wrapped her fingers around Violet's forearm. Violet jerked with a start, her eyes wide as she looked up to find Lando staring at her oddly. It took Lando a second to form words, to let her voice do the work without her mind.

"Let me give directions."

"What?" Violet looked absolutely confused, and Lando couldn't blame her. But if she could give directions while Diane drove, that would free up Violet to do something else that could earn them money, something Lando instinctively knew she was far better at.

"Let me give the directions. Come on." Lando held her free hand out for the computer, not taking her other hand off Violet's arm.

"Why?" Violet shook her head, glancing from Lando to Diane to the storm outside to the computer and back to Lando. "I always give directions."

"So change it up." Lando's lips barely quirked up into a smile. "Let's have it."

Reluctantly, Violet handed the computer over. "Don't get us lost."

"I'm very good with directions, thank you." She stared at the computer, figuring out easily where they were and where they were headed. With one last look at Violet, Lando reached between the seats and grabbed Eli's old camera and shoved it into Violet's empty hands. "Here. Be useful."

"I…" Violet stared down at the sleek black device that had definitely seen better days. She turned it over in her palms and fiddled with the lens. "Is this the only lens?"

"Yeah, sorry. She couldn't find the others, but she said she'd look."

Violet's lips pressed tightly together as she stared dumbfounded at the camera. "Get us as close to the center of the storm as possible."

"I know the drill, teach. You've taught it to me well."

Violet finally flipped the camera on and checked all the settings. She lifted it, took a sample shot, and adjusted it. Lando tried to pry her eyes away, back to the computer sitting in her lap and warming her legs, but she couldn't stop looking at Violet's adept fingers.

"Hey! Where we going?"

Lando bit the inside of her cheek as she glanced at the computer screen when Violet sent her a sharp look. She should have paid closer attention and not gotten so distracted. "Keep going straight. We've got another ten miles before I think we should turn off."

Violet leaned over the center of the seat and looked at the map, no doubt double-checking what Lando had just said. She kept her mouth shut as she shifted back to sitting upright and pointing the camera out the window. Violet didn't take too many photos until Lando guided Diane off into the back roads.

As they got closer to the storm, the temperature dropped. Goosebumps riddled along Lando's arms and the back of her neck as Diane kept her speed up on the dirt roads. The crunch of gravel was loud as Violet rolled down the window to snap a few more photos and get a better view of the sky.

"I see funnels!" Violet called.

"How many?" Diane responded.

"At least two, maybe a third one starting."

No one said anything else as Diane drove. They were in the calm before the storm, literally and figuratively. Lando was going to have to start getting supplies ready to try and catch a tornado, and Violet would have to take over navigation soon. Still, they had made it that far and Lando had given Violet a bit of a break. That was as much as she had wanted that day.

Violet settled into the seat, a smile on her lips that Lando wasn't sure she'd seen since that day in her office. It seemed like months ago even though it was only a few weeks at that point. *When had so much changed?* Shaking the thought, Lando checked the maps. The good thing about Kansas roads was they were largely in a grid pattern. The bad part of that was it made it harder to catch the tornados sometimes as they decidedly did not follow a grid pattern.

"Turn north at the next intersection. It should be coming up in about half a mile."

"Got it," Diane answered.

She had been relatively quiet the entire drive, which was not like her, but then again, the last few times they had truly chased a storm, Violet had been in the front and the two of them had snapped at each other back and forth. She'd almost never seen the two of them together and had it be this quiet.

"We've got a fourth and fifth funnel."

Lando craned her neck to see out Violet's window and catch sight of the twisting clouds as they stretched from the sky downward. She'd always been amazed by the power and beauty in the strength of mother nature. It was something that fascinated and terrified her at the same time. Lando shuddered.

"One's getting ready to touch." Violet's voice rose along with her excitement. Lando pushed forward, trying to get the moment that it touched, but she missed it when Diane turned the Hummer at the next road. Now it was right in front of them, the rope of the tornado twisting as it moved from heaven to earth, connecting the two.

"It's so beautiful," Lando murmured.

"It really is." Violet grinned, moving her gaze from the front windshield to Lando, her eyes lighting with joy.

Lando couldn't help but echo the sentiment. Diane drove, the tornado getting close to being right on top of them. Lando handed Violet the computer as she scrambled in the back to grab the box. She turned the devices on while Violet connected them to her tracking system. Within minutes, Diane parked off the side of the road and grabbed her camera. Violet put a hand on Lando's wrist as soon as Diane was out of the car.

"Remember. Don't lose track of where it's at."

"I won't." Lando winked. "Same goes for you."

Once they were outside, Lando ran around the back end of the Hummer. She'd left the box inside as she figured out exactly where she was going to run and when. Violet stood next to her, camera still locked in her fingers as they stared across the open field. Violet pointed.

"Another one is forming."

"A double?"

"See? A third funnel." Violet turned east, not answering Lando's question.

Sure enough, a third funnel moved closer to the earth, daring to touch the ground and start a rampage on its own. A small white house stood lonely out in the field. Lando squinted, trying to see just how close the tornado was to it, but the distance was hard to navigate when it wasn't on the ground yet.

"How much damage do you think it'll do?"

"No way to tell right now," Violet responded, turning when Diane came around to join them. "I think we need to move farther up the road. We're too far from where it landed."

"I was just thinking the same." Diane gave Lando a pointed look. "Not my usual navigation, so understandable if we made some mistakes."

"No mistakes," Violet quickly responded. "No one's hurt, we're only too far."

They all piled back in, and Diane picked the speed of the car up again as the wheels spun through the dirt. Lando watched as Violet navigated, trying to pick up on any little tips so she could do it better next time. She wanted to be a useful part of the team, and today was the first time she'd felt worthy of being there, that she wasn't a nuisance who had to be taught every little thing.

By the time Diane stopped again, they were right in the middle of it. Luckily all the tornados were on the east side of the vehicle. Lando grabbed her box this time as they got out and stood at the edge of the fence. The wind whipped around them, Violet's hair wildly moving around her face.

Lando stepped up next to her and pointed with her free hand after settling the box on the edge of the fence line. "There's another funnel."

"And one more still." Violet shifted directions. "Don't think that one will touch down, though. It's rare for so many at once."

"This is crazy."

"It's beautiful." Violet said in a whisper, reverence in every single syllable.

"Which one are we going for?"

"This is dangerous, Lando."

Quirking her lips, Lando gave Violet a look with as much confidence as she could muster. "It's what I live for."

CHAPTER 12

THE STORM WAS BREATHTAKING. Violet hadn't been near a storm of this magnitude in years. Her heart thundered as she stood at the fence line, Lando right next to her. One tornado twisted around, dancing. They were still farther off than they should be, but she wasn't sure she wanted to move just yet.

This storm was unpredictable, and the winds kept changing. She didn't need the computer to tell her that, but she could see it from the data. It was almost as if she was in the middle of a surreal movie. Diane snapped another photo, the sound of her boot scuffing the dirt knocking some sense into Violet. She had to figure out where they were going to put the box, which one they were going to go after, and somehow manage to keep track of all the funnels and changing winds.

"Diane," Violet raised her voice to be heard over the wind. "We're going to need everyone on this."

"I know! Where do you want to do it?" Diane settled the camera against the wood of the fencing.

Violet shook her head, her eyes wide as she stared across the field. The tornado was still a good quarter mile off, the funnels popping down and pulling back up at random. Why was it every serious decision seemed to rest on her shoulders when they finally got to the storm? Diane was experienced enough at this point that she should be able to dive in and help out.

"I don't know," Violet murmured, not even sure her voice carried over the rage of the weather. She didn't have an answer. The radio in the car bleeped, and in the distance she caught the echoing and sounds of a blaring siren. They must be close enough to some little town that they had something in place as a warning.

Diane's eyes were wide as she looked at Violet, needing answers. The "what are we doing" question in every second. Violet had to make a choice. Data, or skip it for this one. How much danger was she going to put the team in to get what they wanted? She turned and looked at Lando, who had one thick eyebrow raised, her plump lips parted. *So young.*

"Lando and I will go, you be ready to get us the hell out of there." She said it to Diane, but she stared at Lando the entire time, making sure Lando was prepared and ready for this to happen, that they would work together to do exactly what they had done the time before.

"Keep your radio on you," Diane answered.

Violet twisted on the balls of her feet and dove into the car, grabbing the portable radio and clipping it to her side. She took Lando's and did it for her on the side of her jeans and belt. Hopefully they'd both manage to keep their radios, but at the very least, one of them would have one.

They got back in the car, this time Violet in the front seat. She let Lando have the computer, and she used her eyes to figure out where to go. Diane spun out the tires as she hit the gas. Violet shared a look with Lando, one where she held Lando's gaze and tried to impart how dangerous this really was going to be. A lot of storm chasers would most likely turn around or keep their distance. They wouldn't drive headfirst into the storm, but an entire week without a storm had been enough for her. Violet wanted to make the point that this was what they were there for.

"Turn here," Violet shouted to Diane, her excitement growing.

Lando gripped the box tighter, and Violet held on to the camera like it was her lifeline. She couldn't let it go even though she probably wouldn't take a single picture as she tried to keep track of the tornados and Lando as she ran straight for them. Diane turned north and sped up. The first rope tornado Violet had tracked barreled toward them.

"Stop!" Violet shouted.

Diane slammed on the brakes, jerking them forward in their seats. Lando whistled as she jumped out of the car with the small cardboard box in tow. Violet followed her as Diane stayed near the Hummer. Violet helped Lando over the fence and was shocked when Lando took off toward the tornado. She really was fearless.

Admiration blossomed in Violet's chest as she lifted the camera and snapped a photo on instinct of Lando running straight between two funnels toward one tornado. Cursing, Violet flung herself over the fence and took off as fast as she could. Instant regret hit her as soon as she made it halfway to Lando that she didn't grab a second box to increase their odds.

Her ears roared from the rushing wind as it came even closer to where she was. She moved on instinct, running closer to Lando, who had stopped and glanced up, no doubt trying to figure out where the best place was. Violet looked around, trying to find it herself, but she came up blank.

She reached Lando and wrapped an arm around her back so she'd know Violet was there. Leaning in, Violet yelled, "We need to put it down."

"Where?" Lando shouted.

Violet stood stock still as she swiveled her gaze from side to side. Nothing seemed like a good place, and the tornado to the north was coming straight for them. Violet's heart skipped a beat. "Here!"

"What?"

Violet's eyes widened as the she stared, dirt swirling up around her as the wind speeds in their vicinity increased and then changed direction. She spun around to check where the closest funnel was and make sure they were still safe. Panic swarmed into her belly. Violet tightened her grip on Lando's back. They had no time to drop the box and get out of the way. She leaned in so Lando could hear her. "Drop it."

Lando set the box down and faced Violet.

"Run." They took off toward the vehicle, turning their backs on the tornado, which was never Violet's preference. She wanted to watch, to see the beauty that was in that power as it came ever closer to her, and to know exactly where death and destruction lay. Diane perked up on the radio clipped to her side, but Violet ignored her voice when she sounded mostly calm. It meant the tornado wasn't coming their direction.

The dirt in the air lessened, making it easier to see. With her heart racing, Violet stopped short and spun around to see where they were. Lando came to a halt next to her, her feet sliding in the dirt. Violet breathed deeply, searching for the sign the box had been pulled up. She couldn't see it. She couldn't find it.

"Where is it?" She shouted, hoping Lando could have an answer.

"I don't know."

"Find it. Did it take it?"

Lando stayed quiet next to her as they both looked right at where they'd stood only a minute before. Grabbing her radio, Violet depressed the button to talk to Diane.

"Check the computer, see if it got it." It had to have taken it. The dirt was so dry that it filled the air, Violet breathing it in as she stood on the edge of her seat, waiting for some kind of answer.

"On it." Diane's reply was curt, but Violet expected nothing less. They might fight like cats and dogs most of the time, but when they were out in the field like this, the only thing that mattered was the storm.

Violet stayed right where she was, watching as a third funnel dropped toward the ground. *Wait, no, fourth.* Where was the third? She strained her neck as she tried to find it. Perhaps it had gone back up and she'd missed it. Violet tightened every muscle in her body as she tried to figure out where it had gone. The tornado in front of her danced around, thankfully still going strong.

Lando's hand in hers was a surprise, but when Violet looked over, Lando pointed out to the field where they'd stood. "I see it."

"Shit," Violet muttered. She didn't hesitate or wait. She dug her toe into the ground and ran as fast as she could.

Diane spoke into the radio, but Violet didn't catch a single word of it. Reaching down, she pulled up the sleek black device and held it to her ear to try and listen better. "Wind speeds increased."

Violet snorted. She knew that. She could feel it. She moved as fast as her legs would carry her, but Lando beat her. Lando raced to a halt right at the box and snagged it, coming back to meet Violet. Breathing heavily, Violet swung around to try and find the tornado in question. Warm air hit her, and she cursed.

This was not good.

Grabbing Lando's wrist, Violet ran straight for the tornado in question. She needed to get this one done. They were already out there, it would take too much for them to put the box somewhere new and try again. Lando followed without question as they moved swiftly through the wheat field.

Lando tripped, her arm ripped from Violet's grasp as she tumbled to the ground. Violet jerked, bending down to help Lando up and collect the small devices. She straightened her spine and stopped as she stared directly at the tornado.

Small funnels of swirling air spiked down from the sky on either side of the main tornado, but it looked bigger, as though it was gaining momentum, not lessening or staying. Her stomach dropped. One funnel was super close to the top of the tornado, spinning around and flapping wildly to the side as it desperately tried to find purchase.

Turning on Lando, Violet shook her head. "There's subvortices and a runner!"

"A what?" Lando screamed back.

Violet drew in a sharp breath and yelled. "There's a satellite tornado that's going to touch down."

Lando visibly paled.

"We have to get out of here." As her panic took over, she knew Lando was feeling the same. Violet had been in a storm like this before, she'd seen the devastation it could wreak on the area around. Each one of the subvortices often did as much if not more damage than the main tornado itself, the increased windspeed all working together to do their worst.

Violet gripped Lando's hand, the box tucked under Lando's other arm. She ran toward the tornado, right where it touched the ground. She may be absolutely crazy, but she wanted a record of this. She wanted the be the one who got the data, who made the conjectures from everything they'd collected.

Lando moved with her easily enough. When they were close enough, Violet stopped and ripped the box from Lando's grasp. Even if one of the subvortices took up the devices they would still get some data. If the satellite took and it joined in with the tornado, it would be golden. Violet put the box on the ground and immediately turned and ran back the way they had come.

Wind whipped up around them, making it nearly impossible to see through the dust. Violet breathed it in, sputtering when she got a mouthful. Lando was struggling the same way, but she knew they couldn't take their time. They had to get out of there as quickly as they could. They had to get back to the Hummer and have Diane move. They were too close to stay there with the technology they had.

It was getting harder to run, to keep her feet going forward. Violet knew that the subvortices were gaining ground and getting closer. They really had to get moving. She glanced over her shoulder to make sure Lando was nearby, and she seemed to be struggling just as much. Violet grabbed for Lando's hand so they could move together.

They gripped each other hard as they lowered their heads and shoulders to fight against the wind bearing down on them. They could do this. Violet's radio perked to life, and Diane's voice wavered as she yelled, "Run faster!"

Neither Violet nor Lando answered as they focused on getting to the fence. When they were finally at it, Violet gripped the wooden post hard and helped Lando over the barbed wire first. Lando assisted her, and as soon as they were on the other side, they raced for the vehicle just as hail pounded the ground around them, large hail. Violet ducked behind the door of the Hummer, grabbed the first hailstone she could, and brought it into the vehicle with her.

Lando slammed her door shut, and Diane took off before Violet even had hers closed. Once they were moving, Violet glanced down at the piece of hail in her hand, easily the size of a golf ball. "Lando, get on the phone. We need to tell emergency services what's happening."

"I already called," Diane said.

"Update them." Diane threw her phone at Violet who opened it and dialed the last number. Her heart raced as she stared at the tornado coming toward them. Hail slammed against the roof of the Hummer, against the windshield, but hadn't cracked the glass yet, though Violet suspected they wouldn't get out of this one without damage.

"It took it!" Lando shouted from the back, the computer open in front of her as she stared at the screen.

Violet didn't even have a second to think about that when someone answered the other end of the line. "Hi, we're storm chasers in the area. My partner just called in. There's golf-ball-sized hail, a satellite tornado that has touched ground and still going, and at least four subvortices that I see."

She gave them as much detail as she possibly could, not

knowing what Diane had already told them. They took down all the information. The car jerked sharply, and Violet flung her hand out to the door to make sure she stayed upright. It felt as though they'd been slammed in the side by another vehicle, but when she opened her eyes, they hadn't.

"Shit." Violet twisted around to Lando. "Hang on."

Diane gripped the steering wheel tightly, her knuckles white as she turned into the wind. The tornado was coming right at them and instead of them moving away from it, they were moving toward it. It had changed directions.

Violet spoke into her phone. "It's now moving north-northeast."

"Wind speeds are hitting over a hundred!" Lando yelled up to her.

Relaying the information, Violet stared out the window as Diane navigated, the Hummer creaking against the added stress. She had to trust that Diane knew what she was doing, that she knew where she was going. Violet's heart ran wildly until Diane took a sharp turn and drove south, the wind pushing the car along far more easily than before.

With the tornado behind them, Violet twisted around to face the back of the vehicle. Lando did the same as they each watched the tornado move farther away. Violet finished her call with a few more tidbits of data that Lando shared. Diane finally pulled off the road a quarter mile from where they had been, and they all got out again.

Violet put her hands on her hips as she stared at the tornado, continuing its path of destruction through the fields. They were miles from the nearest town, although she was sure the closest ones were already under shelter-in-place. She walked down the road to get a better view. Sure enough, she could still see the satellite tornado right next to the main one.

"That was insane," Lando said as she stood next to Violet, her hair an absolute mess but her eyes with that wild look to them.

Violet nodded. "See the satellite? I'm not sure I've seen one go this long before."

"How long can they last?"

"No idea. Longest I've personally seen was only a few minutes, but records don't have them for very long." Violet crossed her arms until she felt a nudge. Looking down, she found Eli's old camera in Lando's hands. "You do it."

"Your turn." Lando grinned and forced Violet to take the camera.

Drawing in a breath, Violet lifted the camera up to her face and snapped a few photos. Zooming in as best she could, she steadied the camera and took another one. Hopefully Diane had gotten some good photos because that would land them some decent money with this tornado. She had no doubt that this one was going to take the cake in the news for the next week at least. They were close enough to a large town that people would feel it was a threat but far enough for it to not really be, at least not yet. There was always time for mother nature to do the unexpected.

Diane stood next to them as Violet lowered the camera. "Fancy driving."

Diane snorted. "Don't wait so long next time."

Violet's lips curled upward at the underhanded compliment. They had done what they'd gone out there to do, and that was an achievement in and of itself. She'd wanted nothing less, everything else was simply a bonus.

"Let's follow it," Violet stated.

"On it." Diane chuckled lightly as she went back to the Hummer.

Lando looked confused for a brief moment before she grinned broadly and hopped into the car herself. Violet took one more photo before she followed and got into the back seat with Lando. Rolling down the window so she could have a better view, she took even more photos as they drove. She missed this.

Diane didn't need as many directions this time as they

followed from a safer distance, since their work was largely done. Violet sat quietly in the back of the vehicle while Lando checked the data on the computer. It was the first time since they'd started chasing all those years ago that she'd allowed someone else to read the maps instead of her.

She trusted Lando to do it right. She hadn't even been the best student in the class, but Violet was sure that wasn't because she didn't have the brains to do the work. Classwork was simply not Lando's strong suit. Violet understood. There had been classes she loved and some she hated. Diane took a turn and started north.

"The satellite is gone off radar."

"Good," Violet stated, more to herself than to anyone else.

"There's another one, though."

"Really?" Twisting in her seat, Violet moved the computer so she could see it. Sure enough, another one was starting and ready to touch down. She glanced toward the front of the car. "Want to chase that one?"

"Damn straight."

Smiling, Violet shook her head. "Start heading east hard."

Diane drove, and by the time they got there, the second satellite tornado was already dissipating into the supercell. Other chasers swarmed the roads, some professionals who had vehicles far more expensive than the Hummer they drove, and some who were amateurs just out for a look. Diane wove her way through them like an expert.

They spent the next two hours in and out of the car as they followed the storm across the plains. Violet finally had Diane call it when it looked like the tornado pulled away from the ground and another wasn't going to pop up. They were quiet on the ride home, but it was a satisfied quiet.

Diane stopped at a gas station and snagged beer for their celebration. Violet shifted a glance at Lando and bought some Twizzlers before she got back to the car. They had another hour before they would get back to *Indigo*, and while it was late afternoon at that point, after not sleeping well, Violet was going to struggle to stay up and celebrate.

CHAPTER 13

"That was fucking awesome!" Lando nearly shouted as the excitement in her chest burst. Eli stood in the kitchen, and Lando raced to find her, unable to contain it any longer. Eli cocked her head to the side as she put the casserole in the oven.

"What happened?" Eli asked, washing her hands in the sink before she turned around.

Violet and Diane came in right behind her, chattering, but Lando didn't pay them any mind. "We caught the huge tornado."

"Really?" Eli's eyebrows rose. "That's where you were?"

"Of course," Diane interjected. "We go where the weather goes."

Violet snorted. Lando shot her a curious look, but Violet didn't elaborate. Lando focused on Eli. "Yeah. It was insane. Huge. We followed the storm for a few hours, but the tornado from when it touched down until it left. It was amazing."

Eli chuckled. "I'm glad you had fun. I'll leave the storm chasing to you and stick with hoping it doesn't hit my cattle."

"I got right out in the middle of it. Twice."

"Twice?"

Lando's head bobbed up and down. "Yes!"

Diane settled the beer on the countertop, and Lando's

stomach lurched. She hadn't realized just how much beer Diane had bought. She'd be expected to drink while she joined in the celebration that night. It wouldn't be as easy to get out of it this time.

"The best part was no injuries this time around." Violet gave Lando a pointed look, and heat kissed Lando's cheeks.

Violet was right, however. There were no injuries that time, which had been a good thing. The stitches in her arm were starting to itch, and she wanted to take them out, but she still had a few more days before she could even think about it.

"Right. Violet took some pictures with your old camera. You should show her."

"Oh, they're not worthy of anything."

Lando rolled her eyes so Violet could see, sure the photos weren't absolute crap. But when Violet didn't make a move to pull the camera out, Lando leaned over the counter and focused on Eli. "There were so many funnels."

"How many touched down? I've heard varying reports."

Diane stepped in. "Three total, but there were a lot of subvortices off the main tornado that caused most of the damage."

Eli shook her head. "I have no idea what you just said, but I'll take your word for it."

Violet launched into a long drawn-out explanation about what subvortices were, and Lando tuned her out. She glanced over at Diane, their gazes locking and Diane raising her eyebrows up and down several times and nodding her head toward Eli. Lando balked. She couldn't get away from it, could she? One lesbian meets another and someone wants to set them up no matter what. There was never an end to it, except perhaps where Violet was concerned, though she supposed Diane thought Violet might be too old for Eli. Shaking her head slowly, Lando tuned back in to hear Violet take another deep breath.

Resting a hand on Violet's arm to get her attention, Lando

raised an eyebrow at her. "I don't think Eli needs the entire semester's class slammed into one evening."

"I..." Violet pursed her lips. "I wasn't planning on that."

"Sure you weren't, teach." Lando snorted. Eli's eyes lit up at that. Curious, Lando canted her head to the side. "What?"

"I used to call my favorite science teacher that. She's the one who helped me come out to my parents actually."

"Really? Maybe she'd be interested in Violet's lesson plans."

"Oh, quiet," Violet teased, her tone light. "I'd love to meet her, though."

"Good, because she's arriving tonight."

"Really?" Surprised, Violet leaned forward on the counter, her eyes wide.

Eli knocked her chin up. "Yeah. She and her girlfriend are coming up for the end of spring break."

"Does that mean the other guests have left?" Diane stepped in.

Lando eyed her suspiciously. How much of that week had been planned if Diane didn't even know they were gone? It had her second-guessing everything she'd thought the last few days.

"They were only supposed to stay through this morning, so they left while you were gone. Wanted to beat the storm that you were chasing." Eli's eyes were light with joy. "We've got a new couple and their son in some of those rooms, and then Azalea and Jewel will be here shortly."

"Well, I look forward to meeting them," Violet answered.

Lando felt Diane's tension without even needing to see it lining her face. Eli cast her a quick look too, but stopped. "Dinner should be ready in about thirty minutes."

"Good," Diane answered. "I'm going to go get changed."

"We should, too," Violet murmured, placing her hand on top of Lando's, the one that was still somehow on Violet's arm. "We're covered in dirt."

"Worth it." Lando grinned and was glad to see Violet's

echoing smile. Violet was a truly different person on storm days when they were successful. Lando loved seeing her like that.

While Diane went upstairs, Lando and Violet went back to the Hummer and pulled out the computer and cameras and other tech they didn't want to leave overnight. Bringing the stuff inside and up to their room, Lando grimaced. Diane had taken the shower, meaning Violet and she were going to have to wait.

"How are those bruises?" Lando asked off-handedly as Violet set the computer onto the mattress and rummaged through her suitcase.

"Not bad. Healing well. Yours?"

"Didn't bruise." Lando gave her a broad smile.

Violet rolled her eyes. "Oh to be young again."

"With the way you were running around today? You're not the least bit old."

With her brow furrowed, Violet stood up straight. "Am I supposed to take that as a compliment?"

"Uh…" Lando eyed her carefully. "Yes."

"You don't sound too confident in that answer."

"I was until you questioned it," Lando mumbled, knowing it was loud enough for Violet to hear her.

Chuckling, Violet bent back over her suitcase. "I'll feel it in the morning, I promise you that. My bones are old."

Lando still vehemently disagreed, but she wasn't about to continue the awkward teasing. She sat on the edge of the bed and pulled the laptop closer to her, plugging it in to charge before pulling up the raw data they had collected.

"Want me to start going through this?"

"Sure," Violet said. "I'll give it a good run tomorrow. Tonight, I want food, a hot shower, and some time to revel in what we witnessed today."

"In that order?" Lando fired back.

"No." Violet winked. "Not in that order."

"You take the first shower. Then you can help me wrap up my arm."

"Sounds like a plan."

The water turned off across the hall, and in a minute, Violet was out of the room. Lando lost herself in skimming through the data they had collected, finding all the assumptions they had made about the storm while in the field were mostly correct. Wind speeds were higher than they had guessed, though. The reality of what could have happened out there hit her hard, but she tried her best to push it to the side, fighting the urge to close in on it and let it take over.

She ran down the stairs and grabbed a plastic grocery bag from one of the cabinets after asking Eli where to find it. She was back up in the bedroom in seconds and found Violet leaning over the computer on the side of the bed, only a towel wrapped around her middle and her wet hair plastered to her back.

Lando stopped short, her heart thumping unexpectedly hard. The room smelled sweetly of whatever shampoo Violet had used, and it took over every single one of Lando's senses. She stood awkwardly in front of the bedroom door, closing it slowly. Violet glanced up at her, and Lando held up the plastic bag in silence.

"Come over here." Violet sat on the edge of the bed, tucking the towel in between her breasts so it would stay put.

Lando could not seem to find her voice. Everything she'd said about Violet not being old was absolutely true. Her heart raced as she slowly slipped onto the bed next to Violet and held her arm out. Violet's fingers were damp as she took the bag and wrapped it tightly around Lando's forearm.

"Can't wait until we don't have to do this," Violet murmured.

Lando wanted to say something witty back, but she once again found herself at a loss for words. Violet fumbled with the duct tape, but finally managed to get it pulled. She used her teeth to cut it and wrapped it first around Lando's wrist to block water from entering there. Lando was completely entranced with the way her fingers moved, the delicate way she touched Lando's arm.

By the time she was done with wrapping it, Lando still hadn't found her voice. She took the tape and gripped onto it like it was a lifeline. Violet gave her a soft look. "I bet you'll be happy when those stitches are out."

"Yeah," Lando finally managed. When she lifted her gaze, she couldn't stop from staring at Violet's breasts, then her lips, then her eyes. Violet didn't even seem to notice. A deep breath was her enemy, the scent filling her head even more. She had to get out of there.

Standing sharply, Lando spun around as she searched for her suitcase. Which was stupid, she should know where that thing was. It wasn't like it had moved since that morning. Finally finding it against the far wall, she rummaged around for new clothes and her bathroom supplies. She said nothing as she left the bedroom, embarrassment filling her chest and heating her cheeks so badly that she knew there was no way Violet would miss it that time around. She had to stop doing that.

~

After eating dinner with Eli and her two friends, Lando was pushing on exhausted. She hadn't slept well since they'd gotten to *Indigo* and with the chase that day, it was certainly taking its toll. However, she also didn't want to miss out on the after-party, on a rare chance to see Violet calm and gentle for once. Lando had never realized how uptight and stressed-out her former teacher was.

They all sat in the den, beer covering the coffee table, Lando the only one not partaking—but luckily no one had commented so far. Violet seemed to watch her carefully each time she took a small sip from the one beer she drank while everyone else was on their third or fourth. Jewel pressed into Azalea's side as Azalea and Violet talked about teaching. Azalea had even suggested Violet come teach a day and talk about different careers in science her students could have, breaking down the barriers to women in STEM.

Lando glanced up, catching Eli's gaze. There was something underneath that look that Lando couldn't place, and it unsettled her. The heat from the fireplace was nearly too much, and Lando's cheeks burned as she sat back. She should have felt completely connected to the group, and yet, she felt the odd woman out, as if she wasn't allowed to be in the "in crowd" that day. Not that Diane ever seemed to let her in. There was always a barrier there Lando had to fight against.

Losing track of time, Lando tried to keep up with the conversation, but exhaustion pulled at every fiber of her being. She must have zoned out, because when she looked up, Diane and Violet were slinking away somewhere. She followed Violet's back with her gaze as they walked toward the kitchen, and then heard the distinct sound of the back door shutting.

Left with Eli and her two friends, Lando felt pushed out of the group she was a part of. Eli made eye contact, and Lando shrugged, sipping her hot tea and staring at the beer bottles everyone had left on the coffee table. Not wanting to be the worst guest on the planet, she drew in a deep breath, talked herself up, told herself she could do it, and then stood.

Gathering the alcohol, Lando brought it into the kitchen, dumping out the beer that was left in the bottles, rinsing them, and tossing them in the recycling. Eli came in toward the end to help, but they worked largely in silence until the water was turned off.

"I miss having someone to be with all the time, you know," Eli started.

Confused, Lando looked her over. "You seem like you always have people here."

Eli shook her head. "I mean Sarah. I miss Sarah when she misses out on things like this. I've been trying to get her and Jewel to meet for a year now and they always seem to miss each other."

"She's on tour, right?"

"Yeah. I go out there when I can, but it's not easy feeling like you're the sole one left out."

Lando knew then exactly where the conversation was going. While she appreciated Eli and her wisdom, she did not have a full picture of what the last two weeks had been like with Violet and Diane. Lando's realization of Violet's obsession and Diane's secret affair—if it could even be called that or if it was just longing.

"Where did they go off to?"

"Not a clue," Lando muttered. "But they're not fighting, so that's a step in the right direction if you ask me."

"I'm not sure I could work with two people who constantly fought like that. I get enough of it from the cows when they give me attitude."

Lando snorted. "I wish I had time to figure out your cows."

Eli lifted one shoulder and dropped it, finishing her beer before cleaning and disposing of the bottle. "Cassie's like five cows in one, I swear. I'd start you out easy, maybe with a baby."

"A baby cow?" Lando wrinkled her nose. "I've been interested in a great many things in my short life, but I can't say playing with a baby cow has ever been one of them."

"You should figure out how to talk to them if you're going to be running through random people's fields." The quiet disapproving tone in Eli's voice told Lando exactly how she felt about that portion of their work.

In some ways, Lando didn't disagree. They were blatantly trespassing. On the other hand, they usually only did it when they were trying to reach a tornado, which meant the damage to the field or cattle was already done and one or two people running through wasn't going to make that much of a difference.

"It might be a good skill to have."

"If you end up with time, I'll take you out there."

"I think there's another storm cell coming in tomorrow. I remember seeing it on the map briefly before we got back here."

"Then perhaps another day." Eli stretched her back. "I'm going to hit the sack. Early mornings."

Lando gave a wan smile as she watched Eli walk toward the back door and slip into the basement. Perhaps they were just two lonely souls. At least Eli had someone to spend time with, even if she wasn't around as often as Eli would like. Lando was simply alone, no one to be with her except perhaps Aunt T. Lando cursed.

Grabbing her phone, she stalked up the stairs to her room and called her aunt, something she hadn't done since she'd left. She loved her aunt, but they were not people who talked daily, as much as they said they did.

"Lando, I'm going to kill you if you don't give me a call or a text more often to let me know you're alive."

"Sorry, Aunt T." Lando flopped onto the bed, staring up at the ceiling. "It's been a busy few weeks."

"Right. So...were you at that storm near Colby?"

"We were." Lando clenched her jaw, trying to decide how much to share about what exactly it was she was doing. Her aunt would have a heart attack and order her home for sure, not that Lando would listen. She needed the job, needed the cash, and she wanted the experience.

"Did you catch it?"

"We did." Lando held her breath, wanting to share in her excitement but not quite sure how her aunt would take it.

"So...?"

"It was amazing, Aunt T. I ran right out into that field, twice, and we caught it. There were two satellites and more. It was absolutely amazing. I've never had such a thrill before."

Aunt T snorted. "I swear if you get yourself killed doing this, I'm going to haunt you myself when I die."

Chuckling, Lando smirked. "You would do that."

"I would. Now, how is everything else going outside of chasing?"

"It's...tense. I don't know. I didn't think it would be this hard to live with two people for six months."

"You've never lived with anyone except Nan, really. And she's the easiest person to get along with."

"I know." Lando swallowed, staring at the door and wondering when Violet was going to come upstairs. "It's hard to find time to myself."

"You'll have to make sure you do. I know how you thrive on being alone."

"Yup. But I'm exhausted after today, Aunt T, so I'm going to turn in. I just wanted to give you a call to let you know that I'm alive."

"Well thank you for being so considerate." Aunt T laughed lightly. "Call me more often."

"I'll try." Lando said her goodbyes and hung up. She settled her phone on the nightstand and got ready for bed.

She must have fallen asleep, because when the door opened and the light from the hall shone into the room, Lando was surprised. Violet shut the door as quietly as she could, but Lando was already wide awake at that point. Leaning over, she checked the time on her phone and blinked at it twice. One in the morning.

Violet hissed as she's stubbed her toe on something. Lando frowned and turned on the lamp on her nightstand. Violet spun around, her eyes wide. "Sorry, did I wake you?"

"Yeah, but it's fine. Stub your toe?"

"Ugh, yeah." Violet grabbed her pajamas and stripped right in front of Lando before pulling them on.

Lando's stomach lurched, and she had to pull herself together. The lines on Violet's body in the dim light were stunning. How she could ever think she was old was beyond Lando. She wasn't. She was beautiful, stunning even. Violet slipped under the covers, turning on her side to look Lando over.

"It was a good day."

"It was," Lando answered. "Did you have a good time with Diane?"

"You know, we did." Violet's lips twitched.

Lando wasn't sure where to go from there. She didn't want to pry into Violet's life any more than she already had, didn't want to push the boundary lines, and it was also one in the freaking morning. She wanted to go back to sleep, although she wasn't sure she'd be able to with Violet right next to her, warming the bed, taking up space. Shifting down so her head was on the pillow, Lando turned and watched as Violet did the same. They stared at each other, the silence deafening.

"If only every day could be like today," Violet whispered.

"I think this is the most relaxed I've ever seen you."

"Relaxed?" Violet wrinkled her nose. "I thought you were going to die a dozen times over."

"You're kidding me." Lando's eyes widened.

"I'm not." Violet lips parted. "I've seen it happen, you know. People vanish because of tornados. The damage from vehicles taken up in the wind and spit out somewhere else. The broken bodies."

Her voice broke on that last part. Lando reached out and gripped Violet's fingers tightly, squeezing them. If Violet had been there the day her mother died, then she'd seen her fair share of death and destruction.

"They're not here now," Lando whispered.

Violet nodded. "I know."

"Then don't get lost in the memories."

"I won't," Violet whispered. They stayed quiet for some time, Lando's hand not moving from Violet's wrist. "Were you all right tonight? With all the drinking?"

"Fine." Lando's reply was curt.

"I'll try to keep it to a minimum."

Lando shrugged. It was something she had worked on getting used to in the past two years, but it still wasn't easy some days, especially when she was the only one sober and seemed to be the only one aware. Violet had watched her carefully, and that same scrutiny, while helpful, was also frustrating. She didn't like to be watched as though she was going to break.

"Did you always want to chase?" Lando asked, trying to change the topic.

"Yes," Violet answered. "But I don't think I realized the toll it would take on my life."

"What do you mean?"

Violet blew out a breath. "It's not easy to be in a relationship with someone when you're gone half the year, or so obsessed with something you can't stop thinking about it."

Lando wondered if she was talking about the storms or Diane, but she didn't dare ask that question. "Sounds like you just haven't found the right person."

Violet shrugged. "I gave up looking."

"That's sad."

"It's a choice. I've had my fair share of breakups because of it. I decided perhaps a relationship just wasn't the thing for me."

Lando squeezed Violet's fingers again, trying to shower her with support and comfort all at the same time. "I'd like to get married someday, you know. But I have so much baggage."

"Everyone does, Lando. The hard part is finding someone who will stand with you when that trauma comes back to bite you in the ass." Again that sad final tone was back. Lando wanted to wipe it away, but she wasn't sure Violet would let her.

With no idea how to respond to that last statement, Lando closed her eyes. The exhaustion that had been fleeting when Violet had come in was back, and she struggled to keep her eyes open. She wanted to stay awake, to talk to Violet, this vulnerable person who had shown up instead of the one so built-over with walls that Lando didn't even know where the door was. Prying her eyelids open, Lando gave Violet a half-hearted smile.

"I wish you'd found someone like that."

"Me too," Violet answered. "But I'm pretty sure love isn't for everyone."

"Sure it is," Lando countered. "Everyone is loved, even if it isn't romantic."

Violet laughed, the sound so low and slow that Lando knew she must be just as tired. "I'll give you that one."

"Good. I'm glad I can win one thing with you." Lando's eyelids fluttered shut, and she wasn't sure she was going to be able to force them open again.

"You've won more than one," Violet murmured. It was the last thing Lando heard before sleep took her firmly in its grasp.

CHAPTER 14

VIOLET COULDN'T SAY what woke her, but like she had predicted, every muscle in her body protested. Instead of moving, she stayed perfectly still while she took a mental inventory of her body. Everything hurt. She wasn't sure how long it would take her to get moving that day, but she was going to struggle to go up and down the stairs.

Unfortunately, she needed to rest between storms, which was a newer development she'd noticed over the past few years. Especially when the storm had been as large as the last one. Sighing, she opened her eyes, finding her hand right in front of her face, locked in Lando's fingers. Her brain stuttered.

She hadn't realized they'd fallen asleep like that. The lamp on the nightstand still on, although it didn't make too much difference in the morning light. Neither of them had moved for hours. She wasn't even sure what time it was, but sunrise wasn't supposed to be until close to eight in the morning. Thank God for daylight savings.

Lando's hand was so warm on top of hers, fingers laced together. Her stomach lurched at the thought of their conversation the night before. It had been so soft, so sweet between them. A moment when all the barriers truly were down. She shouldn't be surprised that she'd woken up this way. Lando had all but fallen asleep in her arms.

God, what was she doing? She was there to make nice with Diane, to tell Diane once and for all how she felt, to put her trust in that relationship, and the night before had been a perfect example of what they could be. They'd sat together on the swing on the deck and talked for hours—memories, dreams, excitement about the chase earlier that day. It had been almost like old times, those moments when Violet felt as though Diane loved her.

Yet, here was Lando.

Beautiful, sweet, quirky, strong Lando.

Violet dashed her tongue across her lips, scared to move because she might wake Lando up. She had seemed so tired the night before, not just when Violet had come to bed, but before that. It had been a rough start to the season, nearly two weeks in with two spectacular storms and one serious injury.

It almost seemed like months ago that they'd left the safety of their hometown and school and taken up the task of storm chasing. So much had happened in that short period of time, and Violet could barely even start to untangle it.

Lando's deep breathing brought her attention back around, the light playing on her cheeks as the sun rose higher in the sky. Lando's skin was smooth, begging for Violet to caress it with the backs of her fingers, to ease the palm of her hand against Lando's cheek. Stopping sharply, Violet tensed. *What was she thinking?*

This was Lando, her student, a woman eighteen years younger than her. She couldn't...she didn't want to. She was interested in Diane, who had been her best friend for over thirty years, who had been her first kiss during a stupid game of spin the bottle. That was who Violet wanted. Not this kid who was sleeping so soundly next to her, not the kid she'd saved.

That last thought nearly broke her. Lando had been a kid then, but she certainly wasn't now. She'd faced far more demons than Violet had by the time Violet was her age, and perhaps even now. Violet's heart raced, confused by the emotions and thoughts swirling through her brain. She was a logical person. She often didn't run on emotion except when Diane was involved, and Lando had seen her fair share of Violet's outbursts in the last week and a half.

It was a pity. Violet hadn't meant to be so mean, so cruel. But she'd still allowed it. She'd thrived on it a few times if she was being honest with herself. The constant flirting between Diane and Lando had been her undoing more than once, and yet here they lay, silent in the early morning sunrise, with Lando's hand protectively grasping hers. *What was she supposed to do about that?*

Voices murmured in the room next door, and Violet knew the house was waking up. Eli, no doubt, would have already been awake for hours. Diane most likely was still asleep, and so was Lando. On a whim, Violet flexed her fingers and turned her hand slightly, hoping the grasp Lando had on her would break.

Luckily, it did, so she slid as slowly and as quietly as she possibly could out of the bed. She was changed and ready for the day in a matter of minutes, heading down the stairs to the kitchen to see what Eli had made for breakfast.

Eli had platters full of food on the kitchen counter, filled to the brim with the fixings for a feast. Violet's stomach lurched with hunger. She hadn't realized how long it had been since she'd eaten last, but after skipping food for most of the previous day aside from dinner, she needed the sustenance.

"Can I help with anything?"

"I think we're about ready, actually." Eli flopped a few more pancakes onto one of the plates and set the skillet into the large sink. "Jewel said she'd wake up Azalea, so they should be down in a minute."

"I heard them getting started. Lando is still passed out, I'm afraid."

Eli raised an eyebrow at her, and Violet shuddered. She wasn't sure what to make of the look Eli was giving her, but it was far more than mere acknowledgement of what she'd said. "And Diane?"

"Not a clue, but she usually sleeps late after a chase."

Violet winced as she leaned over the table, her back protesting so much movement. She was just going to have to push through that pain and figure out how to deal with it.

Jewel and Azalea came down the stairs, gushing over all the food on the table. They were shortly followed by another couple. Together, everyone sat along with Eli after she made sure drinks were served. The chatter at the table was strong, but Violet resisted joining in, her stomach still in tangles over how she'd woken up.

It had felt so nice. It had honestly been the best sleep she'd gotten in a long time, even though the hours had been short. The footfalls on the stairs alerted her to the fact that someone was joining, and Violet secretly hoped it was Lando and not Diane. She could use the break from tension.

To her delight, Lando stepped onto the landing and around the corner, sweatpants hanging low on her hips, t-shirt pulled tight on her chest, and her hair sticking up oddly. She was a vision of sleepy and sexy. *Where had that thought come from?* Violet bit the inside of her cheek. She shifted in her chair as Lando sat next to her, grabbing a plate and helping herself to the food.

"Diane still out?"

"I'm assuming," Violet answered, her voice low as if it was a secret, although there was no reason for it. She wanted quiet time with Lando again.

"I'm sore as fuck."

Violet snorted. "Likewise."

"I think we should all take naps today."

"If there's time." Violet took a bite of her pancakes, which were heavenly. Eli certainly had a talent when it came to cooking.

She was halfway through her plate when Diane raced down

the stairs, her eyes wide and her hair wild around her. She must have just woken up, her red cheeks and puffy eyes a sure sign.

"You didn't miss breakfast!" Eli called.

Violet canted her head, trying to figure out what was going on. Diane's lips parted, and she shook her head.

"You're not on your computer," Diane said, most unhelpfully.

"I'm eating," Violet answered.

"There's a storm."

Violet's eyes widened. It was rare Diane found one before she did, but then Violet remembered suddenly she hadn't even checked her computer that morning. She'd only snuck out of the bedroom and tried not to wake Lando. Her stomach plummeted. "Where?"

"South. Strong cell, good activity."

Violet didn't even look at Lando as she grabbed her plate and went to clean up. In seconds, she was racing toward the stairs, Lando hot on her heels. They gathered their gear, Violet's guilt eating away at her that she'd very nearly missed a storm that would be worthy of chasing. She'd wanted to make sure they hit as many storms that season as possible, increasing the chances that she'd be able to retire from teaching and chase full time.

Lando didn't have time to change as Violet begged her to hurry up. They shoved their gear into the packs, Violet staring at the camera on the dresser that they'd left there the day before. At the last minute, she reached for it and shoved it into the backpack along with everything else. Soon they were moving down the stairs, Diane lagging as normal.

For a woman who had been so insistent they hurry up when she told them about the storm, she was taking her sweet time getting ready, and she had less gear to grab than Violet and Lando each. As soon as Violet saw her, she wanted to say something smart, but she held her tongue in check. Diane had taken the time to do her hair and a light coat of makeup before coming downstairs.

Lando and Violet already had the Hummer packed and ready.

Diane sauntered toward them like they had all the time in the world. Violet was about to speak when Eli stepped out of the front door with food containers in her hands.

"I thought you might like these since some of you didn't get to eat much."

Lando stepped forward and took them, cradling them against her chest. "Thank you."

Violet's stomach growled, reminding her that she'd only eaten half her breakfast before running to get ready. Diane got in the driver's seat without a word to Eli. Violet gave a smile, her thanks, then jumped in the back with Lando. There was far more room for her to settle her computer on her lap and navigate where they were going from there.

Her stomach roiled as Diane pulled away from the house and headed down the long drive to the main road. Violet wasn't sure when was the last time it had been graded, but it had certainly been a while, and the recent storms probably weren't helping any. Once they got to the highway, she was able to pull up her computer and check the maps. Except, she was absolutely confused.

There was no storm cell from what she could see. There were small ones here and there, some that would last an hour or two, but nothing strong enough to produce a tornado or hail. Nothing with wind speeds that were going to become catastrophic. She said nothing as she shifted through the programming to try and figure out just what Diane had been talking about when she'd told them about the supercell.

Violet said nothing. Instead, when they hit the main highway and Diane took them south, she shifted the computer over to Lando to let her take a stab at finding this mysterious super storm cell. Lando raised an eyebrow at Violet but took the computer wordlessly. She stared at it, flipped through the maps, changed some of the settings, and then gave Violet a hard look.

"Where is it?" she mouthed.

Violet was glad she hadn't said it out loud because she wasn't even sure what to say to Diane. Violet shook her head and shrugged, putting her hands in the air as Diane drove. She didn't give directions for thirty minutes. They were through the small town Eli called home and on the other side of it when Violet finally came up with something to say.

"I must have missed it. Where's the storm cell we're going to?"

"It's south of Dodge."

"Oh." Violet took the computer back and took a closer look at Dodge. The storm cell there was strong, but it wasn't what Violet would call a super cell. It wasn't even likely to produce hail from what she could tell, maybe small pea-sized hail if it picked up some. No chance of a tornado.

∼

Lando leaned over the middle seat and eyed the screen again, making sure she hadn't missed something. Violet shook her head, more to herself than to Lando. When she saw nothing that would warrant them running out that morning, she touched Violet's hand to get her attention.

Whispering so that hopefully Diane couldn't hear her, Lando asked, "Where is it?"

Violet shook her head but turned the screen so Lando could see better and pointed to something. "I think it's this one."

"Did you find it?" Diane voice filtered to them from the front of the car. "It's not that far south of Dodge. We should be there in about an hour."

"Right," Violet murmured.

Lando was still lost, and she had a feeling that Violet was as well. They couldn't figure out where Diane was trying to take them. The excitement Lando had been trying to find as soon as the word "storm" was out of Diane's lips at the breakfast table completely dissipated. She was exhausted from the day before, but even then, from the night of hardly sleeping until Violet came back in. Then she'd slept like a rock, but certainly not long enough to be considered a good night's rest.

Taking her phone out of her pocket, she typed a quick message to Violet. *"Where is she taking us?"*

Violet shook her head before taking the phone and typing back. *"No clue."*

Lando wasn't sure what else to say, so she kept her mouth shut and watched the shifting patterns in the weather on the satellites Violet was getting her information from. It took Violet another thirty minutes before she broke the silence.

"What images were you looking at when you found this storm?"

Diane clucked her tongue. "The ones on your computer, so whatever you had pulled up. I went to find you in your room and you weren't there."

Lando tensed at that. She didn't like Diane just walking into their room unannounced and messing with the stuff in there. *What else had she gone through?* The thought must have occurred to Violet at the same time, because the line of muscle in her jaw was easily visible.

"What do you mean you went into our room?"

"I needed to talk to you."

"And you just decided to get on my computer without asking or saying anything?" Violet's gaze was locked on the front seat of the car, and Lando was glad she wasn't at the other end of that glare.

Whatever Violet was thinking, Lando was pretty sure murder was top of the list. Lando sunk down into the seat, ready for the argument that was about to break out. She'd been waiting for it, honestly. Violet's countenance had grown tenser by the moment the farther they got from *Indigo*.

Taking the moment for what it was, Lando reached to the floor of the Hummer, grabbed the first Tupperware container Eli had handed her, and popped the lid. Lando popped a piece of sausage link between her lips and watched the argument that ensued.

"I did say something."

"You told us there was a storm, and there is not storm, Diane."

Lando nearly laughed at how Violet said Diane's name, like she was going to rip each letter from it and crush it under her foot. Violet shot Lando a look, meaning she must have snorted too loud and disturbed the angry professor.

"There *is* a storm!" Diane whined. "It's just south of Dodge."

"You keep saying that, and yet nothing on the radar shows it."

"I swear there is," Diane murmured.

Lando finished off another piece of sausage, her stomach no longer protesting loudly at the lack of food. Violet clenched her fist, and Lando was sorely tempted to reach over and cover her hand to ease her anger. While it was somewhat amusing to watch this argument happen, she did not want to be stuck in the car for the hour drive back with it permeating every inch of the Hummer.

"There's a storm, yes, but not one that is going to produce a tornado or even hail." Violet said it so matter-of-factly, as though she had everything under control even though they all knew she didn't. This was Violet unhinged, as Lando had come to figure out.

"It's a promising cell."

"It's not," Violet fired back.

Lando silently ate another sausage link, her gaze fixated on Violet, who barely budged from glaring at Diane.

"There is no storm. You went through my things. Why are we even here?"

"There *is* a storm!" Diane's tone rose, as if getting louder was going to convince them she was right.

Lando looked at the computer. Diane wasn't wrong or lying.

There was storm activity south of Dodge where they were supposedly heading, but it didn't look like there was going to be anything useful to them. And unlike earlier that week when they'd first gotten to *Indigo*, Lando was pretty sure neither she nor Violet wanted to sightsee. Not with as tired as they both were.

"Turn around," Violet demanded.

"I'm not going back."

"There is no point in going forward."

Diane scoffed, her voice echoing through the Hummer as silence came over them. Lando stopped eating and did the one thing she had wanted to from the start. She reached over, covering Violet's tightened fist with her palm. She gave a squeeze, pulling Violet's attention toward her. Lando had never had to play peacemaker before, but it seemed to be her role just then.

She raised an eyebrow at Violet. "We're already most of the way there. Perhaps we can get some good photos that will sell and it will be worth it."

"We don't make money from photos," Violet growled out.

"We make some, don't we?"

Violet drew in a long, deep breath and let it out slowly, clearly trying to calm herself. Lando watched every twitch of her muscles and kept her hand firmly on Violet's, not wanting to let go unless Violet told her she had to.

"We make money off them," Diane added from the front.

Violet rolled her eyes, pushed back into the seat, and pouted. She was all-out pouting. Lando was shocked. Violet's lip protruded, her gaze was downward, and her entire demeanor screamed that she was giving in. Even though Lando had pushed for it, it always surprised her when she saw Violet give in to Diane. This was not the woman she had come to know as Professor Myers. This was an entirely different person, someone who let Diane walk all over her, time and time again.

Violet said nothing as she remained defeated. Lando hated seeing her like this. She rubbed her thumb aimlessly on the side of Violet's hand until Violet's grip loosened. They drove in silence for another thirty minutes until Diane found the storm she swore was for them. Sure enough, nothing had changed.

Lando checked in on the computer, showing Violet every once in a while when nothing had changed that it was still far from being a super cell that would produce anything to cause damage. Diane finally made the call and turned the Hummer around to drive back to *Indigo*.

As they drove, Violet remained withdrawn. Lando had worked so hard to bring her out of her shell the past few days that anger worked in her chest at seeing Violet far off again. Why she kept letting Diane walk all over her was beyond Lando's comprehension. She'd never taken Violet as someone who would roll over and just take it.

Sure they fought, nearly constantly, especially when there was no storm to chase, but this was more than that. Violet willingly let Diane do whatever she wanted, she willingly gave up control and leadership to someone who shouldn't have it. Lando kept the food in her lap, not moving even though she wanted to eat it. She'd rather keep her hand locked on Violet's, giving her what silent support she could.

CHAPTER 15

VIOLET REMAINED quiet the entire drive back, taking comfort in Lando's silent support and strength. Diane had never pulled anything like this before. Then again, Violet had always double-checked everything before they went out. She was the one with the degree, the one who knew what to look for. Diane wasn't trained in that.

They picked around the kitchen for a late lunch, and then Violet was left on her own until dinner. A smaller storm cell picked up in their area, but after the morning they'd had, she wasn't sure it was worthy of their time that she go out to it. Her world was spinning at an odd angle, and she wasn't sure how to tilt it back onto the right axis.

She stared at the stairs where Diane had disappeared after they ate and finally stood up. Lando gave her a cautious glance, but Violet ignored it as she went. She needed to have it out with Diane. It was time to bare everything. At the top of the stairs, Violet ran through the hundred scenarios in her head about what she wanted to say, what she wanted to do to convince her to listen.

By the time she got to the door, she hadn't settled on any of it. The cold handle under her fingertips was a stark reminder that going in unprepared would get her nowhere, but she was already in the middle. Without knocking, Violet stepped into Diane's room and shut the door behind her. They were going to need privacy for this.

Diane shifted on the bed as she made eye contact, immediately going tense. Violet could have cursed because now they were both on edge. She walked into the room and sat on the edge of the mattress, hoping that would ease some of the unnecessary tension.

"What happened this morning?" Violet sounded almost resigned, but she wanted to give Diane a chance for explanation.

"What do you mean 'what happened'?"

Violet cringed at her tone. So much for a calm conversation. "I should have double-checked the readings before we left, but we wasted a lot of time and resources this morning. I know they're slim—"

"There *was* a storm."

Violet gave Diane a soft look. "There wasn't, and you know that as much as I do. But equally, why were you in our room without us?"

"I pay for it." Diane's gaze hardened. "It's our room, and if I need access to the computer—"

"You have your own, Diane. That's the point. Why were you in our room?"

"I told you I was trying to find you."

"And when I wasn't there, you stayed and went through our things?"

"I did not." Diane sat up straight, her back ramrod and her eyes fiery. "I looked at the computer."

Violet wasn't sure whether to believe her or not, and that was part of the problem. While she didn't think Diane outright lied often, she was very good at skirting the truth. "What happened today cannot happen again. We're exhausted from yesterday, and unless there's a real storm—"

"There *was!*" Diane's hands clenched. "You need to get over yourself. You're not the only one who can read maps, Vi. You're not the only one who can figure out where we need to go and when."

Violet cocked her head to the side. "No, I'm not. But *you* can't."

"Yes, I can!"

Violet stuttered to a stop. Diane had never taken this position before. "What's really going on? You've never wanted to make those decisions before."

"You never let me. You're always the one who takes over that, who pushes to do what she wants to do. Well, I'm sick of it. I'm tired of always falling in line."

Violet's mind was blown. It was as if Diane was taking the words right out of her mouth but turning them back around. If anyone fell in line, it was Violet. If anyone conceded, it was Violet. Putting her hand out in front of her, Violet tried to start again, to wrangle the conversation back to where it should be. "Fine, we can have more discussions about what we're doing before we do them and where we're going, but the same goes for you. You can't just up and move us without warning when there are storm cells coming in where we were, without a discussion."

Diane snorted, anger lighting on her face. "I moved us here so we could find storms."

"And we've found one!" Violet nearly screamed at the end, barely able to contain it. "Exactly one, Diane. And what you dragged us out to today was worth nothing."

"This is ridiculous. You're being a fool. Today's storm was a storm, and you've never wanted to avoid them before."

"Yes! Yes, I have." Violet sighed. "We've never gone out to every storm. We've never insisted on traveling so much. Erik—"

"Erik is an idiot, and he followed you around like a lost puppy. I'm sorry I don't do that, Vi, or that Lando doesn't do that, but you have got to get it into your head that you are not the center of everyone's world, that you are not the reason this team functions, and you are not the one in charge."

Violet's jaw dropped. She'd never thought Diane would get this nasty with her. She'd seen it before, seen her push others in this way, but she'd never—they'd never—Violet stopped. "Tell me what this is really about. What happened with Erik?"

"I fired him."

"For what?"

"Not doing his job."

"He did his job perfectly." Violet knew that. She'd even argued for him to get a raise on occasion, and the abrupt change in the team had disrupted the way they functioned. They hadn't found a balance with Lando yet, and Violet wasn't sure they would.

"He didn't. You don't know the half of it."

That was it, wasn't it. Diane ran the show. She might blame Violet for the problems, but she was the one who made the decisions without consultation. She was the one who had fired Erik. She was the one who had hired Lando. She was the one who did everything without warning, without explanation, and without discussion.

"We're a team, Diane. If you're having issues with someone, then you need to come to me about it."

Diane shook her head. "You don't want to know the half of it. You're not built for business or making these decisions. You don't have a head for it. You need to accept your role in this team. You're here for the science, nothing else."

"I...I'm not here just for the science." If anything, having Lando hand her that camera the day before was proof of that. She missed it, missed the creativity, the excitement. Lando had shown her all of that again. "I'm here because I love this, because I love you."

Diane stopped. Violet's breath caught in her throat. She hadn't meant to say that. She hadn't meant for it to come out like that. Panic welled in her chest as Diane's look turned into a sneer, the quiet between them thickening so it was hard to breathe.

"I don't love you." Diane's words were harsh but true.

Somewhere, somehow, Violet had known that all along. She wasn't even sure Diane loved her as a friend anymore or if Diane just put up with her. They stared at each other until Violet stood up and walked out of the room, unsettled. She had gone in there to have that conversation, and it was done. It was over. And she'd gotten the answer she knew she would get.

Violet grabbed the camera from her bedroom and walked straight outside. She needed to be alone. She needed to do something with her hands, focus her mind and her body. She didn't even care that each step pulled at her aching muscles or that she had no place in particular she wanted to go. She found herself at the barn, a storm in the distance. She stopped, lifting the camera to her face and snapping a picture of the oncoming clouds with the bright red barn to the side. She could go in later and make the red brighter, improve the contrast.

"I was just about to head out to the fields." Eli's voice startled her.

Violet spun around on the dirt road, eyes wide, fear in her stomach. She said nothing, waiting for more explanation.

"If you wanted some storm pictures, there are some great places I could show you."

Glancing at the house, the beautiful house that stood stoically, Violet nodded. She piled into the old farm truck with Eli, still keeping silent as Eli drove. Violet didn't pay too much attention to how far they had gone, watching the storm unfold in front of them.

"I like to check the cattle before it hits and after. They say there might be hail in this one."

Violet shook her head. "No hail."

"You sure?"

Sending Eli a sidelong look, Violet nodded. "I'm sure. This is literally what I do for a living."

"I thought weather couldn't easily be predicted."

Violet sighed. "Not all storms can, but this one is relatively calm. We'll get a good dose of rain, lightning, thunder, but that's it."

"How much rain?"

"Half inch, maybe. Enough to get wet but not enough to drown."

"Good." Eli turned off the traveled road and onto the farmland. They drove in the quiet for a few more minutes before Eli stopped. "You can get a good view from here."

Stepping out of the truck, Violet stared out at the fields before her. Eli wasn't wrong. It was breathtaking. They could see for miles, though with the storm coming in that would diminish every passing second. Lightning flashed in the distance, striking down. Unable to resist, Violet adjusted the shutter speed for a long-exposure photo and settled the camera on the hood of the truck since she hadn't brought a tripod.

She spent her time taking photos of the lightning, the bolts hitting the ground. She lost herself in it, consumed by the process of creating. She knew the storm was going to bring that home for her, that she would be able to clear her mind for a few more seconds before she went back and tried to figure out exactly what they were doing for the rest of the season, how she was going to make it through.

Cold air rushed over her cheeks, and she knew the rain would hit soon. She finally looked up and found Eli leaning against the back the truck, waiting on her. Violet calmed herself, turning off her camera. She moved to the bed of the truck to get Eli's attention.

"Thanks for bringing me out here."

"Find what you needed?" Eli raised an eyebrow in her direction.

Violet sighed. "No, but it was a good distraction."

Eli's lips quirked slightly. "Cattle usually are."

"Not the cattle." Violet chuckled. "But the storm."

"Ah, well...hold on to your britches, Cassie's coming."

"Cassie?"

"My favorite cow ever, but shhh, don't tell the others." A large brown cow came over, pressing her nose into Eli's shoulder to get her attention. Eli reached up and caressed her cheek before trying to shoo her away. "She thinks she's the bee's knees."

Violet laughed. "So does Diane, actually."

"Didn't find that storm you were looking for this morning?"

"There was no storm," Violet muttered. "I don't know what she was thinking."

"I might."

"What?" Violet turned on her, ready for any kind of explanation.

Eli shrugged. "Ask Lando. I bet she knows, too."

Confused, Violet didn't push. If Eli didn't want to tell her, that was going to be the end of it. Violet flipped through some of the photos she'd taken on her camera.

"Can I see?"

"Sure." They sat there for a few more minutes, going through the raw images before Violet shivered. "We should go. It's going to hit us soon."

"Yup." Eli stood up and got into the cab. Violet followed. They drove through another field, rain hitting the windshield the whole time. Eli drove back to the house, dropping Violet off before parking down at the barn.

Violet didn't even bother to go inside. She sat on the porch swing with her camera next to her and stared out at the thunderstorm. She was lost. She'd thought she had been before, but she was even more so now. She had no idea what the next day held for them, if Diane would change her tune now that everything was out in the open, now that Violet had confessed...

Lando slipped onto the swing next to her, two mugs in her hand as she pushed one in Violet's direction. "Thought you could use some tea."

"Thanks." Violet took the offered drink and let the hot ceramic warm her cold fingers. Lando stayed relatively quiet as they sat together, the slight sway of the swing from their bodies and the wind, the rain pinging the tin roof of the wraparound deck. "Where is she?"

"Up in her room, I think. Haven't seen her since lunch."

Violet sighed. She didn't want to deal with Diane if she could avoid it. She needed more time to let that conversation settle. "I don't know how much longer I can do this."

"Do what?"

Lando's question may have seemed simple, but Violet knew the answer wasn't. Tears stung her eyes for the first time that day, and Violet wondered where her emotions had been back in that bedroom when she'd talked with Diane. She hadn't felt this kind of pain before, the struggle to just get through the moment. She had no idea why she was talking to Lando anyway. She certainly didn't deserve to have all Violet's problems thrown at her.

"Any of this," Violet whispered, overwhelmed and not even sure where to start.

"Violet," Lando's voice broke. She leaned in, pressing her hand to Violet's thigh, the warmth from her fingers seeping into Violet's cold skin.

The tears broke loose. She couldn't control them as they spilled down her cheeks. Lando grabbed her mug and settled them both on the deck next to the swing, and then she did the unthinkable. She wrapped her arms around Violet's shoulders and dragged her in for a long embrace.

Lando soothed her, running hands up and down her back, trailing her fingers in swirls and random patterns against her spine, her shoulders. Violet even dared to think Lando dropped kisses into her hair, but she wasn't sure. No matter what, she was thankful for the moment they shared. She needed the friendship more than she cared to admit.

Wiping her eyes, Violet sat up and shook her head. "I talked to her about this morning."

"Oh," Lando answered, folding her hands in her lap.

"She swears there was a storm cell, but I think she wanted us out of the house."

"Why?"

Violet shook her head again. "I don't know, honestly. Diane has always been a bit of a mystery to me. She keeps a lot of secrets."

Lando pursed her lips and crossed her arms. Violet caught the move and instantly knew Eli had been right. Lando knew more than she was willing to admit.

"Lando," Violet's voice broke on her name.

"Yeah?"

"Do you know why?"

Lando shrugged noncommittally, which only confirmed to Violet that she at least had some idea. Sighing, Violet leaned into the swing, staring at the rain as it continued to fall. It was a beautiful storm, even if it wasn't one of the big supercells they were always looking for. They fell into the silence, neither moving or leaving, and Violet took comfort in that as well. She was so used to being on her own, alone, that to have someone who stood by her even when they didn't know what was going on was welcome.

"I think Diane wanted us out of the house, too."

"Why?"

"Because she wanted out of the house." Lando stared off into the distance.

Violet had barely noticed how much older she looked than she actually was. Trauma would do that to anyone. She gripped Lando's hand, threading their fingers together and giving her a gentle squeeze. She could give as much comfort as Lando had given her. At least, she hoped she could. "I can understand that desire."

"Can't we all." Lando's lips turned up in a wry smile. When she turned, Lando's gaze dropped to Violet's mouth.

Everything slowed. Violet reached up and cupped Lando's cheek, canting her head slightly. "I wish you'd told me that your grandmother wasn't just your grandmother. You know that's what we're here for—teachers, professors. We're here to support you as much as you need."

Lando's lip quivered, and she nodded. "Thank you, but I'm not your student anymore."

"Because we're here."

"No, because I dropped out."

"Lando." Surprise filled Violet's chest. She had no idea what to say. "Why?"

"Money. Time. I can't do it right now."

Violet sighed, her gaze dropping. Lando was one of her favorite students, one of the ones who did her best whenever she could, one who had a passion for the lessons. "You're one of my best students."

Lando snorted. "Not true, but thank you for trying."

"I'm serious, Lando. I wouldn't lie about that." Violet moved her thumb along Lando's cheek, not knowing why she hadn't stopped touching her yet. They fell into a silence, Violet's eyes locked on Lando's mouth, those lips, the way they were slightly parted.

She wasn't sure who moved first or if they moved together. Their mouths touched. Warmth spread through her, filling every inch of her body. It hit her hard, her chest rising to meet the moment with a breath, her hand sliding to Lando's neck to hold her closer. Lando's lips parting sent her into a panic.

Jerking back, Violet put as much space between them as possible on the tiny swing. Her hands were in her lap, folded together so she wouldn't reach forward and touch again. Lando's expression was pained, and she blinked, her gaze dropping as she blushed with embarrassment.

"I'm so sorry," Lando murmured. "I...I totally misread those signs."

Violet tried to force herself to speak, find something to say to soothe the ruffled feathers, but it was so hard. "You...it's fine. Don't worry about it."

Taking Lando's hand, Violet squeezed it lightly before letting go and putting that wall back up. The past week had been too emotional for her, too much going on, too much arguing. It hurt to be thrust into another one of those moments, but at least Lando wasn't yelling or guilting her.

Eventually Lando bent down and picked up their tea, handing a lukewarm mug over to Violet. They sat together, not speaking, as the rain continued to fall around them. Violet hadn't meant to open up so much, but Lando was there, she was such a good listener, and she was wise beyond her years.

Sipping her drink for the first time, Violet hummed as the flavors burst on her tongue. She hadn't thought of Lando like that, hadn't wanted anything to happen between the two of them, but the feelings from that morning came rushing back. The comfort and care Lando showed her, the calm at being held all night.

Her brain swirled in a vortex of confusion. She'd always wanted that with Diane, had always hoped Diane would be that person for her. They'd known each other so long that it had seemed so natural that a romantic relationship would be their next step. Except Violet couldn't force that on Diane. She couldn't make Diane fall in love with her. It had been a lost dream from the beginning.

With that thought settling in the pit of her stomach, Violet turned her mind to Lando. She had learned so much about this woman in the few short weeks they'd been together. Lando had hidden so well for the year she'd been in Violet's classes, for the time they'd spent together. It really brought home the fact that Violet didn't truly know her students. She knew one very small facet of who they were.

"I'm so sorry about your grandmother," Violet whispered, not sure why she was speaking. "And your mom."

"Thank you," Lando answered. "I never really knew my mom, but my grandmother was my world."

Violet nodded her understanding. "I wish I had the kind of relationship with mine that you did with yours."

"All we can do is change the future, Violet. We can't do anything about the past." Lando looked directly at her, their hands folded together again in silent support and strength.

Lando was right. Violet had to stop living in the world of dreams and what had happened in the past. She needed to take actionable steps toward the future she wanted and needed, not the one that was merely fantasy.

CHAPTER 16

LANDO'S LIPS tingled every time she thought about kissing Violet. They'd stayed out in that storm as long as possible before going inside for dinner, and Lando felt as though they'd reached some kind of impasse, but at least Violet seemed to find a sense of calm. Lando hadn't seen her like that before.

That night, they had both crashed hard, and Lando didn't even remember if they touched while they slept. She wouldn't put it past her. It was damn hard to share a bed with an attractive woman and keep to herself, but she'd managed it so far and would continue to since that seemed to be what Violet wanted.

Still...kissing her old professor had not been in her plans for the season. However, Lando couldn't get the kiss out of her mind. Her lips tingled again as she turned on her back to stare at the ceiling. Violet wasn't there, which was slightly odd. It was barely seven in the morning, so she must have snuck out to get coffee again. Lando normally woke to her leaving, but perhaps she'd really just been that tired, or that caught up in her dreams.

Lando wouldn't put it past herself. Stretching her arms above her head, she readied herself for the day. She already felt better than the day before, less sore and far more rested. After the calm confession from Violet about her friendship with Diane being the pits, they'd built another bridge between them. Lando was glad to lend support when she could.

They should probably talk more about what was going to happen from there on out. Lando hoped Violet had finally found her spine when it came to Diane, but she still had her doubts. Old habits were hard to change. That was something Lando understood viscerally. She scratched at the stitches in her arm before pulling off the gauze to see how it looked. It didn't seem too bad, and it had certainly been long enough. She hadn't wanted to disrupt the peace the day before by asking Violet to pull them out.

Staying in her sweats and T-shirt, Lando walked barefoot to the bathroom before heading downstairs to see if she could find Violet, itching at her stitches again. When had they become so annoying? Violet sat at one of the large chairs near the large picture window by the front of the house. Her leg was tossed over the arm, her fingers clasping a mug of coffee as she stared at the sunrise.

"Hey," Lando murmured, no doubt startling Violet out of her reverie.

"Hey." Violet's voice was still far away, as if Lando couldn't drag her back.

"Do you mind dealing with this? The itches are obnoxious." Lando held up her arm as if to prove her point.

Violet nodded toward her. "Go get the first aid kit. There should be some sharp scissors in there and tweezers."

Lando went back to their room, grabbed the requested items, and made her way downstairs, clutching the box. Violet had moved to the couch in the den, but she'd brought a second cup of coffee for Lando to drink.

"Oh sweet heaven, I need you." Lando grinned as she picked up the hot drink and sipped it.

Violet's lips twitched as she turned the first aid kit in her lap to get what she wanted from it. Within seconds, Lando had her arm outstretched across Violet's lap and her coffee in her other hand. Violet carefully snipped each stitch, pulling it free with the tweezers as it tugged Lando's skin.

"What time did you wake up?"

Violet shrugged. "I was having trouble sleeping. I think I came down here around four."

"Really? I was out."

"I know." Violet's lips curled upward again. "You were snoring."

"I was not!" Lando's cheeks flushed. She hadn't snored, had she? She tried to remember, but of course she couldn't because she'd been asleep.

"It was cute little snorts."

"Jesus." If Lando had a free hand, she would have brought one up to palm her face. She was absolutely embarrassed. "Just hit me next time or something."

"No point in both of us being awake."

Lando set her coffee down and tilted Violet's chin upward so they could look into each other's eyes. "Yeah, sure, but then maybe you could have slept."

Violet's lips parted, their eyes locking, and that same tension Lando had felt yesterday was back. She hesitated this time, though. Violet had moved away so fast the day before, looked as though Lando had hurt her. A kiss was just that, a kiss. It hadn't meant more, but Lando could not stop thinking about it.

"We can't," Violet whispered.

"Why not, teach?" She hadn't meant to ask that, but the question was out of her mouth before she could stop it. "What is there to stop us?"

"We can't," Violet repeated. She moved her head, ducking it so she could focus on pulling the rest of the stitches.

Lando let it drop, not wanting to push Violet into something she really didn't want to do. She wasn't there to upset Violet. In fact, Lando had taken it to heart that her job was simply to calm Violet down as best as she could. Violet got rid of the rest of the stitches in silence. When she finished, she piled them onto a piece of gauze and moved to clean up. Lando settled her hand over Violet's to stop her.

"I've got it. It's my mess."

"It's both ours, really." Violet's blue eyes locked on Lando's face, and Lando couldn't help but think there was a secondary meaning in those words that she was missing. Saying nothing, she gathered up the trash and took it to the kitchen. She washed her arm for the first time in ten days, and it felt glorious. The itching stopped almost immediately.

Before she went back, she took the coffee pot with her, refilling both their mugs before joining Violet again. Calm swept over them as they sat in silence, Violet staring out the window again and Lando watching Violet as if her entire life depended on Violet's next move. Her lips tingled again, but she chastised herself for the thought, knowing she really had to start working on giving that up sooner rather than later. It was clear Violet had no interest in any kind of relationship, even if it was temporary and only for fun.

"Did you check the maps?" Lando finally broke the quiet.

"A couple hours ago. There is a storm headed this way. North of us. It should hit this afternoon if we wait and don't go out to meet it."

"What do you think Diane will want to do?" Lando regretted asking that immediately.

Violet tensed, her gaze on some far-off distant thing, if she was even looking and not pulled back into her own mind. The day before had been fraught with tension between the two of them, and Lando should have known better than to poke it, although they were going to have to talk about Diane at some point.

"I don't know," Violet finally whispered.

Lando was pretty sure she didn't know, that once again, Violet was confessing her relationship with Diane wasn't as good as it first seemed. Lando wanted to reach over and pull Violet into a side hug, but after the conversation they'd just had, she wasn't sure it would be welcomed. Keeping her distance, Lando stayed quiet in case Violet waned to add anything else to the conversation itself.

When she said nothing and it was clear Eli was in the kitchen getting started on breakfast, Lando reached out and touched Violet's arm to get her attention. "Want to go help Eli?"

"Sure."

Together they went into the kitchen, setting their mugs down as the rolled up their sleeves, washed hands, and helped Eli prepare breakfast for the crew at the house. They worked well together, not bringing up anything they had talked about that morning again, and Eli was able to keep the conversation going.

Azalea came down next, looking put together like Lando expected her to. She went for the coffee first thing, starting another pot when she noticed the one was nearly empty. "Jewel will be down in a few minutes. She's just taking a shower."

Eli nodded at her sharply. "These two helped with breakfast, so it went much quicker than anticipated."

"We'll clean up then," Azalea added.

Lando could have laughed. They were at a bed and breakfast, which from everything she'd been taught, meant they were to be served, not helping. She really didn't care, but she found it amusing that everyone seemed to be willing to put in a helping hand when they wanted. Everyone except Diane, that was. She'd yet to see Diane get dirty. She mostly stayed up in her room, away from the rest of them.

Eli tilted her head at Lando, as if expecting to be let in on her thoughts. Lando shook her head, denying the intrusion, and went back to sipping her coffee. She was glad another pot was brewing. She would need it.

They sat to eat, Diane coming down for breakfast last minute as seemed to be her habit. They were halfway through the meal, Diane's gaze shifting awkwardly between Lando and Violet as if she couldn't figure something out. Lando chose to ignore her, and it seemed as though Violet was as well.

"Lando," Eli started. "Did you need help taking those stitches out today?"

"Oh, no. Violet did it earlier this morning. They itched so badly."

Eli chuckled. "I know how that can be. I've had enough stitches to remember that sweet feeling when they're finally gone."

Chuckling, Lando rested in her chair. "Yes. I had some across my forehead when I was an idiot teenager, and trust me, I could not wait to get those things out."

"What did you do?" Violet asked, her eyes wide.

Lando made eye contact with her, debating what to tell her. "I was drunk off my ass, fell down the front steps to the house and bashed my head on the broken step at the bottom. Nan was pretty pissed because I broke it even more, to the point she had to replace it."

"Lando." Pity filled Violet's gaze.

"Stupid teenage antics. I didn't feel a thing until the next day anyway."

"I'm sure." Violet's gentle fingers brushed against Lando's hand before withdrawing suddenly.

Lando clenched her jaw. So touching wasn't completely off the table. *Good to know.* "I also got stitches when I was eight, in my knee. I was running laps for soccer practice and one of the traditions was to jump over the water spigot. Well, I missed and didn't jump quite high enough. Tore a two-inch hole in my right knee. Wicked scar, but three stitches."

Eli laughed. "That sounds like something idiotic that I would do."

"Yeah." Lando eyed Violet up and down again, trying to judge exactly what she was thinking and feeling, though she didn't get far. Diane eyed her solidly. Lando didn't answer. Instead, she let the conversation drop. When they were finished with their meal, everyone brought their dishes to the sink, and Violet volunteered to help clean with Azalea and Jewel while Eli went to the barn.

Lando sat heavily on the edge of the bed. Finally in silence from that morning, a quiet where she could actually think instead of just wonder. Her lips tingled again, and she did have the fleeting thought that if she just waited long enough perhaps Violet would be more amenable to trying something with her. Lando could be patient, and it wasn't like she was going anywhere any time soon.

The knock on the door surprised her. Violet wouldn't knock, unless perhaps she thought that Lando was undressed, but even then, she hadn't done that so far. Standing, Lando opened the door and found Diane on the other side, papers in her hands.

"Hey," Lando said, confused.

"I need to talk to you, and I didn't want to do it while Violet was around."

"Oh, okay." Lando's stomach twisted. This didn't seem like it was going to be a good conversation. "I wanted to talk to you too, actually."

"Good." Diane came into the room, shutting and locking the door behind her.

Lando stared at the lock for a brief moment before shrugging it off and sitting on the bed she'd just vacated. Diane sat next to her and heaved a sigh.

"What's going on?" Lando asked, her brow furrowing.

"I've been trying to figure out how we can make this work."

"Make what work?" Lando's stomach clenched hard, and she knew she wasn't going to like this conversation. She had a feeling about where it was going, but she was not going to make it easier for Diane if she could.

"The team. There's too much fighting going on, and something has to give. We're not getting the work done we need to."

"All right." Lando was still confused. If anyone had been fighting it was Diane and Violet. Lando had largely stayed out of that, but she was also the new kid on the block, so if someone was going to take the blame for something, it would likely be her.

"We need to make some changes so this doesn't happen again."

"I agree with that." Those words would be her damning words, she knew it as soon as she said them. "I think we all need to sit down and have a come-to-Jesus moment."

Diane's lips pulled tight. "Violet and I did that yesterday."

"Oh." Lando bit her tongue. That wasn't exactly how Violet told it, but she supposed Violet could have gotten a few points across that Diane was now taking to heart. "I'm glad. Hopefully it kills some of the tension."

Diane frowned. "We discussed it, and we don't think you're working out on our team."

"What?" Shock rang through Lando's entire body. Violet had said nothing of the sort, but she had been acting odd since yesterday, far more open and less withdrawn. Perhaps it was because Lando was leaving and they wouldn't have to deal with each other any longer.

"We're terminating our contract with you."

"I don't understand." Lando shook her head. "I have an internship. I can't just transfer that to another team mid-season."

"I understand." Diane's tone lowered. "I really am sorry about this, but we have to do what is best for the team and the data."

"And you think you can run as a two-person team?"

"I know we can. It's nothing Violet and I haven't done before."

Lando clenched her fingers tightly into her palm, her nails biting the soft flesh to center herself. She'd been fired before. This wasn't anything new, but she'd never been fired when sober and for seemingly no reason at all. "So what am I supposed to do?"

"Go home, stay here, go somewhere else. That's all up to you,

Lando. Here's your paycheck for the last two weeks. After that we no longer have a working relationship, and you cannot stay in this room any longer."

Lando stared down at the check in her hand. It was minuscule, certainly not what she had earned in two weeks working with them. It wasn't even three hundred dollars. "This...this isn't my whole check, is it?"

"It is, after expenses."

"After expenses?" Lando frowned, unable to move her gaze from the piece of paper in her hands. "What expenses?"

"Here. This is a detailed inventory of everything it has cost us to have you here, and your portion."

"My...portion?" Lando couldn't believe what she was hearing. A second piece of paper landed in her hands, and just as Diane had said, there was a list of everything on it. Half of the room in Oklahoma, Colorado, and *Indigo*, which was expensive. She'd never have stayed here if she'd known how much it was costing them. There were food items on there, Twizzlers that Diane had bought her that first day.

She wanted to cry. She wanted to rage and scream, but all she could do was stare at the information Diane was giving her and say nothing. She just sat there and took it.

Diane patted her shoulder, but it was cold and aloof, not comforting at all. Diane stood up, mumbling something, but Lando didn't even process the words. Her two weeks with them had been worth two hundred fifty-nine dollars. That was it. Her internship had paid everything, the money Diane had taken from it to fill her own pockets.

Her stomach churned with bile. She wanted to puke. She wanted to scream and yell. *God, she wanted a fucking drink.* Tears stung her eyes as she sat in silence, all alone, trying to figure out her next step. After a few minutes, Lando angrily grabbed her computer and pulled up the Internet. She purchased a flight home from the nearest airport, and then hoped she could beg Eli to drive her down there.

She needed to get away, get home, anything that would put some distance between her and Diane, where she could center herself again, not fall into bad old habits. Lando immediately left the bedroom and headed downstairs. She went through the front door instead of the back and took the long way down to the barn. Luckily, Eli's truck was still there, so she hadn't gone out into the fields yet.

Lando stepped inside the open barn and wrapped her arms around herself as she looked around to try and find Eli. Luckily, Eli was right up front, so she didn't have to go too far inside. Eli looked surprised to see her standing there.

"Lando! What's up?"

Lando shook her head, not sure where to begin or what to even say. "Um...do you think you could drive me to the airport?"

"Sure. When?"

"In an hour."

Eli looked confused. "In an hour?"

Lando nodded, her arms still crossed tightly over her chest as if she was trying to protect herself from the world, which she supposed she was. "Yeah."

"Are you not going to that storm today that Violet was talking about?"

Her eyes watered, and her nose scrunched up as she tried to stop the waterworks. "No."

"Lando, what happened?"

"Diane fired me." Her voice was so small and weak. Lando hated it. She wanted to be the bigger person, strong and ready for anything. "And the check she gave me as payment barely even covered the plane ticket."

"Lando." Eli's voice and gaze filled with pity. She stepped in close and wrapped her arms around Lando's shoulders, tugging her in for a hug. "Jesus, what happened?"

"I don't know." Lando plastered her face into Eli's shoulder and held on as if Eli was her lifeline. She needed this more than she'd thought she did. It would have been better if Eli were Aunt

T, but for now, Eli was the next best thing. She was someone Lando had come to like and trust. She cried while Eli rubbed hands up and down Lando's back in a soothing motion.

"I'll take you wherever you need to go, but know you're welcome to stay here for a few days. I have an extra room in the basement if you need some space from them."

"No. I need to go home. I...I probably never should have taken this job."

"Okay." Eli squeezed her tightly before letting go. "Okay. When's your flight?"

"Two."

"You go pack up, and I'll make a phone call. Then we can get going, okay?"

Lando nodded, agreeing to anything Eli said. She needed someone to take control of the situation because if she was left on her own, she wasn't in the right mind to do anything except try not to go find the beer she knew was left over from a few nights ago. It would be the easiest thing to get hold of, she knew that, even if she'd prefer something harder.

"Eli?" Lando cleared her throat.

"Yeah?"

"I need to ask you another favor." Lando looked into Eli's brown eyes, begging for her to understand how serious this was.

"Anything."

Lando nodded. "I need you to not leave me alone for a bit. I can't... I don't want to drink."

"Yes." Eli gave her answer without hesitation. "Yes, I can do that."

Lando stayed with Eli until she finished up what she was working on and made her call to ask a guy Bill for help that day. They walked together to the house, talking about anything under the sun that wasn't related to storms or Violet or Diane or her drinking. Lando had never been more grateful to someone than she was just then.

Eli stood by as she quickly shoved everything she could think of into her duffel and her backpack. Then together, they walked down the stairs and toward the barn where Eli had left both her trucks. Violet was nowhere to be seen, and Lando was grateful for that. The Hummer was still parked out front of the house, so she knew they hadn't gone anywhere. They were probably making plans for the storm that afternoon. Lando slid into the passenger seat of Eli's truck and buckled her seatbelt.

"Are you sure you don't want to leave a note for her or something?"

Lando shook her head. "No. She knows already. Diane said they discussed it."

"And you trust Diane?"

She wanted to say no. Instead, Lando kept her mouth shut, not looking at the house as Eli drove them away. She couldn't stand to look at it, to see what she was leaving behind, because it wasn't Violet, it wasn't Diane. It was her hopes and dreams of being a storm chaser. She wouldn't find another team that season to join with, and she didn't have the time to wait around for it to happen with no income, either.

She would be lucky to get one the next year without a degree and without the experience, and with being fired from the first team she'd ever been on. The prospects were dim, and Lando knew she'd have to make some changes to what she had planned for the future. Her words from the night before came back to haunt her, although she had been right. She couldn't do anything to change the past, all she could do was hope to change the future and make it that much better.

Eli walked her into the airport and then spoke quietly with one of the front workers. When she came back, Eli wrapped an arm around Lando's shoulders. "I hope you don't mind, but I told them you're not allowed any alcohol."

"Thank you." Lando could have cried again. "You're too good to me."

"I think of you kind of like the little sister I never had.

You're welcome back to *Indigo* any time, Lando. I'm serious. You can crash in the basement if you just need a break or whatever."

"Will Sadie be there?"

"Who knows." Eli winked. "But we can always try to line up visits."

Lando chuckled lightly. "I think I'll be okay for now. I know you have to get back to the ranch."

"Lando." Eli turned her by the shoulders so they faced each other. "For the record, I think Diane's got a stick up her ass so big it's gone into her brain."

Snorting, Lando nodded. "Probably accurate."

"Good." Eli hugged her again, kissed the side of her head, and then gave her a sad smile. "I am serious about that offer."

"Thanks. And thanks again for driving me here."

"Anything for you."

Without dragging out the conversation any longer, Eli left the airport and Lando. The building was nearly empty that time of day since there were no flights until hers in the early afternoon. Lando sat in one of the uncomfortable chairs and let out a sigh before she tightened all her muscles again. *How the hell was she going to tell Aunt T?*

CHAPTER 17

VIOLET HAD LEFT Diane's room hours ago after making plans for that afternoon. She'd spent a lot of that time in quiet, trying to figure out what she was feeling. Lando kissing her had been vastly unexpected, and she was still reeling from that. From her soft lips. From the guilt that swam through her gaze when Violet had pulled away.

If she thought about it too long, she couldn't resist the pull of wanting it to happen again. It wasn't just the kiss. That had been nice but nothing significant, nothing mind-blowing. It was the care that Lando had given her before, during, and after. It was the connection the two of them had as Violet lowered the walls she'd built up over the years.

She'd never thought anyone would be able to break down those walls that quickly, and yet, there was Lando. Someone who seemed to be able to do it at the snap of her fingers. It made Violet uncomfortable in her own skin. She wasn't used to that odd kind of vulnerability.

The knock on the door caught her attention. "You ready?"

"Yeah. I just need to find Lando."

Diane's lips parted, surprise but also something else. "Lando won't be coming with us."

"What do you mean? Is she sick?" Violet grabbed her backpack and started shoving the rest of her supplies in it, remembering the first aid kit she'd used on Lando's arm at the last minute.

"No." Diane didn't elaborate.

Violet finished packing and turned to face Diane, hands fisted on her hips. "Then where is she?"

"I don't know."

"What do you mean you don't know?" Violet narrowed her gaze.

Diane straightened her back at Violet's aggressive tone, and Violet instantly regretted using it. She should have taken a softer voice with Diane, that was the best way to get information out of her anyway. "She and I had a talk this morning, and Lando agreed she wasn't right for this team."

Cold rushed through Violet's bones. She shivered as her stomach plummeted at the thought. "I'm not understanding."

"Lando is no longer a part of our team."

"Why?" Violet barely contained whatever emotion rampaged through her. She wasn't even sure she could name it if she tried. Worry, fear, apathy? No, not apathy. Resignation. Somehow she'd known this was going to happen, that Lando wouldn't make it through the season.

"She said she couldn't do it anymore."

Violet pressed her lips together hard, her fingers balling into fists. Diane stepped closer and put a hand on Violet's shoulder.

"I'm sorry. I know you valued her help."

"What exactly did she say?" Violet ground out.

Diane looked surprised, but she didn't comment on it. "I don't remember. It was a quick conversation."

"Where is she now?"

"I don't know." Confusion flashed across Diane's face. "What does it matter?"

Violet raised her gaze, locking her eyes on Diane's. "I don't believe you."

"What?"

"I don't believe you. Lando has worked for years to get to this point, to find an internship, to come out chasing. I don't think she'd readily give that up after two weeks. What did you say to her?"

"I didn't say anything, I swear."

"You had a conversation with her, yes?"

Diane nodded her affirmation.

"Then you talked to her. What exactly did you say to her?"

"Nothing that would make her leave."

"Bullshit, Diane. What did you tell her? Did you tell her we didn't need her? Did you tell her she was fired?" Diane's absolute lack of reaction told Violet everything. Collapsing onto the bed, Violet folded in on herself. "Why the hell would you do that? She's good, Diane. She's better than me in some ways, and you fire her?"

"She wasn't fitting in with our dynamic."

"What dynamic? We argue and fight. She bounced between that. If any dynamic isn't working it's the two of us." Violet glared. "Why did you fire her?"

"It wasn't working out."

"Are you ever going to answer me?" Violet sighed at Diane's hard stare. She'd known better before she asked. Diane would never tell her what was going on. She staunchly kept most of that to herself, hiding it away. Resigned, Violet gripped the strap on her backpack. "Let's go catch this storm."

Diane tried to talk to her while they drove, but Violet wouldn't answer. She stewed. She was pissed, not only at Diane but at herself. Lando had been right. She let Diane walk all over her, and she just took it. There was pushback, yes, but never enough that would require a change from Diane.

They drove for an hour before they found the storm. It wasn't full-fledged yet. Violet stared at the clouds as if they reflected her mood, a swirling dark matter of anger just under the surface, waiting to be let go.

She didn't want to be there. For the first time since Violet could remember, she didn't want to be at the center of the storm. That thought echoed in her mind and her heart as she guided Diane closer. Other storm chasers lined the dirt roads, so Violet knew they were close to the right place.

Biting her cheek, Violet stared out the window. Everything in her protested being there. The love she'd had of chasing gone, and she hoped it was just for the day, although, if she thought about it long enough, her love for chasing had slowly been waning the last few years. She'd found that excitement in Lando, someone who was young and had all those dreams in front of her, someone who brought that excitement with her.

She'd enjoyed Lando's countenance, the energy she brought to everything. Without her they felt like two old women, far past their prime, and nowhere near ready to be chasing that season— or any season.

Diane parked, and Violet stepped out of the vehicle. Wind rushed at her cheeks, pushing her hair away from her face as she squinted through it to see if the funnel they'd been following had touched down yet. Violet took a moment to go the trunk and grab the small box of devices they needed to get into the line of the tornado. She flipped them on and then went back to her computer to make sure they were connected and tracking.

She did everything in silence, not even bothering to talk to Diane about what needed to happen next or where they should be focusing. Diane had her camera to her face, no doubt as a protest to the fact Violet wouldn't even speak to her. Her heart shattered. If Lando had been there, they'd be running off into the field together. They'd be making this plan together.

Violet stopped short, staring at the sleek devices that had been Lando's responsibility. She didn't want to do this without her, but more importantly, Violet didn't want to do it *with* Diane. Everything that season so far had taught her that she and Diane were not a match made in heaven. They needed to not be partners in this, to separate.

The grant money would come with her because she was the one with the credentials. It would leave Diane high and dry, but on some very basic level, Violet didn't care. Diane had dug her own grave on this one, and she wasn't about to pull her out, not when she couldn't guarantee that Diane would ever do the same for her.

Violet rolled her shoulders and picked up the box, turning to face the field to the west. The funnel had touched down, making a very small tornado, but any tornado was worthy for them, especially if it was a rope tornado, which this one was. The bulk of it wound its way from earth to sky, connecting them in a power that Violet wanted to harness and study. She'd always wanted that, but today...today she could have gone back to *Indigo*, curled up in her bed, and stayed there.

No one had ever been able to pound the love of storms out of her before. No one but Diane. Flicking her gaze to Diane as she stood, camera to her face as she snapped photo after photo, Violet acquiesced. They had this one storm, and then she would figure out what needed to happen. For now, she wasn't going to miss an opportunity to find more information, get more data.

Walking next to Diane, they stood side by side and watched as the tornado came toward them, closer as it wobbled in their direction. It was always a miracle that they had any idea where these beasts of power and wind were going to begin with. Violet said nothing to Diane as she walked down the ditch to the fence line.

Crossing it, being careful not to catch herself on the barbed wire, Violet waded through the wheat fields toward the tornado. Her heart raced, and she was determined, but nothing felt the same without Lando there. She wanted to see that excitement reflected in those pale blue eyes—the excitement she'd once had herself.

Jogging, Violet made her way to the center of the field. Wind whipped around her. She glanced back to Diane who had a radio to her mouth, and she realized last minute, she hadn't taken hers.

Cursing, Violet dropped the box at one of the high points she could find and ran toward the Hummer. She made it to the fence before she turned around and found the tornado gone.

"Well, that was short lived," Diane said as she came over, leaning on a fence post.

Violet didn't answer. Short-lived like Lando's participation in their team. It seemed perfectly fitting for a day like today. She walked slowly through the rain to snatch up the box of devices and carry it to the car.

Sliding into the passenger seat, Violet brushed her wet hair out of her face. "I'm done for the day, Diane. Let's go back."

"Are you sure?"

"Yes." Violet didn't give any more explanation than that. Diane would do what she wanted anyway, and all Violet could hope was that she listened this time and took them back to *Indigo*. She wanted to find Lando, figure out where she had gone off to, and then she wanted to talk. Maybe they could still resolve this dilemma and Lando could join their team again. Maybe she could even fire Diane and it could be her and Lando chasing for the rest of the season.

Her lips twitched at the thought. It would be the perfect fuck-you to Diane, although she wasn't sure Lando would want to work with her. She wasn't exactly an easy boss, or person. But for the sake of data, Lando might be into it. Violet zoned out for the drive, her damp clothes chilling her to the bone as they drove. She needed to get changed and warm first thing when they got back.

Diane remained absolutely dry, having taken shelter in the car as soon as the rain started to fall. Typical. Violet inwardly sneered. Everything about Diane had set her on edge lately, all the bad parts about her childhood best friend coming out in full force. They needed a break from each other, but Violet wasn't sure she wanted to carry on that friendship any longer. It wasn't because Diane had told her she didn't love her. Violet had known that—not romantically at least. But at some point, she had to give up the dreams she'd once had and realize what was right in front of her.

The house was quiet when they returned. Eli's truck was nowhere to be found, so Violet figured she was out in the fields somewhere. Gathering her stuff from the Hummer, Violet trudged upstairs. Lando was still gone, but Violet stopped short. She looked around the room, her stomach twisting and sinking fast. All of Lando's things were gone. She was gone. For good.

∼

Aunt T picked her up at the airport, a permanently pitying look on her face as she drove Lando back to the house. Lando could barely look at her, everything Aunt T had said before she left coming back to hit her full force in the face. Sometimes Lando really needed to remember to listen to her.

As they got to the house, Aunt T helped Lando bring her stuff inside and flopped onto the couch. "Tell me the full story of what happened?"

"I don't know what happened, really." Lando collapsed next to her and put her head on Aunt T's shoulder. "One minute I thought everything was fine—tense, but it was always tense—but fine. The next Diane fired me."

"And didn't pay you?"

Lando shrugged, really not wanting to explain that one. She'd already told Aunt T about the abysmal paycheck she'd gotten and how she was going to need to borrow money to pay bills on the house for the next month until she found herself a job that did pay.

"What are we going to do with you, Lando?"

Again, she didn't answer. That day had been the longest day of her life. She grabbed her phone and sent Eli a text, telling her she was home safe, hadn't had a drop of alcohol, and that her Aunt was staying the night with her. But being home again had washed away a lot of those tendencies she'd struggled with when out in the field. She was in her place of comfort, somewhere she knew the people, knew Aunt T would come without a second question if she needed.

"I miss Nan, you know," Lando whispered.

"She'd rip you a new one if she knew about this," Aunt T muttered.

"I know." Lando gave a wan smile. "She would have done it when I left too."

Chuckling, Aunt T wrapped her arm around Lando's shoulders. "Yeah, she would have. And then again every day until you got home. There were a lot of bad decisions that went into this."

"There were." Lando sighed heavily, her head hurting from the stress of the day. "If I fall asleep on you, just shove me off and cover me with a blanket."

"If you're going to fall asleep, go to bed."

Lando grunted, not wanting to explain that for the last two weeks she hadn't slept alone, and the thought of going upstairs to her bedroom by herself was more overwhelming than she'd anticipated. She hadn't thought having someone else right there who could help her with her demons would be so poignant, but it had. Violet had done just that. It didn't matter if she was pissed or annoyed at Lando or at Diane, the silent support was still there.

Aunt T brushed a hand through Lando's short hair, scraping her nails lightly against Lando's scalp. It was something she'd done since Lando was a kid anytime she was upset or melancholy. Closing her eyes, Lando relaxed into the familiar and comforting touch.

"I'm going out tomorrow to get food and look for a job."

"You do that," Aunt T answered. "But also feel free to take a day to mope."

"I don't have a day."

"Lando, you can afford one day."

Keeping her mouth shut so she wouldn't continue a pointless argument, Lando closed her eyes. She was devastated about all that had happened while she'd been gone. It hadn't been very long, but it felt like months.

"Maybe I should get a dog."

"Why?"

"This house is big and empty."

"Are you lonely?" Aunt T turned her chin down. "Because you can always move into the house with me and Kyle and the kids. You know there's a room there for you if you want. We can rent out this place, get some income off it."

Lando had thought about that at one point, more often after her grandmother had died, but she didn't want to intrude. They had a full house already. They didn't need an extra person to deal with, and Lando was an adult. She needed to learn to live on her own and stand on her own two feet.

"No, but I wouldn't mind the occasional sleepover."

Aunt T laughed lightly. "I'm sure the girls would love it."

"Good." They stayed there for another hour until Lando pried herself up and went to bed. She stripped naked and fell onto the blankets she hadn't made up before she left. As soon as her eyes were shut, she was out.

∼

Morning came sooner than she'd anticipated, and Aunt T had woken her early to tell her she was leaving for work, a fresh pair of scrubs already on. Lando couldn't figure out where she'd gotten them from, but then dismissed the thought because it didn't matter.

It took Lando longer than she wanted to admit to pry herself out of the bed and down the stairs. She got to the couch and flopped on it, curling her legs under her body as she grabbed her phone she'd forgotten down there the night before. Unlocking it, she stared curiously and anxiously at a text message from Violet.

"I'm so sorry."

That was all it said. Simply put, firing her hadn't made a bit of a difference. Violet was at least guilty about it. Lando nearly typed out an answer but stopped herself. There was nothing to say. Violet had agreed to fire her but let Diane do the dirty work. Now she felt guilty about it. Deleting the message, Lando closed her eyes.

Job and coffee were the two pervading thoughts in her mind, and not in that order. She was going to have to get back on her feet as soon as possible, and she was going to have to call in a favor she hadn't wanted to. She'd almost done it before she left, but now she was desperate.

Lando stayed put for another five minutes before convincing herself to get up. She couldn't call Bryce that early in the morning. He would flat-out kill her. But she could at least get prepared to beg for her old job back. When she got to the kitchen, she frowned as she stared at her empty cupboards.

She'd gotten rid of just about everything, including the coffee grounds. She'd given those to Aunt T so they would be put to use instead of waste. Groaning, Lando dragged her heavy feet upstairs to her bedroom. She pulled on a fresh pair of cargo pants and a sports bra before tugging a T-shirt over her head. Taking the gel out of her duffel, she went to the bathroom to make herself look at least mostly presentable.

It didn't take long. She was in her grandmother's old Buick, trying to ignore the nearly empty gas tank. Aunt T had gone to get the car for her shortly after she left when she'd had time, storing it at her house until she could get back to it. Lando wasn't sure what she would do without her family around, and in some ways, she'd wondered why she'd been stupid enough to think she could manage without them.

Her first stop was to a drive-through coffee joint. Her second stop was in the parking lot of the big box hardware store she'd worked at most of the summers she had off in high school and college. She'd only taken a leave when her grandmother hadn't been able to take care of herself anymore and needed hospice, then they'd parted ways when the grievance time hadn't been long enough. Lando hadn't wanted to miss a minute of the time they had left.

With a quarter of her coffee warming her insides, Lando dialed Bryce's number and hoped it was late enough in the morning for him. "Lando?"

"What's up?" She put a lot of false enthusiasm into that voice.

"Just waking up for work. Aren't you supposed to be storm chasing?"

Lando frowned. Word had gotten around their small town, and Bryce no doubt had heard that one from Aunt T. "I was. It didn't work out."

He paused, silence echoing. "Are you calling to see if you can have your old job back?"

"Yeah."

Bryce sighed. "Give me a second."

Lando waited patiently, turning her car off so she didn't waste any gas that she might need for something else. She sipped her coffee, letting the caffeine seep into her bones until she felt a little more alive.

"Okay." He came back on the line. "Did you know I never took you off payroll?"

"What?" Lando furrowed her brow.

"I kind of hoped you wouldn't find a team to go out with, honestly, and that you'd always come back after your grandmother..." he trailed off.

"Yeah." That had been her intention, but also the thought of going back there, where they all knew what had happened, was overwhelming. Not to mention, she hadn't been desperate enough just yet. Since then, she'd spent through what little savings she had, and she officially hit desperation.

"I can get you on the schedule for today if you're in town. The hours will be light until I can fully put you back in."

"Can you really?"

"Anything for you, Lando. You're a hard worker. I was sad to see you take a different path, as happy as I was for you."

Lando's eyes teared up. She was finding kindness everywhere she hadn't thought to look. "Thanks."

"Really, I mean it. I'll be in to work in about an hour. Meet me there?"

"Absolutely."

They ended the conversation with a few more pleasantries, and Lando leaned back into the driver's seat of the old car. She drank her coffee, knowing it'd likely be the last treat she got herself for a while. She needed to save up, pay back Aunt T, who would no doubt tell Uncle Kyle to go stock the house full of food while she was at work that day, and figure out what she was going to do for the next six months. Maybe she could start back at school in the fall if she could qualify for some loans—though she really didn't want to take those out.

Her day was already looking up from where it had started. Perhaps she was finally on the right track. Even if it wasn't the dream she had set out to accomplish, it was something, and she was comfortable with the decisions she was making. The tension from the last few weeks was gone, and she was back to her old self—or at least, getting closer to it. With a smile on her lips, Lando stared at the store in front of her. She had a job, she had a house, a car, and she had family. What more could she ask for?

CHAPTER 18

VIOLET COULDN'T SLEEP. She'd spent the night tossing and turning until the wee hours of the morning and well before sunrise when she just couldn't handle it anymore. The room was cold without Lando there, and she missed her, although she didn't really want to admit it and wouldn't to anyone but herself.

Sitting up and leaning against the headboard, Violet pulled her computer up and turned it on, bringing it to life. She searched through the weather radar and maps, finding nothing of particular interest that morning. The small storm yesterday had been worth it, although she had a gut feeling from the start they'd never manage to catch the tornado, mostly because her heart hadn't been in it.

She rubbed her hands over her cheeks and her eyes, closing them. She was exhausted. The last two weeks had been hell, but now she had no light to brighten up her days. That had truly been what Lando was for her. She hadn't realized it at the time, but Lando had brought something new, something interesting to chasing, a distraction from everything Violet didn't want to think about or deal with.

She sighed and bent over the side of the bed to grab the camera. She wasn't ready to go downstairs yet and deal with people. She didn't want to run into anyone she didn't want to talk to. Flipping through the pictures on Eli's old camera, Violet stopped at some of the ones with the huge storm they'd followed for hours. Some of the shots were worth some money for sure. She'd have to doll them up a bit, but it wouldn't be too much work.

She hit the next button again, gasping when she saw the one she'd taken immediately after Lando had taken off running toward it. She was fearless. Lando's strength and energy flowed through the photo and right into Violet's chest. She had run full force toward that tornado without a second thought, and the power in her legs as she moved showed it.

Violet zoomed in on Lando, looking the image over for any flaws. This could very easily be a money shot if she sold it. She'd have to get Lando's permission, but that shouldn't be too hard, especially if she was trying to make a name for herself in the chasing world. Moving the focus of the photo to the tornado, Violet eyed it.

The satellite tornados bursting off the storm cell were just in the beginning of their offshoot, funneling down toward the ground. Violet shuddered. That truly had been a storm of a lifetime for a lot of people. Finding one that powerful didn't happen every year, and finding one they could follow and chase and be in the right place was even more rare.

Turning on her side, Violet lay down in the bed. She moved to the image of Lando. It was her from the back, running straight toward the heart of the storm like she had no care in the world. Violet knew that wasn't true, but that was the sense the photo gave off and she wasn't about to argue with it.

They dared death every day they went out, and they did it so much without allowing fear or anxiety to get through. If they did, it would certainly be the end of all of them. They couldn't fake confidence either. It was something they had to go into each storm with, as if they could wrangle the tornado with their own bare hands even though everyone knew they couldn't, and wouldn't even try.

Violet brushed her fingers over her lips, remembering the way Lando had pressed against her. She'd almost given in to it, almost pushed back and kissed her, taken what Lando offered. Yet, she hadn't. Violet hadn't expected it, hadn't been ready. Still, there she was, days later, still thinking about the warmth of Lando's mouth, the softness of her full lips, the calm and comfort she exuded.

It was all wrong.

Lando should be there with her, should be the one to be chasing storms with her, not Diane. Not someone who didn't seem to care about what they were doing. Sitting up in bed, Violet listened carefully to see if Eli was awake yet. If she closed her eyes, she could hear rustling downstairs.

Grabbing a sweatshirt, Violet pulled it over her head as she made her way as quietly as possible down the stairs. Eli stood in the kitchen, coffee pot in her hand as she filled it with water. Violet's lips quirked up.

"Hey," she said.

Eli jumped before turning around. "Scared me."

"Sorry." Violet shrugged. "I was hoping it was late enough that you'd be awake."

"Late enough?" Eli raised one of her busy eyebrows. "Did you not sleep?"

"Struggled with it. I've been..." Violet paused as she searched for the right word. "...unsettled since you told me Lando flew home."

"Ah." Eli poured the water into the coffee pot and hit the button for it to start. "She was upset."

"I have no doubt of that," Violet murmured. "I would be, too."

Eli cocked her head to the side. "Why?"

"Because it was an unfair termination."

Crossing her arms, Eli leaned against the counter and eyed

Violet up and down cautiously. Violet held her ground, waiting her out. She wanted to know what was going on behind those beautiful brown eyes because there was definitely something swirling in there.

"Did you know Diane was going to do it?" Eli finally asked.

Violet shook her head, pushing away the disgust that wanted to blow up. "I didn't know until we were leaving for the storm yesterday, after you'd already taken her to the airport."

Eli nodded sharply. "You should call Lando."

"Why?" Violet raised an eyebrow, not sure how that would make any difference. "I'm not sure she'd want to hear from me."

"She probably doesn't." Eli turned and grabbed a travel mug for her coffee. "But she thinks you were in on firing her."

"What?" Violet's eyes widened. "I would never... I didn't..."

Trailing off, Violet glanced toward the stairs to the bedrooms. This was unacceptable. Anger burst into her chest, and she curled her fingers, making one of the few rash decisions she ever had in her life.

"Would you have time to take me to the airport today?"

Eli's eyes lit up. "Leaving earlier than planned?"

"Yes, I'm sorry, and the room will be paid for as long as it was booked, I promise." Violet pressed her hand flat on the cold marble counter. She'd never felt so calm before going into an argument with Diane, but it seeped into her. Resolve. That was what it was.

"I can certainly do that."

"Thanks." Violet went to move toward the stairs but a hand on her arm stopped her.

"She was really hurt by it."

"I've no doubt." Violet pressed her lips together tightly.

"If you're going to yell, can you do it outside? I don't want you to wake the other guests."

"Of course." Violet nodded and stepped around the edge of the counter, ignoring the fact that she didn't have coffee yet. It wasn't even on her mind as she quietly walked up the stairs. The first thing she did was pack up her room and get dressed for the day. Then she stood in front of Diane's door and drew in a deep breath.

She would remain calm through this. She wouldn't throw a fit or argue. She wouldn't yell. She had to keep telling herself that. Calm would be the word of the morning as she told Diane off. Violet knocked, but she didn't wait for a response as she opened the door and stepped inside. Thankfully, Diane had left it open.

She was curled in her bed, still asleep. Violet sat on the edge of the mattress and shook her arm to wake her up. Diane looked confused, her brow furrowed as she slowly woke up and figured out Violet was there.

"What's wrong?" Diane asked.

"What exactly did you tell Lando when you fired her?"

"I told her she was no longer working for the team."

Violet clenched her jaw, then her fingers against her thigh. Diane was the master of not answering questions. Nodding to herself, Violet stared out at the sky as it lightened.

"I'm going home," she said, so matter-of-factly that she was sure Diane would be confused.

Sure enough, Diane sat up, grabbing for Violet's hand. "What?"

"I can't do this anymore, Diane. This isn't what I want for my life, and you aren't someone I think I want in it."

Diane looked wildly at her. "You just told me you loved me."

"I did." Violet nodded her agreement. "And I think I was wrong. I don't love you. I don't know how I could, you've never been anything but cruel to me, ever since we were kids. I put up with it because in a town of twelve hundred, there aren't a whole lot of options for friends."

"What are you saying?"

"I'm saying I'm done. I'm not going to chase with you, and I'm not going to allow your cruelty to others. I'm leaving, and I'm going home. I'd prefer if I never heard from you again."

Standing up, Violet made to move for the door, but Diane gripped her wrist and tugged her back.

"How can you just leave?" Her voice rose, as if she was going to yell.

Violet stopped and gave her a hard look. "Because there's nothing here for me anymore, and I want a life where I'm not worried about everything I say and do with you. I want to chase storms with someone who equally wants to be there. I want to find my passion for this again, and I can't do that with you."

Without another word, Violet wrenched her hand from Diane's grasp and left the room. She picked up her bags on the way out and headed downstairs. Eli had pulled the truck up to the house from the barn, and they loaded her stuff into the back. She booked her ticket on the drive, spending an exorbitant amount of money for the last-minute ticket, but she didn't want to spend any more time with Diane than necessary.

She grinned her thanks when Eli handed over a travel mug of coffee. "Thought you could use this."

"Thank you. Don't you need to stay and cook breakfast, though?"

Eli lifted a shoulder and dropped it. "Azalea can figure it out. I left her a note."

"She's your former teacher, right?"

"Yeah. She was my science teacher all through high school."

Violet mulled over the next question she wanted to ask. "When did you two become friends?"

"After I graduated, but she was very supportive when I came out to my family in high school."

"And you never...?" Violet trailed off.

Eli snickered. "No. Azalea, while beautiful, is not my type."

"All right." Violet twisted her hands together in her lap. They made most of the rest of the drive in silence, and when they arrived at the airport, Violet thanked Eli profusely for everything. As soon as she was on her own, Violet rolled her shoulders. It was the first time in years that she felt like she was doing the right thing.

∽

Lando had been officially working at her old job for four days, and while it wasn't ideal, it was a job. She could expect a paycheck, with more hours to fill it up next week, and she would be able to make the utility payments this month. Next month, she could focus on paying Aunt T back.

She climbed into the forklift, checking to make sure everything was in place before she turned it on. Lando drove to the pallet she was supposed to move and set on the floor, following the instructions Bryce had given her the day before since she was scheduled in before him. It didn't take her long to find where she was going and what she needed to do.

Driving slowly through the aisles, Lando took a wide berth so she wouldn't accidentally run into anyone or anything. The store was huge, and often they would move things like this in order to get them there faster. Parking close to the front of the store so she could set out the canopies that were for sale, Lando lowered the forklift so she could access the pallet.

As soon as she was standing next to the large pallet, she took out her box cutter and started to open it. She would set up two of these for the first chunk of her day, setting up the lawn and garden section since it hadn't been done yet, which surprised her. Usually they had it up before the end of February since people liked to shop early for it.

She popped her back as she started in on the first one. The box was heavy and awkward as she moved it by herself to start the stack. She had three more down, but when she stood up to grab the fourth, she froze in her spot. Brown hair, blue eyes, lanky body. Violet was everything she was not, beautiful, strong, confident, stoic. Lando drew in a shuddering breath before she reached forward and grabbed the damn fourth box, saying nothing to her former teacher.

Lando's belly swirled with anxiety and fear. She didn't know if Violet was back for a second firing or yelling or not, though in the back of her mind, she suspected not. Violet wasn't that kind of person, and the two weeks they had spent together had taught her that—well, the year they'd known each other.

"Lando." Violet's tone was soft, nearly pitying.

She couldn't handle it. It sickened her. Lando ignored her as she placed the box on the bottom of the stack and went to grab the next one.

"Lando," Violet said louder this time, as if they weren't standing five feet away from each other and Lando was ignoring her. "Will you please talk to me?"

"There's nothing to talk about." Lando cursed herself for actually speaking. She'd wanted to give Violet the silent treatment, like the last week had been. Except, Violet had texted her. Lando had ignored it, but she'd seen the text, she'd seen the missed calls.

"Yes, there is," Violet insisted. "Please."

"I'm at work." Lando set her shoulders as she leaned over the edge of the pallet she was dismantling. "Unless you want me to get fired from another job—"

"You didn't deserve it," Violet interjected. "It was an unfair firing. It was out of line."

Lando narrowed her gaze, trying to figure out where this was coming from, because as far as she'd known, Violet had been in on it from the beginning. Violet stepped forward and gripped Lando's hand, lacing their fingers together.

"I didn't know that was what she was planning on doing, or had done, until after you'd left and we were preparing to go out for the next storm. I never would have let her—"

"Of course you would have," Lando interrupted. "You let her walk all over you. Anything Diane wants, she gets, and you just hand it to her on a silver platter."

Violet shook her head, raising her gaze until their eyes locked. "That may have been true for most of my life, but it's not anymore."

Lando wasn't sure she could trust that. She wasn't sure she could believe Violet.

"Did she pay you?"

Confused by the turn of conversation, Lando nodded. "Not much, but yes."

"What do you mean 'not much'?"

Lando heaved a sigh. "It really doesn't matter."

"It does," Violet insisted. "For a lot of different reasons."

"Don't you have access to payroll?"

"Not at this moment. Please, Lando."

"A little over two hundred and fifty."

Violet's face fell. "I'll figure out how to get you what you deserve to be paid. It'll take me a little bit of time, but I'll get it to you as soon as I can."

Confused, Lando eyed her suspiciously. "What do you mean? The expenses were taken out."

"There are not expenses. And this is, apparently, not the first time she has done this."

"What do you mean?"

Violet squeezed Lando's hand. "The person who worked with us last year has worked with us for several years. I finally got him to call me back yesterday, and we had a very long talk, but the sum of it is, he quit because Diane didn't pay him. She started pulling expenses from his check, like you say she did for you, and he couldn't afford that. I didn't know."

"Don't you check those things?" Lando lobbed at her.

"I skimmed them. I'm guilty of not paying as close attention as I should have. I trusted her. I grew up with her, so I had no reason not to, but... well, I've learned she's not as trustworthy as I thought she was."

Lando snorted, pulling her hand from Violet's. She grabbed the box she had her other hand on, shifted it off the pallet, and moved it toward the display she was building. She had nothing else to say, nothing else to add to the conversation. The image of Violet she'd had before they had gone chasing together had been absolutely shattered, and she wasn't sure anyone could rebuild it.

Violet didn't leave, however. Lando had meant the move as an obvious dismissal, but Violet hadn't taken it. Instead she hovered near the forklift, as if she wasn't going to move until she got what she wanted from Lando.

Ignoring her, Lando grabbed another canopy and brought it to her stack. She was going to keep working until Violet left. It was the only way she was going to get around it, the only way she was going to be able to make it through her day. By the time she returned for the next one, Violet stopped her with a hand on her arm.

"I'm really sorry for everything that happened. This isn't ... that isn't the way a chase should go, and certainly not your first time being on a team. I apologize for everything. I should have taken a firmer stand with her, for you, for everything."

Lando stared at the floor, not making eye contact. She wasn't sure what to do. She wanted to comfort Violet again, but after doing that over the last few weeks, she wasn't sure she had it in her anymore, or that Violet deserved it this time. In a lot of ways, Violet was every bit as guilty as Diane—even if she didn't know what Diane was doing, she should have. Lando wasn't sure that was something they could easily gloss over.

"I hope you'll come back to school."

Lando snorted. "That I can tell you won't be happening for a while."

"Why's that?"

"No money." Lando gave her a hard stare. "School costs money, and I don't have any. I took time off from work when Nan got sick, and I just started working again. I have back bills to pay, family to pay. I need to focus on that before I can figure out school."

"I was serious when I told you that you were one of my best students."

Lando's cheeks heated. "You can stop with that lie."

"It's not a lie," Violet insisted. "I don't look for students who have the best grades, Lando. I look for students who have passion for what they're learning. You were never lacking in that. When we were chasing, you were the highlight of every storm, I hope you know that. You reminded me how much I used to love it."

Canting her head to the side, Lando stared at her in disbelief. "I suppose not everything about the two weeks chasing with you was bad."

Violet's eyes crinkled in the corners as her lips twitched upward into a small smile. Lando was glad to see it. She was tired of the glowering and pained Violet who stood before her, and she couldn't help but try to bring her some small comfort in their exchange.

"How did you even find me here?" Lando gripped another canopy and moved it.

When she got back, Violet actually looked embarrassed.

"What?"

"Don't all lesbians work at stores like this?"

Lando snorted, then bust out laughing. She clutched her stomach as the sound rumbled through her chest and into the store. Violet's echoing grin was just what she wanted to see. Holding onto Violet's arm, Lando used the other hand to wipe her eyes. "You're dead serious, aren't you?"

"Kind of."

"Have you just been going to every hardware and lumber store trying to find me?"

"First guess," Violet murmured, her voice taking on a hushed tone.

"Oh?"

"I remembered you mentioning something about your job last quarter. I took a chance that you'd tried to get it back."

"Smart woman." Lando squeezed Violet's shoulder and went back to work. "It would be wonderful if you could get me that money, but don't stress yourself too much over it, Vi. I have better things to do with my time than worry or think about Diane."

"Don't we both." Violet's tone dropped. "Thank you, for being so understanding."

"Any time." Lando winked at her. "But really, I have to get back to work if I'm ever going to finish this display before lunch."

"Right. I guess I'll see you around." Violet offered a small smile and her hand.

Lando took it, shaking Violet's hand as if it was going to be the last time they talked. She wasn't sure, but something about it felt so final. As Violet walked away, Lando's chest tightened. She probably should have done or said something else, but she hadn't. Turning around and looking at the display that she'd just started to build, Lando rolled her shoulders and got back to work. Something in her gut told her that she was going to see Violet again, even if it was only at school when she finally got back to working on her degree.

CHAPTER 19

VIOLET COULDN'T STAY STILL. She'd cleaned her entire apartment top to bottom. She'd unpacked and gone grocery shopping. She'd done everything she could think of to entertain herself for the last few days. That first initial look of Lando's when Violet had seen her at work would not shake from her mind. It hadn't been anger or fear, it had been devastation. Violet had broken the flimsy threads of friendship they had by being friends with Diane.

It wasn't until then that Violet had realized truly how much Diane had affected her life, her relationships with others throughout the years. She wondered just how deep and how widely that spread, but as Lando had told her once, Violet could do nothing to change the past.

She checked the radar multiple times during the day as was her habit, but she was tracking a smaller storm that was set to hit their town near sunset. She guessed it would be a beautiful storm, bringing in all the light from the setting sun but also the lightning and thunder that was contained in the power of a storm cell.

Violet needed to relax, and she needed to find her love of storm chasing again. When all was set and she had nothing left to do, Violet packed up her bag and left her computer on her dining room table. She was going to use her instinct and her senses to tell her what was going on with this storm.

She drove out toward the edge of town, where the city left off and the farming picked up. She didn't live in Kansas City proper, but in one of the small outskirt towns. Close enough to the big box stores should she need, but far enough that she lived in what was considered a small rural town. It was the perfect balance for her. Diane, however, had moved straight to the city and hadn't looked back.

Her phone buzzed. Reaching for it at a stoplight, she saw Diane's name and immediately silenced the call. She wasn't sure what to say to her yet. She'd sent a formal email requesting all the files and finances Diane had and that she expected them by the end of the week. Well, it was the end of the week, and she still had nothing.

Violet ground her teeth and drove a little farther out to what used to be one of her favorite spots to storm watch. She used to come here in the middle of the quarter when she was still teaching and couldn't leave to chase. She'd even taken students there on an extra credit field trip so they could do some field observations.

Parking, Violet rummaged in her backpack for her camera, realizing too late that's she'd also brought the one from *Indigo*. She set it on the passenger seat, pulled out her newer camera, and changed out the lens. She would do some wide shots before narrowing in and doing some long exposure to catch the lightning.

Violet lost herself in the moment, taking photo after photo. She got down onto the dirt road, looking up at the sky as it swirled around and the storm clouds came closer, taking photo after photo using the long grass for some contrast. She walked down the road and found a tree, using that to offset the solely sky photos.

By the time she really looked up again, the storm was getting closer to hitting town. Violet walked back to her car and pulled out her tripod, setting up the camera. Lightning had been flashing through the sky for nearly thirty minutes at that point, and she didn't want to miss any more of it.

As she clicked the shutter, Violet stepped back and watched. This was where her passion had begun. Growing up in a small town in rural Kansas had meant that she'd lived through storm after storm just like this. While so many of them seemed similar, they were all different in how they affected her. She'd convinced her mom more than once to take her out chasing when she was little, but it hadn't been as often as she'd have liked.

Still, it had been enough to give Violet a taste for it. She'd gone to school to appease her parents, but mostly so she could learn more about these devastatingly beautiful natural phenomena. She couldn't live without them. The quiet and stillness in the air was perfect, and it soothed Violet's weary soul.

For years she had given herself over to Diane's whims, but the last few weeks had taught her more than she could ever imagine, and she wouldn't do it again. The loneliness that had settled in her chest vanished as the winds picked up and the storm threatened rain. The cold air bit at her cheeks. Violet crossed her arms and closed her eyes, breathing in the deep earthy scent that was her lifeline.

She needed her own team, just her and one or two other people where she was in charge. She had a grant she needed to fulfill. However, it wasn't just to make sure she lived up to her obligations. Storm chasing was her life, and it wasn't something Violet was willing to give up. She needed these moments.

It might take her a month to get going again, but that was something she wanted. She'd call Erik first thing tomorrow and see if he'd be willing to join her without Diane, although she still felt she owed him for the last season. Violet checked the photo before setting up for another one. A few cars came and went, but not many. This storm, to them, wasn't anything special. But to her it was the defining moment in the rest of her future.

A small sedan drove by, the dust from the wheels spinning up. Violet raced to the passenger side of her car and grabbed Eli's old camera. In seconds, she had a photo, the dust creating a surreal effect as the storm came in. It was beautiful. It was an image that described how she felt perfectly. Old, dusty, worn out, but still going. Laughing at herself, Violet straightened her back and went to the camera atop the tripod. Moving it, she refocused the lens and set up for another shot.

"Fancy seeing you here."

Violet tensed, her back going ramrod straight. Turning, she glanced over to see Lando walking toward her, hands shoved into her cargo pants, loose t-shirt fluttering in the wind as it picked it up, her hair unmovable as it was gelled into place. Violet raised an eyebrow. "I thought I could do some storm watching even if I wasn't chasing."

"Yeah." Lando moved to stand next to her, staring out into the sea of fields in front of them as the clouds rolled in closer. "Think hail?"

"Pebbles if any."

"That's what I figured." Lando didn't turn to look at her.

Violet shrugged it off and set up her camera to take another shot. She wasn't sure what to say or do. She hadn't expected to see Lando again outside of maybe another class in the future or when Violet was finally able to pay her back the missed earnings. They stood in silence for some time as they stared out toward the future coming straight at them.

"You talk to Diane?" Lando finally asked.

"Not really," Violet murmured. The last thing she wanted to talk with Lando about was Diane. They had so many other topics of conversation.

Lando shrugged, glancing at Violet before turning back to face the storm. "She's called me a few times."

"You answer?" Violet was kind of curious to see what Lando's take on everything was, though she strongly suspected Lando would prefer to step away from that drama and never be in the middle of it again."

"No. But she's also emailed and texted. Wants me back on the team suddenly. It seems she's in desperate need of someone who knows what they're doing."

Violet snorted lightly. "It would seem that way."

Lando still had her hands locked in the pockets of her pants, as if she was never going to move from her position standing next to Violet. They fell into a silence as the photo clicked completion. Violet pulled it up on the back display and then motioned for Lando to take a look. Violet had managed to catch one lightning bolt that moved straight down to the top of a tree out in the field. It must have been thousands of feet away, but it looked like it was bringing life to that tree in the form of bright white light.

"Nice."

Violet nodded. "Lucky shot."

"Planned luck." Lando's lips quirked up as she stepped away. "You're really good at photography, Vi. I hope you know that."

Violet shuddered. It was only the second time Lando had called her that, and while the first had been another storm of completely different emotions, this one brought with it serenity and warmth, something Violet hadn't experienced in ages from anyone. She wasn't sure what to say to the compliment, and so she kept quiet as she set up for another shot.

"What did you come all the way out here for?"

Lando raised an eyebrow in her direction. "I suspect the same thing you did."

"Which is?" Violet pushed, wanting to know what exactly Lando thought she was doing out there.

"I came for the storm, Vi, nothing else. Well, maybe something to quiet my thoughts." Lando left off there, not elaborating on what thoughts she wanted to quiet.

Violet could only guess. She had wanted the exact same thing, although there was no doubt in her mind that they were both quieting different thoughts. Violet relaxed, enjoying the storm, the quiet, but also Lando's very firm and comforting presence. Lando had always brought that to her, a comfort she couldn't explain, a peace that surpassed all her understanding.

"Lando?" Violet faced Lando, gazing over her profile, the strength in her shoulders, the smooth lines of her cheeks and jaw. It was as if she really saw her for the first time. The roundness of her face, her long lashes, the natural beauty she exuded. Lando didn't need to work to look good, she simply was herself, and she always had been.

"Yeah?"

"I hope you don't give up on chasing."

"I won't, teach." Lando winked. "But it may be a few years before I can get back out there."

Violet nodded her understanding. She had a much better view of Lando's life after two intense weeks together, and she was sure Lando had a deeper view into hers—one that was full of hopes that had already been dashed, in pining that wasn't worth its salt.

The winds changed again. Violet could see off in the distance as the clouds let loose and rain poured from them onto the dry earth, forcing dust to rise into the air from the force of it slamming into the ground. The dust cloud slowly moved toward them. She could smell it a minute later, that beautiful before-rain scent that she had tuned herself to for years.

"How long are you going to stay out here?" Lando asked, breaking Violet's reverie.

"Probably until I have no other choice but to go in. I need this."

Lando nodded sharply. "I do, too."

Silence fell over them again as they stared off into the distance. Why was it so hard for her to say and do anything when it came to Lando? In some ways it seemed so easy to open up to her, to let Lando in to see the demons that raged inside her, but other times, the simplest of conversations was the most difficult.

Another vehicle drove by, breaking the silence and Violet's thoughts. The rain was even closer now, the thunder rumbling so loud that it echoed in her chest. They weren't going to be able to stay out there much longer unless they were going to stand in the rain and hail. Still, Violet didn't move to put her camera away. She reset photo after photo in the quiet, showing Lando the photos as she took them.

They found a balance. Perhaps this was the apology both of them needed. Lando for leaving, but mostly Violet for everything that had happened while chasing. The anger, the fighting, the unsafe environment, the tension, the firing—all of it. Violet reached out and touched her fingers to Lando's arm. Lando immediately loosed her hand from her pocket and Violet curled their hands together.

"I'm so sorry about everything, Lando. I should have protected you better."

Lando's brow furrowed. "You did protect me, but more than anything, I don't think I'm the one who needed protection."

"Why do you always seem to say exactly what I need to hear? Hmm?"

Lando's lips blossomed into a smile. "I must be really good at listening to what isn't said."

"I suppose you are." Violet squeezed Lando's hand and went to move, but Lando held on firmly. Looking into Lando's pale blue eyes, Violet waited for an explanation.

"I don't blame you for anything. I hope you know that. There were decisions you could have made that would have bettered everything, yes, but the same goes for me. We're both not without mistakes, but don't let those mistakes take you down. You deserve better than that."

The weight in Violet's chest lightened. She hadn't known how much she needed to hear that. She hadn't even realized just how much tension she held within her, for years. Not everything was her fault, but some of it was. Violet nodded and stepped in closer to Lando, their warm fingers still pressed tightly together. She forgot about the camera, about the storm coming in as she moved.

"If there's one thing I've learned in my twenty-three years, which sounds so odd to say."

"You've lived a lot of life in those years," Violet commented, shifting in closer.

"Yeah, I have. I don't like to think about it."

"I don't suppose anyone would."

Lando turned her chin, raising it up so their gazes met. "Exactly, but if there is anything that I have learned, it's that life is short, life sucks, and if we want it to be good, if we want it to be better, then we're the ones who have to do the hard work. The good things in life aren't just handed to us."

"Sometimes they are." Violet smiled, thinking that one of the last few things Diane had done, probably to piss her off, had been for the best. Inviting Lando to join them in chasing had changed so much in Violet's life, and she didn't want to let that go by. At Lando's confused gaze, Violet elaborated. "When Diane hired you, I'm pretty sure it was to piss me off."

Lando laughed. "No doubt of that."

"I'd told her not to hire you."

"Why?" Confused, Lando shook her head. "You never explained why you didn't want me to go chasing with you."

"Right." Violet dashed her tongue against her lips. "I don't think I knew why."

"How do you not know?"

"Because unlike you, Lando, I'm not very good at figuring out what I'm feeling and when. I go with my emotions a lot of the time because it's easier than resisting, but when asked exactly what I'm doing and why, I can't give a concise answer. At least, not usually for a good chunk of time until I've had a few weeks or months or years even to dissect it all."

Lando scrunched her nose. "What are you even talking about?"

"Diane saw something in my office that day that I did not see. Not until the other night when we were on the porch swing. Actually, to be fair, it was that morning."

"That morning?"

Violet nodded and gave Lando's fingers a tight squeeze for emphasis. "When I woke up and you were still holding my hand."

Lando reached up with her hand and scratched the back of her head. "I'm still confused."

"I know you are." Violet tugged Lando's hand slightly. "Diane is very good at observation and figuring out what makes people tick. She has always been good at that. When we were growing up, she used it to her advantage even then, played her parents against each other, played teachers against each other. She made the world bend to her will, and she did that solely through reading people."

"How manipulative."

Violet shrugged. She didn't really care why Diane did it. It was more a fact—that was who Diane was and always would be—but Violet was finally untangling herself from that web. She'd cut herself out, and she firmly wanted to be somewhere else, with someone else. "Lando?"

Lando raised her chin up, their eyes locking.

"She saw there was more to our relationship than a simple student and teacher."

"There was never anything—"

"We never did anything, no. We never talked about doing anything, or even acknowledged it, but can you deny that you felt something else for me all those months when you took my class? Because I can't deny that. You're my favorite student, Lando, and I have always maintained it's not because of your grades, and it's not."

"What are you saying?" Lando's voice wavered.

Violet held her ground. Reaching up, she curled her hand around Lando's cheek, her soft skin. She brushed her thumb along Lando's chin, and then her lips. She'd done this before, but this time all those barriers were down, this time, there was nothing holding her back.

"I'm saying I have always felt more for you than I should." Violet stayed as close as possible to Lando, holding their gazes as she waited to see what Lando would say and do next. They both needed to be in this together if anything was going to change. It might ruin their futures or it might open them to amazing possibilities. For years, Violet had repressed what she deserved, and she was tired of it. She wanted this, and she wanted Lando to experience it with her.

"Vi," Lando's tone dropped. "I don't think—"

"Regardless if you want it or not," Violet interrupted. "I need you to know that I do. I want you."

Lando drew in a ragged breath, saying nothing. Violet wasn't sure how long they stood there. The storm would be there in minutes and they wouldn't have a choice but to move, but Violet couldn't tear her gaze away from those eyes. Lando was so much wiser than she should be, so much stronger than Violet was herself. She wasn't going to back Lando into a corner or force her into anything she didn't want. If she said no, Violet would step back and learn to live into the relationship they had built over the last year.

If that was what Lando wanted, so be it. But Violet couldn't deny, at least for now, that something had shifted the second time she'd met Heather Sutherland. She'd always favored her, always put in the extra time and energy to make sure she understood the lessons, always enjoyed it when Lando stopped by for office hours.

The rain hit them, splattering onto their heads and faces. Startled, they separated sharply. Lando laughed and gasped, grabbing the camera on the tripod and unlocking it before handing it to Violet. She quickly and efficiently closed the tripod and ran for Violet's car with Violet hot on her heels. They shoved the equipment into the back seat.

Violet closed the door and let out a grin as small pea-sized hail fell on top of them. It was nothing like being out in the middle of a tornado and being slammed with hail. This was pleasantly fresh, light. She laughed as she held up her hands to see if she could catch any and was surprised when Lando clasped her hand tightly.

With no words, Lando leaned in and pressed their mouths together. Violet gasped, wrapping her arms around Lando's back as she held on tightly, pressed between Lando and the car. Lando's entire body was warm and firm against her. Her heart raced, rain pouring and drenching them. Violet moaned, nipping at Lando's lip before parting her own and letting Lando enter her.

They stayed there for who knew how long. Violet eventually flipped them, pushing Lando into the car, running hands over her drenched T-shirt, feeling her firm breasts in a sports bra, pushing their hips together. Violet didn't want to let go. She wanted to stay there forever, kissing the woman she'd grown to love. That thought settled into her chest, and it felt so right. It felt perfect, like a future she could grab hold of and run with.

Lando broke the embrace, smiling at Violet and blinking away the raindrops. "You're shivering."

Violet shook her head. "I didn't even notice."

"Get in the damn car."

"Don't want to." Violet bent down again, their lips brushing. "I'd rather stay right here."

"You're freezing. Let's go someplace warmer where maybe I can get you out of these wet clothes."

Violet liked that idea. She kissed Lando one more time before pulling away. "Fine. You win."

"Get in your car, and I'll follow you wherever."

Narrowing her eyes, Violet looked around for Lando's car but didn't find it anywhere. It hadn't even occurred to her before to ask how Lando had gotten there. "Where's your car?"

"I live just down the road from here." Lando straightened her shoulders. "I often walk this road when there's a storm coming in."

Violet parted her lips in surprise. "Let's go to your place."

"Are you sure?"

"Yes. Get in the car, Lando."

Lando kissed her hard before stepping around the back of the vehicle to get inside. Once they were settled, Violet turned the engine over and waited for Lando to tell her where to go, but one thing she knew was she couldn't wipe the smile off her face. Whatever was happening between them, it was something Violet wanted, desperately.

CHAPTER 20

LANDO STARTED water for tea as she waited for Violet to get changed into the dry clothes she still miraculously had stashed in her car. Lando was going to change next, but she wanted something warm for them to drink.

She was in her room, tugging her wet T-shirt off and dropping it into the laundry basket near the door to her closet. She was just about to unbutton her pants when her phone rang. Cocking her head at it, Lando picked it up. *Diane.* Clenching her jaw, she debated whether or not to answer, but she figured it was time to finally tell her.

Answering while she continued to undress, Lando said, "Hello?"

"Lando, it's Diane."

"Uh-huh." She shucked her pants to the floor, picking them up and tossing them into the basket.

"Look, I wanted to talk to you and apologize for what happened out here in Kansas. Violet never wanted me to hire you."

Well, Lando knew that much was true, but her stomach tightened as she waited for Diane to drop the next lie into her lap. She hadn't thought she was so manipulative as to blatantly lie, but Lando had been proven wrong on that one already.

"So when we got into the field, she was less than enthusiastic about you being here."

That was equally another truth, although Lando was pretty sure Violet had warmed up to her since then. Her lips tingled at the thought of what they'd done only thirty minutes before. She bent over her drawers, trying to decide what to wear but settled on her basic outfit of cargo pants and a T-shirt.

"I didn't want to fire you."

Lando snorted, and she didn't even try to hold it back. She let Diane hear it for all its glory. Whatever Diane had to say, unless it was a flat-out apology for what she had done, not what Violet had supposedly done, and a paycheck, Lando didn't really want to hear it.

"So I talked to Violet, and she's no longer working on the team either."

"Oh really?" Lando feigned innocence, wondering if she could get away with lying as well as Diane. It would be a feat, but she could try if only to have a nice fuck-you moment in about three minutes.

"Yeah, she left shortly after you did, actually, and I'm left without a team and someone to help me fulfill the requirements of the grant."

Lando knew without a doubt that Violet had been the one to receive the grant, which meant Diane couldn't actually run a team with the money from it without asking for a change in leadership, which she wouldn't have gotten in the week they'd been gone.

"You were so good at catching the storms and tornados, that I was wondering if you'd be willing to come back and work for the team."

Lando really wanted to ask what team, since it seemed to just be Diane.

"Since Violet is gone, I can pay you more."

Diane had no shame about anything, did she? What had Violet ever seen in her? "You mean more than a hundred and twenty-five bucks a week? Gee, I might hit the threshold for poverty level."

Silence echoed through the receiver, and Lando wasn't surprised. Her comment had been particularly harsh. Lando tugged a dry pair of pants on but left them unbuttoned as she fiddled with the phone.

"Diane, while I appreciate the offer..." She did, mostly. "...I have a new job, and I need to stick this one out. I don't think you can out-pay them, so just quit while you're ahead. Thanks! Bye."

Hanging up, Lando dropped the phone onto the mattress. She grabbed a dry sports bra and was just about to pull it over her head when the door to her bedroom suddenly opened. Violet stood still, her hand on the doorknob, dry clothes on, and her eyes locked on Lando's chest.

"Vi, my eyes are up about twelve inches."

"What? Oh..." Violet blushed, her cheeks beet red. "Sorry."

"Don't be." Lando raised an eyebrow, trying to be more confident than she felt. She dropped the sports bra back onto the mattress and put her hands on her hips, realizing all too late that she still hadn't buttoned her pants. "Like what you see?"

"I thought you'd be done by now."

"I started water for tea."

"I thought..." Violet trailed off, her gaze dropping again. "I didn't...well, yes."

"Yes what?" Confused, Lando furrowed her brow and stayed still. Violet had a death grip on the doorknob and hadn't moved, but her gaze raked up and down Lando's body, sending a shiver through Lando's spine. She liked this openly appraising Violet. For the two weeks they'd spent locked together, Lando had been so careful to maintain privacy and not overstep boundaries, but there was none of that to mess around with anymore.

"Yes, I like what I see."

"Then come here already." Lando stayed put as Violet left the door and walked into the bedroom. She stopped right in front of Lando, her eyes still locked on Lando's breasts. Reaching up tentatively, Violet brushed her fingers over Lando's collar bone and then lower as she murmured reverently, "You're so beautiful."

Lando had never thought of herself as such. Handsome, perhaps, awkward and a little chunky even more, but the way Violet said that word, with so much appreciation in it, it felt right. Placing a finger under Violet's chin to raise her gaze, Lando looked her directly in the eye. "You're allowed to touch me if you want."

"I've wanted to for a while."

"For a while?"

Violet nodded so subtly, Lando almost missed it. "Since that one night..."

"At *Indigo*?"

"Yeah."

Lando moved in slowly, pressing their mouths together in a tender kiss. "I thought about touching you before that, on and off, depending on your mood."

Violet's lips curled. "I suppose I'm not the easiest person to get along with."

"Easier when certain people who won't be named aren't around. That's for damn sure."

"Mmhmm." Violet kissed her this time. "We should turn the water off."

"It's an electric tea kettle. It turns itself off."

"Even better." Violet slid a hand around Lando's back, the warm skin of her arm against Lando's still cool flesh a contrast she wanted to remember forever. Their mouths melded together, and Violet rolled Lando's hard nipple between her fingers. Lando moaned, pushing into Violet and turning so they landed on the bed.

She didn't care if they'd only just started something up, she'd wanted this for as long as she could remember. She'd thought about what-ifs with Violet, never with the notion they would actually happen. Violet pulled herself backward on the bed, her mouth never leaving Lando's for longer than a few seconds before she tugged Lando back to her.

Following Violet's lead, Lando hovered over her, their tongues tangling as Violet ran her fingers up and down Lando's back to her ass under her pants, and back up. Violet spread her legs so Lando could rest in the cocoon of her body. They kissed slowly, unlike out in the middle of the storm. This pace was so different, so perfect for exploration.

Lando rutted against Violet, their clothes between them causing friction. Violet moaned and brushed her hands through Lando's short hair. She tugged and got Lando's attention. Violet kissed down Lando's neck to her collarbone, swirling her tongue over Lando's skin.

"Tell me what you like and what you don't like." Violet's voice was a soft command.

Goosebumps raged along Lando's arm and chest, her nipples tightening even more. She'd never been asked that before by a lover, and the sultry tone to Violet's voice was breathtaking.

"I've already touched your breasts, but did you like it?" Violet scraped her nails oh so lightly along Lando's sides, every touch on Lando's body as tender as the last.

Pressing her forehead into Violet's shoulder, Lando took a deep breath as she figured out what the hell to say. "You can do whatever you want to me, Vi. I trust you."

Violet hummed, nipping at Lando's chin. "But do you like it rough? Soft? Hard?"

Lando whimpered. This woman was going to undo her with fucking words. No one could compete with this, ever. Kissing Violet's neck, Lando breathed in her scent, focusing her mind.

"I will do whatever you want, and I mean that, I'm not just saying that."

Violet smiled up at her. "Yes, but what do you want?"

"Anything, really."

"Lando, you're not exactly helping me make a decision here."

Chuckling, Lando bent down and kissed Violet's neck. "What's something you like?"

"Whatever you were doing with your hips a few seconds ago was amazing."

"Yeah?" Lando raised an eyebrow as she kissed Violet's neck again. "Would you be opposed to using a strap?"

Violet shuddered. "Never."

"I have one."

"I'd hoped as much." Violet cupped the back of Lando's head. "But before we do that, since it has been a while for me, why don't we do something else."

"Something like what?" Lando used the tip of her tongue against Violet's neck, making designs and patterns that made no sense. Violet's skin was salty, and she nipped lightly at it, kind of hoping she'd leave a mark. Violet scraped her nails against Lando's scalp in response, so Lando did it again.

"Yes...that," Violet breathed out the words, wrapping her legs around Lando's hips to keep her in place.

"Do you perhaps like sex a little rougher?" Lando murmured. "A little more passionate."

Violet whimpered. "Yes, but I will do anything with you. Please don't stop."

"I'm not planning on stopping anytime soon." Lando reached down, found the edge of Violet's shirt, and tugged it upward enough to get her hand underneath. Violet's skin was so smooth, exactly like she'd thought it would be all those times she'd seen it. Moving her hand up higher, Lando found the dip at Violet's waist. She brushed her thumb back and forth as she moved to take Violet's mouth in another bruising kiss. "I don't want to get out of this bed anytime soon either."

"The feeling is mutual," Violet murmured, her lips brushing against Lando's. Violet skimmed her hand down Lando's chest, bypassing her breasts, to the lower part of Lando's belly. "May I?"

"God yes." Lando kissed Violet's cheek.

Violet didn't hesitate as she pushed under Lando's underwear. Lando flopped onto her side, pushing at her pants so she could wiggle out of them while Violet slid her fingers between her folds. It was awkward and messy, but Lando wouldn't have it any other way. That had pretty much been everything with Violet since they'd met over twenty years ago.

When she was naked, Lando spread her legs to give Violet the best access possible. Violet bent her head and sucked Lando's nipple into her mouth, swirling her tongue over the tight nub. Lando ran her fingers through Violet's damp hair, tugging slightly and moaning. She hoped Violet liked it when she was loud.

"That feels so good," Lando murmured.

Violet changed the pattern of her thumb against Lando's clit, and Lando writhed in response. She'd wanted Violet to touch her like this for weeks—well, months, if she was being honest—and had never let herself fully fantasize about it because Violet was her teacher, because they were sharing a room, and then a bed.

Lando's lips parted, her breathing quickening. The thunderstorm raged outside, rain pelting the windows, lightning flashing, and thunder roaring, but all Lando could think about was Violet's hand between her legs, Violet's still clothed body pressed against her side, Violet's mouth on her breasts.

"Vi." Lando swallowed hard, trying to find her voice that seemed to have suddenly disappeared. "Vi...oh." She scrunched her nose up as the last boundary holding her back broke. Violet moved into her, and Lando rose higher and higher until she fell.

Violet softened her kisses, slowed her hand, but let Lando ride out her orgasm for as long as she possibly could. The kisses moved from each of her breasts, up her neck, to her chin, and then to her lips. Lando sighed into the embrace, holding Violet as close to her as possible, their tongues tangling lazily together as they each sought comfort and familiarity.

This was entirely new territory, but it didn't seem that way in the grand scheme of things. Over the past three weeks, Lando had gotten to know Violet so well, every tic, every strength and weakness. Three weeks together had been intense and filled with enough drama to last them a lifetime. Lando pulled back, grinning up at Violet.

"You're quite talented."

Violet wrinkled her nose. "Wait until you see what I can do with my tongue."

"See? Or feel?" That comment got the rise of color to Violet's cheeks Lando had hoped for. Chuckling, Lando pulled at Violet's clothes and tugged her shirt off before starting to work on her pants. "Come on, I want to feel you against me."

Violet complied and helped Lando to remove her clothing. By the time they were done, Lando couldn't stop kissing her. It was just as good as chasing. Once they had started, Lando hadn't wanted to stop. She wanted to stay in the bed with Violet naked next to her as long as she possibly could. Lando straddled her, grinning as Violet raised her arms above her and gripped onto the bars on Lando's ancient bed.

"Wanting something in particular?"

"Your mouth first. If you will."

"Absolutely." Lando shimmied down the bed, happy when Violet raised her knees up. Lando took her time, swirling her tongue, tasting, figuring out exactly how she wanted to do this. It was only going to be the first step in her plan, because if she had her way, they would be up all night and outlast the storm itself.

Violet reached down, griping the short spikes of Lando's hair and tugging sharply. Her hips moved along with Lando's tongue, her stomach pulling tight as she got even closer to exactly where they both wanted her to be. They'd spent weeks wrapped up in tension, and they were both finally getting a release.

Cooing as she finished, Violet smoothed her fingers through Lando's ruffled hair and shifted to give each of them some space. Lando wiped her mouth with the back of her hand. She pressed gentle kisses along the inside of Violet's thigh, keeping as much momentum as possible. As Violet relaxed, her body easing and her legs straightening to stretch her muscles, Lando slid off the edge of the bed. She fiddled with the top drawer of her dresser, digging way in the back where she made sure to hide anything she needed to from Nan and pulled out the strap she hadn't worn in nearly a year.

Fuck, it really had been that long. She hoped she still had it in her, though she suspected it would be like riding a bike and she'd figure it out in no time. Violet watched her carefully as she slid her legs through the straps and made sure the fit was firm.

"Do you want any lube?" Lando asked, pulling the strap as if it were her own cock.

Violet's eyes widened before she had a seductive look on her face. She trailed her fingers between her legs, dipping them into her body before pulling them out. "Don't think I need it."

"Fuck, that was sexy," Lando muttered as she got on her knees on the couch. "I think someday I'd just like to sit here and watch you do that to yourself, repeatedly."

"Well, I think we can arrange that, some day." Violet pushed herself up, pressing their lips together and holding Lando tight. "I'm ready whenever you are."

"Oh good." Lando was nervous. Anxiety bubbled in her belly, and she couldn't exactly figure out why. They'd already done this once each, why was this so different? She stared down at her hands, trying to figure out what to do and say next, but her mind drew a blank.

Violet's fingers on her cheek pulled her back to reality, the soft look on her face steadying. "Are you ready?"

Lando shook her head for a second.

"Tell me when you are or if you want to do something else."

"I want to do this," Lando whispered. "It's just...it's been a while."

"It's been a while for me, too, Lando. But I'm still here, still wanting this."

"You're not going to leave?" Lando didn't dare look at her. Everyone she had ever loved left her, except Aunt T. It'd been her downfall since she'd started dating and why none of the relationships she'd had in the past had lasted very long.

Violet's brow furrowed, and she seemed concerned. Moving so they faced each other properly, Violet cupped Lando's cheek and tilted her chin up so they could look in each other's eyes. "What do you mean?"

Lando's cheeks heated with embarrassment. She hadn't meant to say that, hadn't meant to let any of it out. Hell, it was their first night together, and she didn't want to ruin it by getting all emotional on the woman she probably loved. The first woman she'd ever loved in this way.

"Lando," Violet drew her attention back to the conversation at hand. "What are you thinking?"

"That I love you," Lando whispered, apparently no longer able to control the words falling from her lips. She hated herself for it. She should be so much better at controlling herself by this point. She couldn't even bear to look at Violet, knowing exactly what she would say and do.

"You know," Violet started and stopped. "Will you look at me?"

It took Lando longer than she'd wanted, but she did finally bring her gaze up to Violet's eyes.

"Thank you. You know, I was thinking that same thing earlier today, when we were out in the storm."

"Were you?" Lando's voice was dark, and her stomach dropped. She didn't want to lose the woman she loved, someone who was so important to her, who had taught her so much.

"Yeah, I was. And to answer your question, I'm not going anywhere unless you want me to."

Lando nodded, but leaving the house hadn't really been what she'd meant, and she wasn't quite sure how to explain it. She'd never had to before. Licking her lips, Lando took the plunge. "I didn't mean tonight."

"What did you mean, then?"

"Every person I have loved has died. And I can't...I don't know what I would do if that would happen again."

Violet remained quiet, only the sound of the rushing storm outside as their companion. Lando wasn't sure what to do, but she was fairly certain she had ruined whatever mood she'd wanted to keep. Instead of saying anything, Violet kissed her, surprising Lando out of her despair.

"Lando, I can't promise you that I won't die. I'm not exactly in an un-risky line of work, and if you want to chase storms, you aren't either. Accidents happen. People die when they chase. And I am much older than you. I will probably die before you do. We both know this. I'm not going to lie to you."

"I appreciate that." Lando played with Violet's fingers, still unsure of where to go from there.

Violet pulled her in for another kiss, this one longer and deeper. "But I don't want to leave you. I want to love you. In fact, I'm choosing to love you. I hear your fears. You haven't had an easy start to life, or easy middle to it, but I'm here, and I want to be here with you."

"Why? Why would you? I'm a drunk, I'm a drug addict, and I have no family."

"You're one of the kindest, most peaceful people I know, and whether that comes from such a rocky past or not, I don't know, but I have never known you to be someone who is spiteful, or miserable, or hates solely because it's fun."

"I would never—"

"Exactly. You're sweet, you're so incredibly strong, and in the last few weeks, the more I have gotten to know you, the more that has proven to be true."

Lando's lips parted in surprise. *Did people really see her like that?* She whispered, "Thank you."

"I wasn't fishing for thanks. I was stating facts, and you know how much I love to live in the facts."

Grinning, Lando nodded. "I do. You and your data I think are closer than we are."

"Never." Violet pulled Lando in for a deeper kiss, drawing her back into the moment. Allowing herself to be lost in Violet's strength, to lean on her in that moment, Lando pushed her down on the bed, covering her as their lips remained locked.

Lando pushed into Violet, her hips sliding and pulling slowly at first and then speeding up. Violet reached between them, her fingers flicking over her clit in a successive rhythm with each pull from Lando. Her back arched, and her eyes closed. Lando watched as she fell beautifully into her orgasm: the lax muscles in her face, the smile that brightened her lips. It truly was love, and love in a way she'd never experienced.

Hours later as they lay tangled together and the storm was off in the distance, Lando kissed Violet's shoulder, ready to fall asleep. Violet held Lando's arm around her front, their fingers twined together as they breathed into the silence.

Finally, Violet broke it. "Would you ever consider chasing with me again?"

"What? Chase with you?"

"Yeah," Violet's voice trailed off. "I think...I know I want to find my passion for chasing again. I miss it."

"I don't know," Lando answered honestly. If it was anything like last time, it would be a hard no, but without Diane thrown into the mix, Lando wasn't sure what it would be like. She wanted to get to know Violet better than that. "I'll have to think about that one."

"Please do," Violet answered. "It's not anything we have to decide tonight."

Violet brought their hands up to her mouth and kissed the back of Lando's. Tightening her grip, Lando closed her eyes, breathing in Violet's scent and memorizing it. She never would have guessed that this was how her first season storm chasing was going to go. Never in a million years would she have thought she'd find herself in bed in her house with Violet in her arms. In a dream perhaps, but this was beyond any dream Lando had ever imagined. This was damn near close to perfection.

CHAPTER 21

THE LAST MONTH seemed to fly by. Violet had been amazed at how quickly it had snuck up on her. One month she and Lando had been together, and the majority of the time, she'd spent it at Lando's house, to the point Lando had given her a key and more than a drawer all to herself.

While she hadn't gone back to work, since she was still technically on leave, Violet hadn't been doing nothing. She'd taken on Diane, fighting to get control of her grant again. Every day that passed, she couldn't figure out why she'd allowed Diane to have so much power over her life. She should have broken that friendship and business relationship years prior.

Instead, she'd spent the last month threatening legal action until Diane had caved. But she had everything now, and figuring out how much was owed to Erik and Lando had been tedious but rewarding work. Writing the checks had made it all the better, though Erik's had to come from her personal funds since that grant money was gone.

Worried it might affect her ability to get a grant in the future, Violet did her best to right all the wrongs and made sure there was a paper trail in place. She could argue her own stupidity, but also argue trying to fix everything—including firing Diane and never hiring her again.

Brushing her hand through her hair as she stared down at the two checks, Violet rolled her shoulders and stretched her back. She was sitting at Lando's kitchen table, her computer and an abundance of papers surrounding her. She'd always had so much paperwork while teaching that she'd taken the respite from it during chasing season. Not her first mistake, and surely not her last.

However, Violet was determined not to let those mistakes follow her. Lando would be home soon, and she wanted to prepare something special for the both of them. Cleaning up would be her first task. Her phone ringing surprised her. Violet picked it up, staring at Diane's name as it lit up the screen.

She almost didn't answer, but habits and guilt pushed her to do it. "Hey."

"Vi, I'm so sorry," Diane started. "I just... I want to talk to you."

"About what?" Violet crossed an arm over her chest in a knee-jerk protective reaction. They had talked several times on the phone over the past month, but most of it had not been pleasant, and the last two weeks, Violet had stopped answering, resorting to legal forms and letters to do the work for her.

"Everything." Diane sighed. "I miss my best friend."

"I'm busy, Diane."

"Please. I want to apologize. Properly."

"Then apologize. I'm listening."

"No, I want to see you."

Violet's stomach churned. She hadn't quite anticipated that one. She hadn't thought about when she'd see Diane again since they lived in different cities and didn't run in the same circles outside of chasing—which was a small community, but Diane wasn't exactly popular in it.

"I don't think that's a good idea."

"Please," Diane begged. "I promise I won't try any funny business."

Violet doubted that. Diane would always try something. It was more a matter of whether she could push past it and stand her ground. "This will be the last time I see you."

Diane was slow to respond, and Violet was pretty sure she was trying to work through what she'd said. "Can I meet you at your place?"

"I..." Violet looked around the kitchen she sat in. She absolutely would not allow Diane there. She did not want her knowing that they were together. "Yes. I'm not there right now."

"I know. Your car's gone."

Violet stiffened. "I can be there in fifteen minutes."

"Okay."

Hanging up, Violet cleaned up the table quickly, grabbed her keys, and raced out to her car. She was at her apartment in ten minutes, and there was Diane in the Hummer, parked in front of her building. Violet tapped on the window with her knuckle, startling Diane.

"Hey," Violet said, surprised that the tension in her belly wasn't there this time. Maybe the last month had really been what she needed.

"Hey." Diane gave her a pitiful look. "Thanks for talking with me."

"Yeah. Let's go upstairs." They took their time walking to her apartment. Violet unlocked the door and let them in, immediately starting water for tea because those ingrained hospitality habits were never going to be rid from her.

"Thank you again for talking with me."

"You said that, Diane. What did you want to talk about?" Violet leaned against the wall between the kitchen and the living area, waiting for Diane to start in on everything.

"I'm so sorry about everything that happened this season. It was...not a great start, and I apologize. I should have told you I was hiring Lando."

"You should have." Violet drew in a deep breath. "Just like you should have told me you didn't pay Erik last season."

Diane's lips quivered, caught in another deception. Violet could read her, finally, like she'd never been able to before.

"You also should have talked with me about making decisions. This was my grant, Diane. You put that in jeopardy, you put my job and my reputation in jeopardy. And for what? Because that I haven't figured out."

Stepping closer, Diane put a hand on Violet's arm. "I didn't mean to. I wasn't thinking, and I got caught up in the stress of it all."

"In the stress?" Violet raised an eyebrow in disbelief. "You could have asked for help if you couldn't handle it. That's the entire point of being on a team. Instead, I'm here fixing your mistakes from a year ago. I'm not out chasing this season like I wanted to be, like I took a leave of absence for."

"Then come back," Diane murmured.

"What?" Violet's eyes widened.

"Come back. Let's go chasing, just you and me, and it'll be just like old times again. We can use what's left of the grant, find tornados—come on."

"Are you serious?" Violet canted her head to the side, flitting her gaze all over Diane's face as she dared to find the lie in it.

"Yes. I miss it. I miss you. You're my best friend, and this past month... I don't know. I've done a lot of thinking, and I can't live without you. I can't live without chasing." Diane's eyes looked sincere, but Violet still had doubt raging in her belly.

"You can't live without chasing? You don't do anything except drive the damn car." Violet's harsh tone took Diane by surprise.

Diane's lips parted, and she moved back, giving Violet some much-needed space. "Are you angry with me still?"

"Yes!" Violet stepped away from the wall and turned the kettle off, deciding they weren't going to need it after all. "And the fact you think I wouldn't be is absurd. You toyed with people's lives, Diane. You let them risk their lives for no benefit at all. You sat around and watched them run into oncoming danger and think you're a part of the team? No. The team was only ever me and Erik or me and Lando. You were nothing essential."

"I don't know what to say."

"Good." Violet glared at her. "Because I'm tired of cleaning up your messes. I'm tired of fixing your mistakes and watching your back and getting nothing in return. I'm tired of being your bitch."

Diane's jaw clenched tightly, her brows drawing together. She was either going to lash out in anger or she was going to walk away. Taking the decision for her, Violet stepped toward the door to her apartment and opened it.

"It's time for you to leave, Diane. If you call me again, I won't answer. And if you show up here to talk to me, I'll call the cops. Get the hell out of my life."

Diane hesitated, but she eventually walked by Violet and out the door. Closing and locking it, Violet put her forehead against the cold metal, closed her eyes, and sighed. It felt good and awful at the same time, but most importantly, she felt lighter. The weight of the relationship was gone, and Violet had never been so free. She should have done this decades ago. Smiling to herself, she thought of Lando, a perfect idea forming in her head.

She waited in her apartment for another thirty minutes to make sure that Diane had left and they wouldn't *accidentally* run into each other in the parking lot. Closing up her apartment, Violet drove straight for the grocery store. She was going to make them a nice meal that night, have a semi-proper date, and then she would ask Lando the question that had been burning in her mind for weeks. Finalizing her break from Diane only brought it into reality even more, and she didn't want to wait any longer.

~

Violet was just pulling dinner out of the oven when Lando came in the front door from her shift, right on time. She'd gone in early to get some extra hours in but knew she was going to stay for the full length of her shift. Violet let the casserole dish filled with pork chops and smothered in a homemade barbecue sauce sizzle as Lando came into the kitchen, dropping her jacket onto the back of the chair.

"It smells delicious."

"I thought we could do something special for tonight."

Lando cocked her head at Violet, definitely trying to read what was underlying those words. "Is there something to celebrate?"

"Well, it's been a month."

"It's not that." Lando pulled off her uniform shirt, leaving her only in a sports bra. Violet both hated and loved when she did that, but she understood Lando's desire to get out of her dirty work clothes first thing. "I'm going to grab a quick shower, and I'll be down for dinner."

"Take your time." Violet pressed her lips together hard, eyeing Lando's hips and breasts as she turned and walked out of the kitchen. She was completely enamored, that much was obvious, and Violet was fully willing to live into that. She was enjoying it, actually.

As the pork chops cooled and the sauce set, she pulled out some fresh green beans she'd purchased and snapped the ends after washing them. She threw them into a large cast iron skillet that Lando had told her had been her grandmothers from when she'd gotten married, thus it was perfectly seasoned and she'd never get rid of it. Violet threw some butter and salt into the mix, letting the green beans cook slightly before she tossed in some chili powder on top for a hint of spice.

Her mother had been the one to teach her to cook, forever in the kitchen, and always telling her that as a woman, she needed to know these things. Sighing out the unwanted feelings,

Violet focused on their meal. Lando's warm hands around her middle surprised her, but the kiss on her neck was perfect.

"What did you get up to today?"

Violet stiffened at the thought of Diane, and then had to force herself to relax. "Well, there is something for you on the kitchen table."

"Oh?" Lando left her.

Violet snuck a peek over her shoulder as she pulled the cooked beans off the stove top and went to grab plates. Lando found the check, which Violet had left in a sealed envelope on top of her computer. Lando looked confused as she opened the back of it, her eyebrows raising as she read what it was.

"What is this?" Lando stated.

"What you should have been paid for the two weeks you worked for us." Violet set the plates on the counter and turned around to face Lando fully. "And I apologize again that Diane didn't do that to begin with."

"I don't know what to say."

"Say nothing. It's what was owed to you. I'm also mailing Erik his check in the morning."

"I bet he'll be happy to get that."

"I hope." Violet sighed.

Lando dropped the check back onto the table and moved against Violet, pressing into her so their mouths touched in a sweet kiss. Her skin was still damp from the shower, her hair wet and clinging to her head. "You didn't have to pay me though."

"Actually, legally, I did."

Laughing, Lando winked. "Fine, you win that one. I don't have to deposit the check."

"That is your choice." Violet kissed her quickly. "And it would be a stupid decision to make."

"I know. Thank you, for making it right."

"I needed to."

Lando kissed her again, this time lingering. Violet had gotten used to this over the last month, Lando coming home from work, making love, and spending the rest of the night together. She honestly couldn't remember the last time she'd slept at her apartment, and more and more of her stuff was ending up at Lando's in the meantime.

"Want to go upstairs and save dinner for later?" Lando whispered, her hand firmly on Violet's hip.

"Yes," Violet murmured.

Lando kept their hands locked as they went up the stairs. Lando was already stripping off her clean clothes as she entered the bedroom and walked toward the bed. Violet smiled to herself as she followed Lando's cue and pulled her shirt over her head and snapped her bra off.

"Sometimes I think you would rather stay in bed all day every day than go to work." Violet climbed onto the bed and straddled Lando's already bare hips.

"Sometimes?" Lando raised a bushy eyebrow. "Oh, Vi, that's every day. But I suppose I do enjoy work some days."

Chuckling, Violet bent down and captured Lando's mouth with her own. "Go get the strap."

"Yeah?"

"I wouldn't have said it if I meant otherwise."

Lando got up, and Violet finished undressing. Instead of lying on her back, Violet moved to the foot of the bed and held onto the footboard, her knees pressing into the mattress. She looked over at Lando, curious if she'd figure out exactly what she wanted.

Slathering the lube on with her hand, Lando came over and grinned. "I like it this way."

"I know you do. I do, too."

Lando moved in behind her, rubbing sticky hands over Violet's breasts and teasing her nipples. She dropped kisses along Violet's back, down to her ass, nipping lightly before moving upward again. Violet stayed right where she was, loving the attention Lando lavished on her.

"I've grown quite used to coming home to you," Lando whispered into her ear, sending a shiver through Violet's body.

"I won't deny that I've grown fond of it as well. I was at my apartment earlier today, and I can't remember the last time I slept there."

"Three weeks ago, Tuesday," Lando stated, so matter-of-factly.

Violet furrowed her brow, giving Lando a hard stare. "How do you remember that?"

Lando shrugged. "I'm good with dates."

She was just about to respond when Lando pressed her hand between Violet's legs, finding her clit between two of her fingers and scissoring them. Violet groaned, her entire body rocking forward at the sudden pleasure coursing through her.

"Like that?" Lando asked, a tease in her tone.

Violet wasn't sure she would be able to speak, so she grunted and clenched her eyes shut. Lando brought her up almost to the edge of her orgasm before pulling away. With a hand on each of Violet's hips, she knew what was coming next—the slide of the strap into her, the press of Lando's hips against her ass. It was a slow intrusion, but it was the perfect pause in the teasing.

Reaching between her legs as Lando began thrusting, Violet resumed the teasing on her body that Lando had stopped. She pushed back into Lando with each thrust, finding the rhythm and gentle waves washing through her. She had gotten so used to this, to the comfort, the peace that she felt when they were together, the heights and pleasure Lando would bring her to before soothing her on the way down.

"Lando," Violet said, her voice nearly breaking on the name.

"I've got you." Lando wrapped an arm around Violet's waist and held on until she crashed.

Violet slipped onto the bed, Lando lying next to her and trailing her fingers over Violet's body in soothing patterns. Violet smiled, facing Lando and kissing her fully on the lips. When she pulled away, the words spilled from her lips.

"Will you go chasing with me?"

"What?" Lando was confused, rightfully so. Violet hadn't prepped that conversation in the least and instead had dived straight toward the end. "I've been thinking, and the season's not over. I need to finish out my grant, which means I need to go out again, but—will you come with me?"

"You want me to go chasing with you?"

"Just me." Violet turned on her side and curled her hand against Lando's cheek. "I want to steal your love for storms."

Lando flushed, flopping onto her back and putting a hand over her eyes. "You do pick the most random times for these conversations. Not over dinner, not when I get home, nope, after I've fucked you senseless. Maybe that's what the problem is, all the sense has left your head."

Giggling, Violet moved in closer and kissed her way down Lando's neck to her chest. "I think I finally found my sense."

Lando peeked an eye out at her. "I don't mix business and pleasure, Vi."

Confused, Violet leaned up on her elbow. "If I remember correctly, you're the one who kissed me first, in Kansas, at *Indigo*, while we were working together."

"Not what I meant." Lando gripped Violet's hand and laced their fingers together. "I have a job."

"Yeah, but I can pay you more, especially if it's only the two of us."

"Where would we go?"

"Where the storms are." Violet was confused now. There was no other place they needed to go, but she did need to catch at least one more storm to collect data.

"That's not what I meant." Lando scratched her head. "Did you think you could butter me up with sex before asking?"

"No," Violet answered honestly. "I didn't really plan to ask you this way. I thought we'd have dinner and then talk, but I should have anticipated this, since it seems to be our routine."

Lando blushed. "You're right about that. Except normally there's a bit more reciprocation before serious conversations."

Violet's lips bowed upward. "Oh, I see. You don't mix business with pleasure."

"I don't."

Starting with their still tangled hands, Violet moved her way down Lando's body, pressing as many kisses as she possibly could. She pulled at the straps as soon as she got to Lando's hips, divesting her of the toy and tossing it to the head of the bed. She nipped the supple flesh on the inside of Lando's thighs before finding her way back up.

"How would you like your pleasure today?"

Lando laughed. "Whichever way you want. Then I want to eat."

"I thought that's what I was about to do."

Jerking upright, Lando gave her a hard stare. "Are you stealing my lines?"

Violet shrugged, giving Lando a direct look before she moved her tongue in a circle around Lando's clit. Lando gave up and fell back to the bed, her arm thrown over her eyes again. Violet trailed her hand up to join her mouth, inserting one finger and swishing it back and forth as she sucked and moved her mouth.

Lando cried out, her moans growing louder as she got closer. Violet continued, wanting to give Lando as much pleasure as she'd just received. They could easily do this for hours, but Violet knew they wouldn't that night. She wanted to talk, to plan out the rest of the summer.

As Lando's body clenched against hers, Violet continued until Lando's soft hand on her head beckoned her to stop. Violet moved so they were pressed together again, kissing Lando deeply just as Lando's stomach rumbled loudly.

Laughing, Violet shook her head. "Did you forget to bring your lunch again?"

"Yeah."

"We've got to find a better solution to that."

"Like working together?"

Violet parted her lips, then nodded. "Yeah, if that's something you would be interested in. We can go out whenever you want."

"Tomorrow?" Lando asked, but the tone of her voice told Violet she was only teasing.

"There's no storms within driving distance tomorrow."

"Fine." Lando rolled her eyes. "I would like the opportunity, just so that is clear."

"Good." Violet kissed her. "I promise it'll be just be the two of us."

"No Diane?"

"No." Violet ran a single finger down Lando's chest. "You and me."

"Just the way it's supposed to be."

Violet raised her gaze to look Lando in the eye. "I love you. You know that."

"Yeah, but I like to hear you say it. Often."

Grinning, Violet moved in to kiss her. "I love you."

"Good, because I love you, teach. And I trust you." Lando brought their mouths together, her stomach rumbling loudly again.

"And you're hungry." Violet shook her head. "Come on, let's go eat and we can figure out details over dinner."

"Is this what you in the business call a working dinner?"

Violet chuckled softly. "Yes, and get used to it, because when we're out in the field, every meal will be a working meal."

Violet crawled out of the bed and grabbed her shirt and pajama bottoms to semi get dressed before heading down the stairs. Lando followed suit, except all she wore was her sports bra and a pair of basketball shorts. Violet inwardly groaned because she knew how much of a distraction that was going to be.

"You'll have to teach me your ways, oh wise one."

"Oh good Lord," Violet muttered. "Is this what working with you every day is going to be like?"

"Well, if I don't have to play peacemaker, it means there's far more room for jokes."

They headed down the stairs, but just before Violet grabbed the plates she had set on the counter nearly an hour before, Lando came up behind her and wrapped arms around her waist. Violet turned in the awkward embrace and kissed Lando.

"I love you," Lando stated.

"I love you, too."

"I would love to chase with you again. As stressful as those two weeks were, they were probably the best two weeks of my life."

"Why?" Violet would never have guessed that one.

Lando grinned. "Because I got to know you."

Violet's chest warmed with the sentiment. As much as Lando had been through in her life, she always seemed to find the silver lining.

"It was quite a storm."

"But not the best storm."

"Never." Violet kissed her again then moved to plate their dinner, shoving each plate into the microwave to reheat it before setting it on the table. Since she'd met Lando again, she'd known there was something different about her. But Violet never would have guessed that this would be where they ended up.

ABOUT THE AUTHOR

Adrian J. Smith has been publishing since 2013 but has been writing nearly her entire life. With a focus on women loving women fiction, AJ jumps genres from action-packed police procedurals to the seedier life of vampires and witches to sweet romances with a May-December twist. She loves writing and reading about women in the midst of the ordinariness of life.

AJ currently lives in Cheyenne, WY, although she moves often and has lived all over the United States. She loves to travel to different countries and places. She currently plays the roles of author, wife, and mother to two rambunctious toddlers, occasional handy-woman. Connect with her on Facebook, Twitter, or her blog.

INDIGO: LAW

One accident. One nurse. One choice.

For years Bridget has hidden who she is from her small hometown. A democratic lesbian wouldn't very easily be elected Sheriff in the Bible Belt, and she doesn't want to give up her dream of working in law enforcement.

When a freak accident with a combine throws her life into chaos and nearly kills her, she must learn to rely on friends and family she wasn't sure she still had. With a desperate call to Eli, Bridget comes home, to a new world, a new life, and a new love. She is ready to come out and face the consequences.

This is the final installment of the Indigo B&B series.

ALSO BY ADRIAN J. SMITH

Romances
Memoir in the Making
OBlique
About Time
Admissible Affair
Daring Truth
Indigo: Blues (Indigo B&B #1)
Indigo: Nights (Indigo B&B #2)
Indigo: Three (Indigo B&B #3)

Crime/Mystery/Thriller
For by Grace (Spirit of Grace #1)
Fallen from Grace (Spirit of Grace #2)
Grace through Redemption (Spirit of Grace #3)
Lost & Forsaken (Missing Persons #1)
Broken & Weary (Missing Persons #2)
Young & Old (Missing Persons #3)
Stone's Mistake (Agent Morgan Stone #1)
Stone's Homefront (Agent Morgan Stone #2)

Urban Fantasy
Forever Burn (James Matthews #1)
Dying Embers (James Matthews #2)
Ashes Fall (James Matthews #3)
Unbound (Quarter Life #1)
De-Termination (Quarter Life #2)

Release (Quarter Life #3)

2022 RELEASES

Indigo B&B

Indigo: Law (*November 7, 2022*)

Crime/Thriller

Alone & Lonely - Missing Persons #4 (*December 1, 2022*)

Urban Fantasy/Speculative Fiction

Beware - Quarter Life #4 (*October 1, 2022*)

Dead Women Don't Tell Tales (*October 21, 2022*)

Printed in Great Britain
by Amazon